ALONE!

One more kiss, sweet and tender, and he was flying down the platform with the other last ones, swinging on the train and waving from the step with a real smile on his lips, forced there in answer to the bright teary smile with which she was waving him farewell. And then the train passed out of the car shed and into the darkness of the night.

He was gone!

Tyndale House books by
Grace Livingston Hill
Check with your area bookstore
for these bestsellers.

Grace Livingston Hill

ALL THROUGH THE NIGHT

LIVING BOOKS®
Tyndale House Publishers, Inc.
Wheaton, Illinois

This Tyndale House book
by Grace Livingston Hill
contains the complete text
of the original hardcover edition.
NOT ONE WORD
HAS BEEN OMITTED.

Printing History
J. B. Lippincott edition published 1945
Bantam edition/1968
Tyndale House edition/1989

Living Books is a registered trademark of Tyndale
House Publishers, Inc.

Library of Congress Catalog Card Number 88-51665
ISBN 0-8423-0018-X

98 97 96 95 94 93 92 91
10   9   8   7   6   5   4   3

DALE Huntley finished labeling and tying the last of the packages. The expressman had promised to call for them before ten o'clock. She gave a quick glance at the clock, and finding it was only half-past nine she sat back with a sigh of relief and closed her eyes for just a second.

It had been a hard time and she had not stopped for a moment to think of herself or her own feelings. But now, were all the little nagging duties accomplished that Grandmother had left for her to do before the relatives should arrive? With her eyes still closed she went swiftly down the list that was keen in her mind.

"Put all personal gifts, jewelry, heirlooms, private letters in the safety-deposit box in the bank." That had been done last week while Grandmother was still alive and alert to all that was going on about her, intent on leaving her world all in order for her going, interested in each item as if it were a game she was playing.

"You know," she told Dale with one of her old-time twinkles that gave her such an endearing look, "those cousins of yours that have been anything but cousinly in their actions, are liable to turn up as soon as they hear that

I am gone, and they'll do their best to search out anything that could possibly be interesting to them, and make your life miserable if they think you want it, so it is best not to have anything around to make trouble for you."

Grandmother was always so thoughtful for everybody.

But she must not think about that now. This was going to be a hard day and she would not be able to go through with it if she gave way to tears at this stage. At any moment those relatives might arrive—the telegram had said Tuesday—and she must not have traces of tears on her face. Oh, of course, tears were natural when one had lost a dear one, but she was in a position where she must be more than just another relative. She must carry out Grandmother's plans. She must meet the cousins quietly, and with some measure of poise. That would be the only way to offset any arrogance, and desire to manage, on their part.

Dale had not seen these relatives for years. Not since she was a small child, too young to be noticed by them. Young enough to be calmly swept aside for the pretty spoiled cousin, Corliss, who had to have everything her little heart desired, even if it upset everybody else in the house. Corliss had taken great delight in making Dale the butt of all her tantrums. It was natural, therefore, that Dale did not look forward to the reunion with pleasure. Still, she told herself, perhaps she was not being fair in feeling this way. After all it was a good many years ago, and Corliss had been only a baby then, some months younger than herself. There was a good chance that through the years Corliss might have changed, and would perhaps be a charming young woman by this time. It might even be quite possible that they could be friends. Though from Grandmother's description of her when she last saw her, Dale did not think so. Grandmother had at times given little word-sketches of her grandniece, witty and sarcastic, but altogether good-natured. However, these sketches were most evidently given in the way of warning lest Dale be taken unawares, and thereby lose out.

It was for that reason that Dale was really dreading the arrival of these unknown relatives, and had carried out the little details of Grandmother's plans most meticulously, schooling herself to a calmness which she was far from feeling. Not until these relatives were come and gone could she relax, and give attention to her own personal plans. By that time perhaps she would be used to the fact that the dear grandmother was gone and that henceforth she was utterly on her own.

She was interrupted in her troubled thoughts by the sound of the doorbell.

Hastily assuming her habitual quiet demeanor she hurried to the door, giving a worried glance toward the little stack of packages waiting for the expressman. Oh, if only this was he instead of the dreaded relatives. Then she opened the door, and glimpsed with relief the express car standing on the curb.

"Oh, you've come, Mr. Martin! I'm so glad! I do want to get these packages off on the first train."

The expressman grinned.

"I told ya I'd come, didn't I? I always keep my word when I can. Especially in a case like this where there's a funeral. I always like to help out. Especially when it's an old friend like 'Grandma Huntley.' I know she ain't here, and can't see but somehow I think where she is she'll know."

Dale's face lighted tenderly.

"Yes, I think she will," she said softly.

The old expressman got out a grubby handkerchief and blew his nose violently, then turned on his grin again:

"Okay!" he said getting into alert again. "Where's yer packages?"

"Oh, yes. Right here by the dining-room door. All of them."

"And you want these here things all prepaid, you said, didn't you? Okay. You can stop by the office and settle the bill when you come downtown again. I'll have 'em weighed and be ready for you."

Dale drew a breath of relief as she watched the truck drive away. Now, no matter when Aunt Blanche and Corliss came there wouldn't be anything for them to question about. Grandmother had made it quite plain that they would likely resent her giving anything away before they arrived, if there was any evidence about that it had been done.

So Dale was free now to go about the arrangements for the day and her undesired guests, realizing that she was going to have need of great patience and strength before this visitation was over.

Hattie was in the kitchen. Dear old Hattie, who loved Grandmother so much, and whose lifework from now on was merely to be transferred to the granddaughter whom Grandmother had loved so well.

Hattie had had experience in former years with the coming relatives, and would know how to deal with them. Grandmother had talked it all over with Hattie, and prepared her, made sure that she fully understood and could arrange an adjustable firmness, with courtesy, so that no clashing would be necessary. But when Dale came into the kitchen and found Hattie standing disconsolately looking out the window into the kitchen garden, the old woman said sorrowfully, "I dunno, I dunno, Miss Dale! Grandma said I was to be real sweet and polite, and not stir up no strife. But ef you had a-knowed them peoples the way I did, you'd know that wasn't just physicumly possible. I'd like to carry out your Gramma's wishes, an' I'm sure I'll do my best, but I know I can't really do it. I've tried before and it didn't work, and I don't seem to believe it'll work this time, but I'll do my best."

"Why, of course you will, Hattie. You'll be all right.

And don't you worry about it. If they say anything you don't like just put it aside and don't think about it."

"Yes," sighed Hattie, "that's what Gramma advised me. She said I was to remember that the Lord was listening to me, and He would know what was going on, and would be expecting me to act to please *Him,* not them."

"That's right, Hattie," said Dale with a little tender smile on her sweet lips.

"Miss Dale, if-en that's so, and the Lord can watch an' see what I do, do you 'spose p'raps *Gramma* can see too? If I thought *she* would be watching I could do a great deal better."

Dale smiled.

"Why, yes, Hattie, perhaps she will be able to see. I think it would help us both to think of her watching, and I'm sure the Lord will care and will be watching, and be pleased if we do the right kindly thing."

"Okay, Miss Dale, I'll 'member that. I'll do my best to please the Lord, and *her!*"

It was a busy morning. There were orders to give, telephone calls to answer, telegrams and letters to read, and the dinner to plan for the possible guests that evening. There were callers to meet, old friends of Grandmother's to talk to, a hundred and one questions to answer. The minister came to talk over the arrangements that Grandmother had made with him. There were flowers to receive and arrange for keeping, and there were tender precious messages from friends. Everybody had loved Grandmother for years, and she was going to be greatly missed.

Then, suddenly, late in the afternoon, when the company dinner was beginning to send forth delicious odors, there was a stir in the street, and a taxi drew up at the door ostentatiously. They had come! The waiting was over.

Dale cast a quick look out the door, caught a glimpse of a golden-haired haughty girl with very red lips, and drew a deep breath to quiet the sudden thumping of her heart.

She knew that it would not do to yield to excitement, for if she did there would be no poise, and no quiet dignity in her meeting with her guests, and she must remember what Grandmother had desired.

With another deep breath, and a lifting of her heart for help above, she went to the door, with the nearest to a real welcome in her eyes that she could summon. She came down the walk to the little old-fashioned white gate to meet them.

Aunt Blanche was having an argument with the taxi driver about the fare and didn't notice her at first, and Corliss, who was engaged in staring about at the neighborhood, did not at first see her either.

But finally the aunt finished her argument with a sharp bit of sarcasm and flung herself out to stand on the pavement and look around.

"Oh, is this you, Dale?" she said as she almost tripped over her niece. "Why, you've grown tall, haven't you? I expected to find you short and fat the way you used to be."

Dale had been prepared to greet her aunt with a brief kiss, but it appeared the aunt had made no provision for such a salutation so she contented herself with a brief handclasp, and turned to Corliss.

But Corliss was standing there staring at her. Apparently for some reason she was not at all what Corliss had expected, and it required some adjusting of her preconceived ideas to help her correlate the facts. It had not yet entered her mind that any form of definite greeting would be required between them, so Corliss took no notice of Dale's smile or the hand held out in greeting. She simply stared.

And behind her loomed a boy whom she knew must be Corliss' younger brother, Powelton. How cross he looked! Such frowning brows! She sensed on the boy's lips the grim distaste for the errand on which they had come.

She tried to reassure him by smiling, but he only summoned a wicked grin.

Dale spoke pleasantly:

"You are Powelton, aren't you?" she said with real welcome in her voice. "I haven't seen you since you were a baby."

"Aw, ferget it!" said the insolent youth. "Just call me Pow. That's what I prefer."

"Now, Powelton!" reproached his mother. "You promised me—"

"Yes, I know, Mom," said the boy, "but that was when you said there was going to be a lawyer here. You can't make anything out of this little dump, I'm telling ya!"

"Powelton! Be still! Driver, you can bring the luggage into the house."

"No ma'am, I can't! I ain't doing that no more. These is war times and I can't take the time to lug in suitcases. I put 'em on the sidewalk and you can lug 'em in yereself, ur let that spoiled boy o' yours do it. I gotta get back to the station. I'm overdue a'ready," and he started his car definitely.

"Oh, we can manage the luggage," said Dale pleasantly, gathering up three of the smaller bags. "Come on, boys and girls, each of you gather up a handful and we'll soon be all right."

The annoyed aunt stood in their midst and protested, but Dale had started on with her load of bags, and there was nothing for the rest to do but follow.

As they came up the steps to the white doorway the boy flicked his cap over the exquisite delicate lilies that were fastened to the doorbell.

"Why the weeds?" he said contemptuously, turning a sneering glance at Dale.

"Oh, please don't!" she said, planting herself in the way of a second thrust of the ruthless cap.

"Well of all silly customs," sneered the young man.

"Mom, I wouldn't stand for that if I were you. Tying a whole flower garden on the house we're expected to stay in all night."

Dale took a deep breath and tried to summon a calm expression.

"Take the suitcases into the living room," she said quietly. "Put them right on the floor by the door and then we can easily sort them out for the different rooms."

"Okay!" said the lad disagreeably, and he dropped the luggage he was carrying and turned to walk into the living room and look around.

"Some dump!" he commented disagreeably, casting a contemptuous look at the old steel engravings, and ancestral portraits in high stocks with their hair combed in a roach. He gave a semblance of a kick toward the fine old polished mahogany sofa with its well-preserved haircloth upholstery.

But Dale paid no attention to him. She put down the bags she was carrying and hurried out to the walk to get more, though she noticed that nobody else was like-minded, for they were surging into the house and staring around.

"Heavens, Moms," said Corliss, "I don't see what you wanted of a shanty like this! It really wasn't worth coming all this way over for."

"No," said Powelton, "it wouldn't even make a good fire."

His mother cast a reproving look at him.

"You'll find it will sell for quite a tidy little sum," said his mother. "You see, I didn't come all this way over here without knowing plenty about the situation. I found there is a project on to build a large munition factory right in this neighborhood, and a few strings properly pulled can make it possible for this place to be included in the center of things. A little judicious maneuvering will bring us in a goodly sum if we hold out just long enough."

Dale coming in with the final load of bags happened to

overhear this last announcement, although her aunt thought she had lowered her voice. But Dale put down the baggage with no more sign than a quick pressure of her pleasant lips into a straight line.

"Now," she said looking up at her aunt and endeavoring to speak pleasantly, "will you come upstairs, Aunt Blanche, and see what arrangements I have made for you? Perhaps Powelton will bring up the bags you want right away."

"Not I, my fair cousin," responded the boy. "I've carried just all the bags I'm going to carry today."

But Dale thought it best to ignore that remark. Let his mother deal with her boy. It wasn't her business. So she led the way upstairs.

A straight easy flight of broad low steps led to a landing in a wide bay window, overlooking a pleasant landscape. The sun was just setting, and the scene was very lovely. But Dale was in no humor to pause or to call her aunt's attention to the sky decked out in glory. She hurried up the stairs, trying to make her voice steady as she spoke.

"I thought you would like the old room where you used to be when you last visited here."

"Oh! Indeed! I really don't remember anything about it," said the aunt in a chilly voice. "I'll see what you have arranged and then take my choice. I'm rather particular about my surroundings."

Dale threw open the door at the head of the stairs, and indicated the room within.

"I hope you'll be quite comfortable here," she said as pleasantly as she could over the anger which made her voice tremble.

The aunt cast a cold look over the pretty room with its starched muslin ruffles, its delicate old-fashioned china, its polished mahogany.

"H'm!" said the woman, "I don't remember it. Have you anything else?"

Anger rolled up in a crimson wave from Dale's delicate throat and spread over her face, and for an instant she thought she was going to lose control of herself. She was being treated as if she were a servant in a rooming house. Then it suddenly came over her that Grandmother had drolly described what her daughter-in-law was like and given her a clue to just such actions, and she caught her breath and gave a little light laugh.

"Yes," she said brightly, "I thought the room next would be nice for Corliss."

"Which one? That next door?" asked Corliss sharply. "No, I won't have that. It hasn't but one window! I want that room down at the far end of the hall. It looks out to the street, and I'm sure it's much larger and sunnier." She turned and sped toward the room she had craved, and Dale caught her breath and cried out softly. "No! No, you couldn't have that. That is Grandmother's room."

"Nonsense!" said Corliss sharply. "What's that got to do with it? I say I want that room," and she hurried down the hall, her hand already on the doorknob before Dale could reach her, and she was only deterred from flinging open the door by the fact that it was locked.

"What's the meaning of this?" she almost screamed. "What right have you to lock the doors? I suppose you are keeping this room for yourself because it is the best room, obviously. Answer me! Why have you locked this door?"

Dale was by her side now, and her voice was low and sweet as she answered gently: "Because Grandmother is lying in there."

Corliss dropped the doorknob as if it had been something terribly hot. She turned frightened eyes on her cousin.

"What do you mean?" she almost screamed. "Do you mean that you have kept a dead person in the house and then let us come here to stay? Why how perfectly gruesome! I think that is ghastly! I couldn't think of staying in the house, going to sleep, with a dead person in the next room. I should go mad! Mother, are you going to allow this to go on? For I won't sleep here. I simply won't. Not with a dead woman in the house. You'll have to do something about it!"

Then Aunt Blanche came to the front.

"Dale, you don't mean that Grandmother's body has not taken to the undertaker's yet? Why, I cannot understand such negligence. Who arranged all this anyway? Did you, a young girl, presume to do it?"

"No, Aunt Blanche, Grandmother made all the arrangements. She said she wanted to stay here till she was taken to her final resting place, and she sent for the undertaker herself and made all the arrangements."

"How horrible!" said the aunt. "Well, it's evident we shall have to get another undertaker, and have the body taken away at once. We can't let this go on. Corliss is a very nervous temperamental child. The doctor says she must not be excited unduly. Suppose you call up another undertaker and I will talk with him and have this thing fixed. We'll have the funeral in some funeral parlor. I somehow knew I should have come yesterday."

But Dale stood quite still and looked at her aunt.

"I'm sorry you feel that way, Aunt Blanche, but it will be impossible to change the arrangements."

"Nonsense! Leave it to me. I'll cancel the arrangements quick enough. I'll just tell the man we'll not pay him, and he'll get out quick enough."

"He is all paid, Aunt Blanche. Grandmother paid him herself. She wanted to save us from having any trouble at the end, she said."

The aunt turned a face of frozen indignation.

"All paid! How ridiculous! Grandmother must have been quite crazy at the end. She had no right to do this. I shall refuse to let this house be used for the service."

"I'm afraid you wouldn't have the right to do that, Aunt Blanche."

"Not have the right? What do you mean? The house will of course eventually be mine. I certainly have the right to do what I will with my own, and I do not intend to have any funeral here to spoil the sale of the house. You see I have found a purchaser for it already. Someone I met on the train, and he's coming here tomorrow morning to look the house over. We certainly can't let him see a funeral and dead people here. He would never want to buy it under those circumstances, so gruesome."

A wave of color flew up into Dale's cheeks, and then receded suddenly as she remembered her promises to her grandmother not to get angry in talking with her aunt, but to remember to take a deep breath and lift her heart in prayer when she felt tempted. Grandmother had been so anxious that all things should be done decently and in order, and she must have known, too, just what provocative things might be said. So Dale drew a deep breath with partly closed eyes for an instant, and a lifting of her heart to God for help.

"Why, the house isn't for sale, Aunt Blanche," she said quite sweetly, in a pleasant tone.

"What do you mean?" screamed the lady. "Do you mean to say that the house has already been sold and Grandmother was only renting it? I always understood that it was her own." But just then Corliss raised her voice from the foot of the stairs.

"Mother, if you stand there and chew the rag with Dale any longer, you won't get anything done, and I simply won't stay in this house tonight the way things are. I feel as if I was about to faint this minute. Where is my medicine? I'm going to faint. I am! Come quick!" And Corliss slumped down on the stairs, and dropped her head back on the step above, rolling her eyes, and gasping for breath.

Her mother flew wildly down the stairs wafting back angry words to Dale: "There, see what you've done now! You'd better send for a doctor. These spells of hers are sometimes very serious. Powelton! Powelton! Where are you? Go out in the kitchen and get a pitcher of cold water, and a glass and spoon, and then look in my black bag for Corliss' medicine. Be quick about it too."

Corliss was presently restored to sufficient consciousness to talk again, and she began to whine at her mother.

"Moms, you've simply got to get things going. You can't have night coming down and all this funeral stuff around. I simply would die to be in a house with a dead body."

Then Dale stepped up quietly and spoke with dignity and sweetness.

"Corliss, if you would just come up into the room and see Grandmother, how sweet and pretty she looks, just like a saint lying there with the soft lace about her neck and her dear hands folded, and the loveliest smile on her gentle lips, you wouldn't feel this way."

But Dale's plea was interrupted by a most terrific scream of utter terror that must have been heard throughout the neighborhood.

"No! No! No! I won't! I won't ever see her. How perfectly horrid of you to say that. Take me out! Take me out of this house!"

This was followed by a quick exit to the front porch, and a flinging of the girl's body down in a chair, where she sat moaning and wailing in a tempest of hysterics.

Then her mother came back to the house to Dale.

"Dale, you'll have to tell me some place where I can take her until you can make other arrangements. Corliss will be a wreck unless we can get her out of here."

Dale with a quick uplifting breath, thought rapidly.

"Perhaps you would like to take her to the Inn," she said coolly. "I think they might have a room there. At least they would have a reception room where she could lie down on a couch till you could find a room that would do. I'm sorry I don't know of a boardinghouse that is not full to the brim with defense workers just now. Or, it might be one of the neighbors would let her lie down in the parlor till she gets control of herself. But certainly it is impossible to make any different arrangements here in the house. These are Grandmother's own arrangements and I intend to see that they are carried out. If Corliss cannot get used to the idea she might stay at the hotel, or down at the station till the service is over. Now, if you'll excuse me, Aunt Blanche, I think I'm needed in the kitchen. The dinner will be ready in about a half hour. Perhaps Corliss will feel better after she has had something to eat."

"No!" screamed Corliss, uncovering her sharp ears. "I'll not eat a mouthful in this house! I'm going to the hotel." But Dale went into the kitchen to face an indignant old servant.

"Leave her go to the hotel!" said Hattie furiously. "We don't want her screaming around here, desecratin' Gramma's house fer her when she ain't fairly out of it yet. We don't want 'em here. Let the whole kit of 'em go. We don't want to house 'em nor feed 'em nor nothin'."

"There, there, Hattie," said Dale. "Remember what Grandmother said."

"Yes, I know, only Miss Dale, it ain't fair fer you. You workin' an' slavin', to make ready fer 'em, an' then they make like this! It ain't reasonable."

"Yes, I know," said Dale wearily, "but it will soon be over and they'll be gone."

"Yeah?" said the old woman. "I wonder, will they?"

And then Dale could hear her aunt calling loudly for her and she went back into the living room to see what new trouble might have arisen.

She found her aunt most irate.

"Dale, what in the world was that you said about the house just as Corliss was taken ill? Did I understand you to say that you thought this house was not for sale? What did you mean by that?"

"I meant just what I said, Aunt Blanche," said Dale firmly. "The house is definitely not for sale."

"But how could you possibly know that?" asked the aunt sharply. "Grandmother didn't rent it, did she? I always understood that she was the full owner."

"No, Aunt Blanche. Grandmother did not own the house at all. It was just to be her home while she lived, but she had no ownership in it."

"Well, she did own the house once, I'm sure of that. I remember perfectly well. I think my husband engineered that. I think he paid part or perhaps it was the whole price for it. And of course it was to be mine after Grandmother was gone."

"I'm sorry, you have misunderstood, Aunt Blanche," said Dale quietly, "but that was not the case. Grandmother never owned the house, or even a part of it. The house is mine. My father bought it for me before he went away on business. Later, he was killed, and there was a proviso that Grandmother was always to have a home here as long as she lived. The house was left in trust for Grandmother and me until I should come of age, and that happened just a year ago you remember."

"How ridiculous! That's a pretty story for you to concoct out of whole cloth. I suppose the real truth of the matter is that you coaxed Grandmother into signing some papers and giving the house over to you, but a thing like that will be easily broken. And of course it will not be hard to prove that your father never had any money before he went to war. He was a sort of a ne'er-do-well, as I understand it, and couldn't have bought a house if he wanted to. As for you, you were only a babe in arms when he went away. I don't believe that even Grandmother could have helped to get up a story like this, much as she disliked me."

Dale summoned her utmost dignity.

"Aunt Blanche, don't you think perhaps we had better leave this decision until after dinner? Hattie has just told me that the dinner is all ready to be served, and I'm sure you must be hungry. If Corliss doesn't care to eat in the house would she like to have a tray brought out to the side porch? It is pretty well shaded with vines and nobody would be likely to see her, and wouldn't it be well for us to sit down now and postpone this discussion until tomorrow after the service? You know a little later the friends and neighbors will be coming in to see Grandmother, and we wouldn't want to be eating then."

"Oh, for heaven's sake! Is that going to happen, too? I think we better go over to the hotel right away. This certainly is a queer reception you are giving us."

"I'm sorry, Aunt Blanche. We have a nice dinner, and surely you must be hungry!"

And just then Hattie swung the kitchen door open letting in a delicious smell of roasted chicken. Powelton arrived in the doorway and sighted two plump delectable lemon meringue pies on the sideboard.

"Oh gee!" he said. "Let's stay, Mom. I'm clean holler, and if you don't stay I'll stage a scene too, and then see where you'll be!"

So Dale seated her recalcitrant guests about the table that had been stretched to its fullest extent for the occasion, and there was a sort of armed truce while they ate.

But Dale felt as if she scarcely could swallow a bite as she sat trying to be sweet and pleasant, and not think of what was going to happen next. Perhaps she should have insisted that they go to the hotel. But she wasn't entirely sure there were rooms there, and certainly the neighbors would think it very queer that Grandmother's relatives would be sent off to a hotel. Still what would they think if a public argument about the house, and the funeral in general should be staged that evening in their presence? Well, she couldn't help it. What had to come must come. But she prayed in her heart:

"Dear Lord, please take over, for I can't do anything about it myself."

So they were presently served, the visiting aunt under protest, though she was hungry. She sat down with a face like Nemesis, as if she were yielding much in so doing, and snapped out her sentences as if she were a seamstress biting off threads.

Outside on the pretty white porch sat the petted unhappy Corliss, accepting ungraciously the plate of tempting dinner, surveying it with dissatisfaction, and tasting each separate article tentatively, with a noise all ready to turn up, and lips all ready to curl in scorn. But after the first taste she gobbled it all down in a trice and called out for more.

But before anyone heard her outcries, her roving glance suddenly lighted on the lovely spray of lilies that was fastened so gracefully to the doorbell, and she arose from her improvised dinner table with a clatter that rattled all the dishes. She flung down her knife and fork and spoon noisily to the floor, she pranced angrily over to the front door, where her frantic fingers wrenched the beautiful flowers from their moorings, then snatching them up she marched into the dining room.

"So you thought I'd eat my dinner beside a lot of funeral flowers, did you? Well, I *won't,* and that's *flat!*" she finished and flung the lovely blossoms across the room.

There was an instant of utter silence while the angry girl stood surveying them frowningly, and then Dale arose from her seat and slid quickly over to pick up the flowers and vanish into the kitchen to discover how much damage had been done. These flowers were sent by Grandmother's close friend, Mrs. Marshall, the lady who lived in the finest house on the hill above the town, and had her own conservatories and wonderful gardens. They must go back in place and must not be missed for a moment by the neighbors or anybody in town.

Dale found that fortunately the blossoms were rein-
forced by wire about their stems, and had not been badly
broken by their rough treatment. She straightened them
carefully, and going out the back door went around to the
front and put the lilies back in place again. Then just as she
fastened the last bit of wire, and felt that the flowers were
going to be all right after all, Corliss appeared in the front
door with a dish of Hattie's exceptional apple pudding
brimming with delightful hot sweet gravy. With thunder-
ous fury on her brow she stood and screamed. "You *shan't*
put those horrid flowers back on that door. Not till I've
finished my dinner!" and she stamped her dainty foot re-
soundingly. Then she followed her wild words by another
piercing scream, which brought her mother to the door at
once.

"Well, now, what are you doing, Dale Huntley? You
certainly act possessed! Are you determined to make my
little girl suffer?"

Dale turned as calmly as she could, though she was
trembling from head to foot.

"I'm sorry, Aunt Blanche, but these flowers were sent
down by Mrs. Governor Marshall, from her own conservatories. She cut them with her own hands for Grandmother, for she loved her very much, and she is due to
arrive here any minute now, for she was anxious to see
how the flowers look, and I could not let her see that they
were not in place. I'm sure you will understand that, Aunt
Blanche. And —here she comes now—!"

A shiny limousine drew up before the door, driven by a
chauffeur in livery, bringing a lovely lady of unmistakable
breeding.

Aunt Blanche stared aghast and then suddenly turned
and vanished inside the house, herded her children together and out to the kitchen.

2

MRS. Marshall's car had been gone only a short time when a handsome naval officer came slowly down the street with a package in his arms, looking carefully at the numbers of each house.

Corliss emerged from her hiding in the kitchen just in time to see him in the near distance. She remained within sight to watch him. Such a personable young man in uniform she had not seen since she came east to attend this awful funeral of a grandmother she had seldom seen, and had not been taught to love.

Corliss went nearer to the open window the better to see him, and wondered if it would be too obvious if she were to go back to the chair in which she had eaten her only half-finished dinner.

But the young officer was stepping more quickly now, and was actually turning in at the gate. He was coming *here*! What was he? A florist? Surely not, as he was in uniform! Of course not.

Corliss gave a quick pat to her golden curls, adjusted a smile of come-hither-ness on her fierce young features, and got ready to go to the door when he should knock. She had no intention of letting an opportunity like this pass her by.

But Corliss was reckoning without her hostess, for Dale had lingered on the porch to straighten out the evidence of the recent meal served there, before more people should arrive, and she went forward with a quiet little smile as the officer came up the steps saluting her.

"Is this where Miss Huntley lives, Miss Dale Huntley?" he asked with a grin of recognition. "I thought I'd find you. You wouldn't remember me, would you?" and there was a wistfulness in his voice which it was most fortunate that Corliss was not outside to hear. "I'm just the guy that helped you wipe dishes about a month ago at the Social Center. I had another short furlough and I thought I'd run in on you and see if you were still on the job."

"Oh yes, I remember you," said Dale with a sudden lighting of her eyes. "You are David Kenyon. Isn't that so?"

"That's right. You've got a wonderful memory. All the fellows you must meet at that Center."

"Oh, but that night you were there was the last night I've been to the Center. You see we've had sickness here, and death—"

"Yes, I know," said the young man with a sudden gentle sobering of his expression. "They told me. They said your grandmother was gone. And I remembered how you spoke of her. You've lived with her for a long time, and it seemed as if you must love her a lot. I thought perhaps you wouldn't mind if I brought a few flowers, just to show my sympathy."

He held out the florist's box he carried, almost shyly.

"Oh, how very kind of you," said Dale, quick appreciative tears springing to her eyes at such thoughtfulness in a young stranger. "Do you know, I told Grandmother about you when I got home that night. She had been a little worried about my staying out so late, and she was so grateful that you had walked home with me. Of course she wanted to know what kind of a man you were, and I told her how you came out in the kitchen and helped me wash up the last dishes after the other helpers were gone. She enjoyed hearing what we talked about and she said 'If you ever meet that young fellow again you tell him I thank him for being helpful to you, and for bringing you home. And tell him I like his name, David!'"

"Say! I appreciate that," said the young man. "You described her so pleasantly I was quite disappointed when I heard she was gone. I had hoped I might be able to find you and perhaps have the pleasure of meeting her. You know my own grandmother died while I was overseas the first time, and she was the last of my family, so I have missed her greatly this homecoming."

"Oh, I'm sorry you couldn't have met my grandmother then. She would have loved it I know. She was so keen and sort of young for her years. She could enter right into talk with anyone and seem to understand them. Would you—care to—see her now? She looks so sweet, lying there, just as if she is glad to be seeing Heaven."

"Yes, I'd like to see her," he said gently, "that is if you don't feel I would be intruding."

"Intruding? Why of course not! I'd love to have you see her. We'll take your flowers up and give them to her. Come!"

She brushed bright tears away and led him into the front door and up the stairs. Right past the curious Corliss who had hastily and arrogantly arranged herself where they would have to brush by her; and could not, she was sure, fail to see her in her recently repaired make-up.

But David Kenyon did not cast an eye in her direction, although he passed so near he almost had to *push* by her, following Dale up the stairs. Dale had not even noticed that she was there until she had started up the stairs, and then she could only pray in her heart that her young cousin would not be moved to scream or otherwise mar the quiet atmosphere of the home from which the moving spirit had fled.

Corliss stared up after them until they vanished toward the room where the grandmother lay, and then she flouted herself out on the porch and met her brother who had just come whistling up the walk from the street.

"Hi, Cor, didn't I see a navy man coming in here? What's become of him, and how come you're not flirting with him with those big wistful eyes of yours?"

"Oh, get out! You're a pest if there ever was one! That navy man is a flat tire. He's gone upstairs with Dale, acts as if Gram was *his* relative. It makes me tired, all this carrying on about a dead person. When you're dead you're dead and that's the end of it, isn't it? Then why all the dither? Where've you been? Isn't there a movie house around here where we could go see a picture or something? I'm simply fed up with all this funeral business. And where is that hotel Dale talked about? I think it's time we found it and moved on. Go find mother and tell her to come out here. I can't see going into that house again. It makes me sick to smell those flowers. I'd like to pull them all down and scatter them on the sidewalk. I wonder what Dale would do if I did, now that her precious Mrs. Marshall has been and seen them. I believe I will."

"You better go easy, Cor, that's the undertaker coming now. He'll give you ballyhoo if you touch 'em, and he looks as if he could wallop you good if he got mad enough."

"Oh, get out, you bad boy! You know perfectly well he wouldn't dare!"

"Wouldn't he though?" mimicked the loving brother. "Wait and see! Just you wait till I tell mother what you said about those flowers. Now she's seen the dame that furnished 'em she wouldn't let you get by with an act like that!"

So the bickering went on out on the porch, with rising angry voices floating around the neighborhood.

"Isn't that perfectly awful!" said little Mrs. Bolton next door peering out behind the curtains, and then pulling her window down sharply with a bang to let the young people understand she was hearing them.

But upstairs Lieutenant David Kenyon and Dale Huntley were standing quietly before the sweet dead face among the flowers. The sun was slowly sinking behind the distant hills, and made a soft rosy light on the quiet lovely face of the old lady, lighting up her silver hair and giving a glory that was not of earth, as if God's sun would touch her brow with a hint of the heavenly glory that dear soul was wearing now.

"Why, she's beautiful!" said the young officer in surprise. "I've seen a lot of death lately, but I never saw a face glorified like that. I didn't imagine death could be beautiful!"

"She is beautiful, isn't she?" said Dale softly. "She was like that in life, lovely of expression. Only there's something different about it now. Something not of earth. Something heavenly. Doesn't it seem that way to you?"

"It does," said the young man reverently. "It seems—" he hesitated, and then went on, "it almost seems as if she were standing right in the presence of God, and had just looked at Him for the first time. Only I suppose she must have known Him well before she went away."

"She did!" said Dale, brushing the quick tears away. "Only I suppose it is different when one gets there and really sees Him in His beauty. The King in His beauty. She used to say that sometimes, smiling to herself, those last few days. 'The King in His Beauty!' I wonder what it will be like when we first see Him."

"Well, she's seen Him now," said the young man with conviction.

"Yes, there's no doubt about that!" said Dale, with a

smile like a rainbow through her tears. "Oh, I'm so glad you came up! It's good to have someone who understands. A great many loved her, but very few knew her as she really was. She was reserved and quiet, just a touch of fun and a twinkle in her eyes. She had a great sense of humor too, but they didn't all understand how real Christ was to her. But you are a Christian then, aren't you? I didn't know."

"One could scarcely be anything else to be where I've been for the last two years," he said gravely, "unless one turned into a devil and grew hard. Coming near to death every day puts a different light on life and what it means. You find out that you need a Saviour, when you are surrounded by death. But somehow I never realized that death could look like this."

They talked a few minutes, while Dale opened the box and took out the lovely flowers he had brought.

"Lilies of the valley!" she said. "How lovely! And Grandmother was so fond of them! But I thought it was too late for them!"

"I guess it is late," said the officer, "but somehow they seemed the fitting thing for a grandmother gone home. I could not send flowers to my own grandmother's funeral for I did not know in time, so I thought I would like to bring them to this one!"

"Oh, that is so kind of you!" said Dale, lifting a lovely smile to his eyes. "It seems the most beautiful thing that anyone could do. We'll put them in her hands. I can see just how she would have enfolded them in her lifetime."

Dale lifted the white hands that were folded across the breast and put the mass of delicate little blossoms in them, just as the dear old lady might have picked them and held them to her to smell their exquisite perfume, and then the two stood back a little looking at the sweet picture it made.

"It seems," said the young man, "as if there must have been somebody else's flowers that should have priority over mine; as if I were stealing in where I have no right to be, so very close to her. I am only a stranger to her, you know."

"No," said Dale quickly, "you are not a stranger. You are someone whom God has sent, and it comforts me to see your flowers there, because you understand. And there are no flowers she loved as much as those lilies of the valley."

"Thank you," he said. "I'm glad I could help a little."

And then there were sounds from downstairs of more people coming, and the young man drew back, feeling that their quiet time together was over.

"When is the service?" he asked wistfully.

"Tomorrow afternoon at two o'clock," said Dale. "I wish you could be here. Grandmother arranged it all. She wanted the service to tell the story of salvation, if there should be somebody here who did not know the way."

"I shall be glad to be here," said the young man, "if I won't be intruding. I am afraid this may be my last leave before I go back overseas, but I have till midnight tomorrow night. I was hoping I might have another word or two with you before I leave, but I suppose you will be very busy."

"Not too busy to talk to you. I shall be so glad if you will come to the service, and I can give you time after the service. You will help to tide me over the first hard hours knowing that she is gone."

He looked down at her tenderly and smiled.

"Thank you," he said quietly.

And then they could hear those other people coming up the stairs with Aunt Blanche's clarion voice leading them on self-consciously, as if it were entirely her funeral, glory and all, although she had not as yet come upstairs to see the grandmother.

David Kenyon put his strong warm hand on Dale's with a quick clasp like a benediction.

"Thank you, and good-by till tomorrow. I'll be praying for you all through the night, for I know it will be a hard one for you."

Then with a smile like a blessing he was gone, down the stairs alone, out the door, and into the street, before Corliss realized that he was coming. He vanished so quickly that she looked down the duskening street in vain to see a stalwart officer, whom she had fully intended to accompany on his way to get a little better acquainted with him.

"What got with that navy guy, Cor?" asked her brother looking up from the funnies over which he had been straining his eyes in the fading light.

"That's what I'm wondering," answered Corliss surlily. "I thought I was watching him every minute. I was going out to speak to him, but he just came down from the porch, swung out that gate, and disappeared before I could tell he was even there. He must wear seven-leagued boots. I never saw anybody go into nothing as quick in my life. It certainly wasn't very flattering to the family, when he must have seen us all sitting here on the porch."

"Mebbe he had to catch a train," said the boy. "Say, how long is this line goin' ta last? I'm about fed up with it. Why can't we go to the movies somewhere?"

"No," said his mother sharply. "We've got to wait till Dale comes down and arranges for us to go to the hotel. She'll have to send for a taxi, and I do wish she'd hurry up. All these fool neighbors coming in and staying so long! I can't see any sense in it."

"Well, why can't we go and find a taxi ourselves? Can't you phone for a taxi? Ask that servant out in the kitchen. She'll know where to get a taxi."

"No," said their mother. "It's better to stay right here till I can have it out with Dale. I've got to find out about that funeral, what time it is set, and when I can have the man here to see the house. I'm afraid she's going to be hard to handle about this. She seems to think the house is hers, and it isn't, I'm quite sure. I'll have to find that lawyer our Mr. Hawkins told me about and look into things tomorrow."

"When are we going home, Mom?" asked the bored boy. "I'm fed up with this funeral business, and if you are going to hang around here any longer I'm going home by myself."

"No!" said the mother firmly. "You are not going home alone. You are not going until the rest of us go. I may need you here to carry these things through. You aren't of age of course, but there is nothing like having the family in evidence. We may be able to make some money out of this. You'll be glad of that I know. And if there *is* any money, we don't intend to be cheated out of it. I'm quite certain that your father told me he had furnished the money to buy this house for his mother, and if that's true the house is mine."

"But I heard Dale say it was hers."

"It doesn't matter what she said. She's probably got that story up herself, or else Grandmother has told her some fairy tales. Of course even Grandmother may not have known where she got the house. She may have fancied it was from both brothers, but I've always heard that Dale's father was a sort of a ne'er-do-well. I really never knew him you know. He went overseas before we were married, and just before your father went, and Dale's father never came back. He was killed, you know."

Just then there was sound of footsteps coming down the stairs, several people, and Dale's voice could be heard gently. Aunt Blanche stopped talking and sat up abruptly.

"*Now,* we'll see," she murmured in a low voice to her children, and promptly there was an arrogant question in the very atmosphere, so that it was almost visible to the neighbors who came slowly down the stairs and out to the porch.

The neighbors lingered several minutes on the porch,

just last tender words about the woman they loved who was gone from their midst. Aunt Blanche and her children, in spite of their avid curiosity, grew more impatient before the last kindly woman said good night and went out the little white gate.

Then Aunt Blanche, without waiting for them to get beyond earshot, arose to her feet and pinned Dale with a cold glance from her unfriendly eyes.

"And now, if you have got through with all the riffraff of neighbors that seem to have so much more importance in your eyes than your own blood relations, just what are you going to do with us?"

Dale turned troubled eyes toward them.

"Oh, I'm sorry," she said gently. "I suppose you are tired after your journey. Would you like to go up to your rooms now?"

"No!" screamed Corliss with one of those piercing shrieks with which she had lorded it over her family since she was born. "No! I will *not* sleep in this house, not with a dead person here! My mother knows I won't do that! Not *ever!*"

"Well, in that case, what do you want to do? Go to a hotel? I didn't know but you had already arranged to do that. Of course you knew I wasn't able to get away just then."

"I don't see why!" said her aunt sharply. "I should think guests in your house would be of the first consideration. But I don't suppose you've had the advantage of being brought up to know good manners from bad ones, and ought to be excused on that score. But how would you suppose I could do anything about a hotel? I don't know any hotels around here."

"I'm sorry," said Dale again, "but I thought you would probably ask Hattie about them. She would know, and any hotel in this region would be all right of course, provided you could get in. You know this region is rather full of defense workers, and most hotels and boardinghouses are full to overflowing, just now in wartime."

"So, you would expect me to go to a servant for information, would you? Well, that is another evidence of your crude manners. However, now you are here, what are you going to do with us?"

"Well, what would you like me to do? Your rooms are all in readiness upstairs of course, and since you do not choose to occupy them I wouldn't know just what to do. Would you like me to order a taxi to take you around to the different hotels, to see if you can find a more desirable place for the night?"

"No, certainly not," said the irate aunt. "After I've come along journey I'm not going around hunting a place to stay. I'm too tired for that. I think it's up to you to find me a place."

"I'm afraid I don't think so," said Dale firmly but pleasantly. "However, I'll be glad to call up and inquire whether there is room anywhere. I can call the Oxford Hotel. It's rather expensive, but it would be very nice, if they still have room. And being expensive they might be more likely to have a room left. Or would you rather I try the cheaper places first?

"I should think that would be entirely up to you, whatever you want to pay. We are your guests you know."

Dale stared at her aunt in slow comprehension.

"Oh, I see," she said slowly. "Well, I don't see that it's my affair at all. If you are my guests you will occupy the rooms I have arranged for you. But since they do not suit you I think the choice would be all your own. I couldn't afford to pay hotel bills, you know."

"Then you could have sent for the undertaker and had Grandma taken away. It isn't too late to do that now."

"No," said Dale, "I can't do that. But if you won't stay here I can call up and find out if there are any accommodations left anywhere. Or, if you and Powelton are satisfied to stay here I can ask one of the neighbors to take in Corliss. The old lady who just went away asked if she could do anything for me. She has a little hall bedroom that is plain but immaculate, where I think Corliss could be very comfortable. I could call and ask her. Would you like that, Corliss?"

"Me? Go *alone* to some little old *stranger's* house? Not on yer life!" said Corliss hatefully.

Dale gave her a steady look, and then turned into the house and went to the telephone, followed by the three guests.

"What are you going to do?" asked Corliss impertinently. "You needn't think you can force me into anything like this. I'll *scream!* I'll make a scene! You haven't really heard me scream yet!"

Dale did not answer. Instead she called the number of the Oxford Hotel and asked for the manager, while the three invaders stood in a semicircle around her belligerently. Dale, as she caught a glimpse of their three unpleasant faces, could not but think what a contrast they were to the sweet placid face lying upstairs with the glory of Heaven upon it.

A few clear-cut questions she asked, showing that she was well versed in making business arrangements.

"You have a room? Only *one* room? What floor is that on? The second floor? What price? Ten dollars a day? Is there a double bed? Twin beds you say? And where would the young man sleep? The fifth floor, you say? A small hall bedroom? Five dollars a day. Oh, you say there is another larger room on the fifth next to the small one? The price is seven-fifty a day? Thank you. The lady will probably be around there to look at them. Yes, it's a lady and her daughter and son."

Dale turned.

"You heard what he said, didn't you? Would that be satisfactory or do you wish me to ask at other places?"

"Yes," said Aunt Blanche. "It's best to find out what is

available. Yes, call up three or four more hotels."

Dale smiled.

"I'm afraid I don't know that many hotels anywhere near here. There is the Longworth, and the Kenmore. No others this side of the city. Unless of course you want to go all the way in town, and that would cost you a good deal in taxi fares."

Dale turned back to the telephone, called up the Longworth, but was told curtly that they had no available room at any price. Then she tried the Kenmore, and found one large double room, where a cot could be put in for the young brother.

Dale gave the result briefly, and then said:

"Now, please excuse me a minute while I talk with Hattie. There are some plans for tomorrow she will be waiting to know, and you can talk this over and see what you want to do. When I come back I'll call a taxi for you."

Then Dale vanished into the kitchen.

"The very idea!" said the indignant aunt. "Well, I guess she'll find she'll have to pay for this. I'll have all bills sent to her."

Dale returned and ordered the taxi. She was relieved to get her unaccommodating guests off finally and be alone in the quiet of her sorrow.

"They ain't no kind of relatives fer a dear lady like our Gramma to have," grumbled Hattie as she locked the back door and turned out the kitchen light. "I'm right glad they're outta the house, so I am, and I wish they didn't hevta come back. They don't care nothing about *her*—just what they can get out of it!"

"Well, there, Hattie, don't let's think such thoughts about them. That wouldn't please Grandmother, and I'm quite sure it won't make it any easier to get along with them while they are here."

"Yeah. I know that. But human nature can't stand *every*thing, you know."

"No, but we haven't had to stand everything, Hattie. And besides Grandmother's Lord can help us to stand even everything."

"Oh, you's just a saint, Miss Dale, an' no mistakin'," sighed the old woman, "I couldn't never be as good as you, no matter how hard I tried."

"Well, just tell the Lord about it, Hattie, and then forget it. Do you know, I don't believe they know the Lord, and that's what's the matter with them, but if we act unpleasantly to them they won't have much opinion of the way we serve the Lord either. We've got to think of that you know, Hattie. Grandmother always said our business on earth was to witness for the Lord."

"I know, Miss Dale, yes, I know well enough, but I ain't so much on the doin'. Say, Miss Dale, do you reckum they will come to breakfast?"

"I don't know, Hattie. I told them breakfast would be at eight, and we were having lunch at half-past twelve to get everything cleared away in time for the service, but Aunt Blanche didn't answer, so we'll just have a simple breakfast and lunch, and if they come we can always cook another egg. Dry cereal, coffee, toast, jam and orange juice. Then that nice soup you made for lunch, and hot muffins with applesauce. If that doesn't suit them they can go back to their hotel. But I don't much believe they will come till lunch, or perhaps only in time for the service. However, don't worry about it. Just plan simply and have enough so if they do come we don't need to be embarrassed. Now, good night, Hattie, and thank you for the way you've carried on today, and made things easier for me."

"Oh, you blessed little lady, I ain't done nothin'. I jest wish I coulda made things easier. Good night."

And then the two went quietly to their beds to rest for the day that was ahead, and to ask keeping all through the night, and the days that were to follow.

3

THE next day dawned brightly, a fitting morning for an old saint to leave this earth on her way to her Heavenly home. Dale arose quite rested and ready to face the trials that would undoubtedly come to her that day.

She had a passing wish that she could go in there and stand by her sweet grandmother and tell her all that had passed, for somehow she felt her beloved presence was still here. Well she knew that if she were here she would only laugh at some of the things that happened, and press her lips and shake her silver head at the whole attitude of those unwelcome relatives, and she would finally say, "Didn't I tell you, Dale, dear?"

Then she knelt by her bed and thanked the Lord that her grandmother was away out of it all, not here to hear the unpleasant words, nor guess at the insinuations that Dale was having to bear. "I thank you, dear Lord," she prayed, "that You have taken her Home, out of all the unpleasantness of earth. And please help me to keep calm and sweet and bear everything gently as You would have me do."

She went down the stairs slowly, singing softly to herself the words of a little chorus that the soldier's words had brought to her mind, a song she had often sung in young people's gatherings.

> All through the night, all through the night,
>   My Saviour has been watching over me.
> He saves me so sweetly, so fully and completely,
>   And washes in His own atoning blood;
> My sins are all forgiven, I'm on my way to Heaven,
>   I'm walking in the smile of God.

Hattie looked up from her work at the stove and smiled: "You-all feelin' better, Miss Dale?" she asked in her most motherly tone. "You look real rested. Now sit you down and eat your breakfast. You ain't got no call to wait to see if them relatives come. They'll surely understand that people will be comin' and goin' and you couldn't wait around to be stylish."

Dale glanced at the clock.

"Yes," she said thoughtfully. "I believe you're right. They'll probably like it better that way anyway. And then, you know, they may not come."

"I shorely hopes they don't!" breathed Hattie almost like a prayer, as she slammed out in the kitchen to bring in the coffee and toast, and Dale felt her soul echoing an Amen to that prayer.

But they came. All three of them. With an eye to Hattie's delectable cooking they remembered. It was a quarter to nine before they got there, and the table was all cleared off, except for the cloth. But when Hattie heard them say they hadn't eaten yet she whisked the dishes on, and remembered to keep a pleasant face as she had promised Dale she would do.

There was orange juice for them all, coffee and toast in plenty.

"Is this all?" asked Powelton insolently. "We'd better have stayed at the hotel. If I had known—" But Hattie hurried out into the kitchen, thus moving the audience to further insolence.

Hattie returned presently with a platter of neatly fried eggs and set them down with a finality. Powelton surveyed them unpleasantly and asked:

"Haven't you got any bacon? I like bacon with my eggs."

But Hattie in a greatly controlled tone said quietly:

"Not today, we ain't. We couldn't have the smell of bacon when there's folks coming and going."

"Nonsense!" said the boy in his imperious voice. "Go cook me some bacon."

Hattie looked at him calmly an instant, with close-shut lips and then marched back to the kitchen, shutting the door definitely. She did not return, and Powelton finally finished the eggs and went out to the front porch to smoke endless cigarettes, growing more and more peeved at the idea of the funeral that was imminent, and from which his mother had absolutely refused to let him absent himself.

"You know you have got to make as good an appearance as possible," his mother had said. "The will hasn't been read yet, and it may mean something to you if the lawyers are in your favor."

So the spoiled boy sulked on the front porch and smoked and watched the undertakers bring piles of folding chairs into the house. And when he went into the house to get a drink of water he found them taking the leaves out of the dining room table, closing it up and shoving it to the far corner of the room.

"Hey!" he said arrogantly, standing in the doorway. "You can't do that! We've gotta have lunch here before the funeral!"

The undertakers glanced at him curiously, and looked to their own head who answered Powelton curtly:

"Those were the orders, young man," he said, and paid no further attention to him.

So the guests discovered, when Hattie called Aunt Blanche to the hurried meal, that lunch was to be served in the kitchen. A couple of small neat tables covered with snowy napkins, were set in the far end of the kitchen, with steaming bowls of soup for the three, cups of coffee, a pitcher of milk, plenty of bread and butter, and applesauce with a plate of sugary doughnuts. But Dale was nowhere to be seen.

"She's in the livin' room, fixing the flowers," explained Hattie when questioned. "She said she couldn't come now."

Aunt Blanche stiffened and sat down in the neat chair after inspecting it to see if it was really clean.

"Well, if I'd known I was to be treated so informally," she sighed, "I certainly shouldn't have come."

Hattie pursed her lips grimly together and refrained with effort from saying, "I wisht ye hadn't uv."

But they ate a good lunch, and not a crumb of the big plate of doughnuts remained, for Powelton and Corliss made a business of finishing them, meantime going out-side to observe developments.

"Well," said Aunt Blanche arrogantly, as she arose from the kitchen chair, "that's the first time I was ever served a meal in the kitchen in any place where I was visiting."

But Hattie again made no reply, and very irately and a trifle uncertainly the guest withdrew.

They found when they entered the hall that the casket had been arranged in the living room opposite the door, and the sweet silver-crowned face was visible among the flowers.

Corliss gasped, and ducking her face down in her mother's neck got ready one of her terrific screams. But her mother, well knowing the signs, put a quick hand over her mouth and uttered a sepulchral order:

"Shut right up! Do you hear? There are ladies coming in the front door. And there comes a sailor!"

It was that word "sailor" that stopped the scream in its first gasp. Corliss lifted her frightened angry eyes and caught a glimpse of a uniform coming in the front door.

Wide-eyed Corliss ducked behind her mother, slunk into the corner out of sight of the doorway and shut her eyes. If she had to endure this torture, at least she would make it as bearable as possible. She wouldn't *see* any more than she *had* to see of the horror of death.

The people were stealing in quietly now, going into the living room for a solemn look at the face of the old friend who was lying there, and then with a downcast eyes settling down in an unobtrusive seat. A few of them stepped across to the open dining room. It seemed to be quite a sizable gathering, mostly old ladies, a few uninteresting looking men, thought Corliss, as she peeked out between the fringes of her lashes and observed Grandmother's friends contemptuously. The seats were almost full and the minister was arriving, according to a sepulchral whisper of the woman who sat just in front. And then suddenly there came more people, hurrying in as if they knew they were late, filling up all the chairs in sight. Behind them came a good-looking young man in a gray business suit, who walked straight out of sight over to where the minister had gone, by the foot of the casket. Corliss wondered who he was and stretched her neck to try and see him, wishing she had taken a better seat while there was still room. But there wasn't a vacant chair in sight, and even if there was she couldn't well get by, the chairs were crowded so closely.

Then, just at the last minute like that, came the officer, the same one who had been there the night before with the flowers that they had put in Grandmother's hands, they said. She hadn't seen them. She wouldn't go and look. Silly lilies of the valley, what you gave to a baby!

But the officer walked quietly in and one of the undertakers placed him in a chair in the doorway, where he could see into the living room, and best of all where Corliss could watch him. She decided that this funeral wasn't going to be so stuffy after all, and straightened up in her chair, opening her eyes as effectively as she knew how.

Then gentle notes on the piano startled her into attention, and a wonderful voice began to sing. It seemed to Dale as she sat quietly by the casket as if an angelic voice were announcing the arrival of a soul in Heaven, and a sweet smile hovered over the lips of the girl who was being so terribly bereaved.

"Is that Grandma's song?" whispered an eager neighbor to Hattie who was standing up just behind Corliss.

"Yes ma'am," Hattie whispered audibly. "Mr. Golden always sang it for her when he come to see her. She just loved to hear him sing."

"Open the gates of the temple, Strew palms on the victor's way, Open your hearts ye people," sang the golden voice, thrilling triumphantly through the rooms, and startling even Corliss into attention. That man really had a voice if he only would sing something decent. But this song was quite an old chestnut. Why didn't they pick out something real? Why, there wasn't a word about Heaven even in that song. Or was there?

Then suddenly the golden voice brought out the tender triumphant affirmation:

"I know—I *know*—I KNOW that my Redeemer liveth!"

Oh, so that was it, was it? Religious stuff! Of course, that would be it. Grandmother was that way. Corliss turned back to lean against the wall and close her eyes again.

But the golden voice went on: bringing out the words with such conviction in the tone that Corliss had to listen, had to know that there was really something in this song that others beside Grandmother believed in. A hint crept into her heart that it might somehow be true, at least to a

certain extent. It was conceivable that she herself *migh.
have* to pay some attention to such things *some* time. But
not now. She was young. When she got to be as old as
Grandmother it might be all right, if people still believed in
such things as a Redeemer. She wasn't at all sure *she* did.
Yet the voice of that good-looking young man sounded as
if *he* did. That golden voice like a piercing blade of a golden
sword that was cutting deep into her soul and frightening
her, in spite of all her opposition, in spite of all her unac-
knowledged sin!

Suddenly she turned toward the officer sitting across
from her, sitting where he could see into the room with the
golden voice and the casket. Was he taking it as some sort
of a mockery, just a form of words? Or even a joke? She
hoped he was.

But no, the man was looking straight toward the voice,
a warmth of sympathy and conviction in his face. It really
was quite attractive in a service man, a look like that. She
hadn't thought it would fit with a uniform, but it did. And
he didn't look like a sis either. He looked as if he could fight
hard if he tried, throw bombs, and shoot, maybe dance
and have good times. Corliss sat back and studied him
through half-closed lashes. She decided he looked pretty
nice, and she would stick around and see if she couldn't
date him for the evening. It oughtn't to be hard to do. If
she only could get out of riding to that old cemetery!

There were exercises going on all this time, but without
benefit of Corliss' attention. She was studying the young
officer. Maybe she could work it around for him to ride in
the same car to the cemetery, if he went. If he didn't she
would stay at home herself and see if she couldn't follow
him down the street and pretend to sprain her ankle or
something. She was determined to get to know him.
Maybe make him take her to a movie or a dance tonight.

Wonderful scripture was being read that Grandmother

Huntley had herself selected, but it made no impression upon Corliss. She was studying the profile of the splendid-looking officer.

But the man was giving interested attention to the service, and was utterly unaware of the girl who was watching him.

Corliss was disappointed that he didn't ride in the same car with them. Instead he was put with Dale and the minister and the young man singer. That was mean of Dale to manage it that way. And there was some old woman in the car with her mother and brother and herself. If there hadn't been so many people around she might have tried the screaming act, but on account of the good-looking singer and the navy man she didn't consider it. Perhaps there would be some way to get to talk to him after this ride was over. So she gloomed through the remaining ceremonies, and was glad indeed when the car drew up at the house again, and she saw that the navy man was getting out and going into the house with Dale. He probably wouldn't stay long, and she would plan to talk to him somehow. So she settled herself on the porch to wait for his coming out. He seemed to be over by the desk in the living room writing something for Dale. What in the world could he want of Dale? Some business probably connected with the funeral. He certainly couldn't be interested in her. She was awfully plain and not stylish at all according to Corliss' tastes.

But Corliss grew impatient before the interview at the desk was ended. Dale was writing something too. Some address probably, or maybe signing a paper. Only they seemed so awfully interested in what they were saying. A sharp jealous look went over her young face. It had always been this way with Dale, thought the young cousin. She seemed to think because she was older she could manage everything.

But at last the two young people arose from the desk and came to the door. Corliss arose precipitately and scuttled to the other side of the door where she could easily slip down the steps after the man when he should go; and so, she missed the look in his eyes when he took Dale's hand briefly and said good-by.

Then he was gone, with a quick bright smile back at Dale standing in the doorway. But Corliss missed getting the full effect of even that, for she was hurrying down the walk nonchalantly ahead of him, sliding behind two old ladies who were going into the house next door, and nearly knocking one of them over in her haste. Her main object was to catch that "navy guy" before he should vanish again as he had last night, for he was walking now with long quick strides, and looking at his watch as he went, as if he were afraid he was going to be late somewhere. She mustn't appear to be walking too fast either. She mustn't dare to run, or her mother would call her to account. She had already endured one long sharp lecture from her mother on the subject of decorum at the time of a funeral. But as soon as the two old ladies went into their own gate she pressed by them and hurried on, dismayed to find how far ahead the man had already gone. Then, as he turned a corner, she did begin to run. She wasn't going to let him escape this time. A moment later she brought up by his side, quite out of breath, and accosted him.

"Oh, I say, what's your rush?" she panted. "I've nearly run my legs off to catch you."

"Oh, I'm sorry!" he said, coming about-face and looking at her startled. "I didn't leave something, did I? Was there some message from Miss Huntley? Should I go back?"

"Oh no, no such luck," laughed Corliss. "I just wanted to talk to you. I like service men, and I especially like you. I wanted to ask you if you wouldn't make a date with me for this evening? We could go to the movies first and then you could take me dancing. I'm just sick to death of all this funeral business and I want to have a little fun. I thought you would show me a good time."

The young man gave her a puzzled look.

"That would be impossible," he said. "I have to catch a train back to the barracks."

"Well, miss your old train then and stay with me. There are always more trains. Besides, I want you! I'm fed up with all the solemnity, and I've got to get out and see some life. Miss your old train. Come on!" There was wheedling in the blue eyes lifted to his, but there was only firmness, almost severity in the eyes of the young officer.

"Haven't you heard that there is a war?" he said. "When one is in the service one does not miss trains. Here comes my bus. Good night!" and he was gone.

Corliss, baffled, angry, stood and watched the bus disappear around the next corner and then went furiously back to the house to see what other deviltry she could think up.

Meantime Dale had dropped into a chair near her aunt, getting ready to take over the burden of this uncongenial set of guests; hoping against hope that they would see their way clear to going home on the midnight train, yet not daring to believe that they would.

But her aunt broke the momentary silence:

"Who is this naval officer who seems to be so much in evidence?" she asked, withdrawing her gaze from the place where her daughter had disappeared in pursuit of the uniform.

Dale came to attention at once, bringing back her mind from a consideration of what she ought to do or say next.

"Officer? Oh yes? Why, he's just a friend."

"Oh! Only a friend. He must be a very special friend to go out of his way to come to a mere funeral."

Dale hesitated. How should she explain?

"It was kind of him, wasn't it?" she said pleasantly.

"You see he was interested in Grandmother. A great many people were interested in Grandmother, you know."

"So it seems," said Aunt Blanche sarcastically, as if the fact annoyed her. "You certainly had a mob here today. One wonders what satisfaction people like that get out of a funeral. It must be just morbid curiosity."

"Curiosity?" said Dale with a perplexed frown. "What could they possibly be curious about? They were most of them very dear old friends who have been here constantly during the years, and who loved Grandmother very much."

"Oh, I see!" said the aunt dryly. "Well, I suppose the poor things have very little else to do. But I can't understand a young naval officer coming. He must have seen plenty of death in a more dramatic form, if he *really has* been overseas."

Dale's eyes suddenly flashed, but she turned her face away so her aunt would not see, and taking a deep breath she suddenly rose to her feet, changing the subject sharply:

"Now, what are your plans, Aunt Blanche? Are you returning home tonight, or do you wish to go back to the hotel? In which case would you like me to send for a taxi?"

The aunt looked at Dale with an annoyed manner:

"I don't see any rush about it," she said, offended. "I thought perhaps we'd stay here now and take those rooms you prepared for us. Corliss of course thinks she would like to have Grandmother's room. She is sure that is much the best room in the house, and the outlook is much pleasanter I suggest you send Hattie up to clean it thoroughly right away, and open all the windows wide."

Dale paused and looked at her aunt steadily.

"No!" she said firmly. "Nobody is going to occupy Grandmother's room at present, and certainly not Corliss, after the way she acted. I wouldn't like Grandmother to be dishonored that way."

"*Dishonored?* What do you mean? Can't you understand

a young girl being afraid of death? Don't let's have any more argument about it. Just call Hattie and tell her to thoroughly clean Grandmother's room, and put it in order for use. If you don't *I will*. I'm not going to live through another night like last night, and Corliss is all upset. Will you tell Hattie, or shall I?"

Dale drew another long breath and looked at her aunt quietly.

"Hattie isn't here," she said.

"Isn't here? Where is she? She was at the funeral, wasn't she? I saw her myself. I thought it was awfully queer, too, letting a servant come in with the family. Where has she gone now?"

"She has gone to see her sick sister. I told her to stay as long as she thought it was necessary, that I would get along all right. She has been wonderfully good staying here through it all, though her sister really needed her. But she wouldn't leave me alone till the funeral was over."

"Oh! She wouldn't, wouldn't she? And you actually *let* her go while *we* were still here?"

"Why, I wasn't sure whether you were here or not. You have been staying at the hotel, and I never heard you say whether you were going back west right away or not. But anyhow, that made no difference, Hattie *had* to go. I think she did a good deal to stay till the stress was over."

"*Stress?* Well, I'm sure I don't know what you mean. We're still here, and since the objection to staying here is now removed I don't see why you should jump to the conclusion that we were going to the hotel. Of course having come so far to look into business matters I shall not be going back until I am finished. And now, what are we going to do about that room? It *must* be cleaned *thoroughly* or we never can get Corliss to enter it, and I cannot blame her. Is there some one else you can get to do this cleaning, at once?"

"I am sorry to disappoint you, Aunt Blanche, but that

room is not a consideration. It has already been thoroughly cleaned of course, but it is *not* to be used at present, by Corliss, or anyone else. I have other plans which I am not willing to change. And please, Aunt Blanche, I am very tired tonight. It has been an exceedingly hard day. Suppose we don't talk any more about such things. I am not going to get another cleaning woman and there is no house-cleaning to go on here, either tonight or tomorrow."

"But Dale, you are unreasonable. I told you that the man who is thinking of buying this house is coming to see it. I reached him last night on the telephone and told him to come tomorrow morning at eleven instead of today, so whatever has to be done toward cleaning *must* be done tonight."

Dale turned suddenly and faced her aunt.

"Listen, Aunt Blanche," she said firmly. "Nobody is going to look at this house tomorrow or any other day with a view to buying it. The house is definitely *not for sale!* I thought I made you understand that yesterday."

"We'll see about that!" said the aunt hatefully. "You are not beginning very well for the favors I was planning to give you. I had decided to ask you to come and live with us. I know you have no money to live on, and you are scarcely prepared to earn your living in any way, so I thought it was really my duty to look out for my dead husband's only niece. But you certainly do not give the impression of being very good-natured or adaptable, and we shall have to have a thorough understanding before I can go on and make the offer I had intended. But this first thing must be understood. *I* am taking over in this matter about the house. It will eventually be mine and I do not intend to lose the opportunity of sale to a man who is willing to pay a good price."

Dale faced her aunt with steady calmness.

"You will do nothing about this house, Aunt Blanche,

because you have no right to do anything. Tomorrow morning my lawyer Mr. Randall Granniss will be here at ten o'clock, with all the papers which will show you how impossible your claims are. I called him last night and arranged this, and he said he would bring all the data relating to the house."

"Oh, *really! You* presume to have a lawyer? Well, that's ridiculous! A girl of your age having a lawyer."

"He is the lawyer whom my father left in charge of my affairs," said Dale quietly.

"Yes? Well you'll find you'll have to prove all this."

"Yes, certainly. Mr. Granniss will bring the proof."

"Well, if you are going to such lengths I shall certainly have to call up the lawyer to whom I was recommended. Just excuse me and I'll call him."

"Certainly," said Dale calmly, and then sat down and covered her tired eyes with her hands. How right Grandmother had been when she had warned her about this aunt, and had prepared for all such contingencies as were happening one by one.

Out in the hall at the telephone she could hear her aunt's sharp voice demanding to speak with a certain Mr. Greenway Buffington. Then the voice lowered into a confidential scream. But Dale resolutely held her weary eyes shut, and in her heart began to pray. "Oh, God, be with me. Protect me through all this unpleasantness. Help me not to be a false witness. Help me to show these people who in a sense belong to me, that I have a Saviour who is able to keep me. Guard my tongue that it may speak the truth in quietness and peace, and not let anger come into the conversation. Keep me calm and trusting."

In a little while Aunt Blanche came back into the living room and announced:

"My lawyer will be here tomorrow afternoon. That will make it possible for me to expose to him all the machinations of the man you say is your lawyer."

"Very well," answered Dale quietly, without opening her eyes, and her aunt flounced down into a rocking chair and fairly snorted in anger. After a few minutes Dale heard her get up and go upstairs. She heard her walk the length of the hall to Grandmother's room and try the door, but failed to get in, though she rattled and shook it. Dale sat still. She had locked that door, and had the key in her pocket. Moreover she had gone through the adjoining bathroom and *bolted* the door from inside, and then locked the bathroom, so it was impossible for her aunt to enter the room without actually breaking down the door. She sat still for a few minutes and then went up to her own room and lay down on the bed. She was very tired and it just did not seem she could stand any more argument.

She was awakened a few minutes later by a loud determined knocking on her door.

"Yes?" she said, sitting up sharply and trying to get her senses back from the deep sleep into which she had fallen.

It was her aunt's voice that answered her.

"Aren't we going to have an evening meal? Or hadn't you thought of that?"

Dale got to her feet and staggered to the door.

"I'm sorry," she said, putting her hand to her eyes and trying to make her voice pleasant. "I should have told you. I didn't realize I would fall asleep so soon. I really was very tired, you know."

Her aunt gave her an unsympathetic glance.

"We *all* are!" she said coldly. "And of course we *are* guests, so we couldn't do anything about it."

"Well, if you don't mind foraging for yourselves this once," Dale said pleasantly, putting her hand up to her forehead. "There are sandwiches and salad in the refrigerator, also a pitcher of iced coffee, and plenty of milk. You'll find an apple pie in the pantry, or if you prefer custard you'll find some in the refrigerator, and there's a sponge cake in the cake box. I think if you don't mind I'll just sleep this off. I'm rather dizzy."

"Oh!" said the aunt ungraciously. "Well, I didn't expect to have to do the housework when I came, but if you're *really* sick, of course we'll do the best we can."

With a deep sigh, as if she were being ill-treated, Aunt Blanche summoned her children and they went out to the kitchen and certainly made hash of Hattie's neat kitchen and pantry and refrigerator. But for once Corliss had a chance to sample everything in sight.

4

DALE went back to sleep, being thoroughly worn out by the strain of the last two days, and the sudden realization that her beloved grandmother was gone from her and she was now on her own. But she was too near the breaking point to do any more connected thinking now, and hearing only dimly the sounds of slamming refrigerator door and the breaking of a dish or two, she sank quickly into a deep sleep.

It was several hours later that she awoke with a sudden start to a realization that a tremendous storm was in progress, lightning, thunder, wind and rain, and the wind was blowing rain fiercely from the open window into her face. The lightning made her room bright as day.

Dale brushed her wet hair away from her face and hurried wildly across the room to shut her window. Then turning as the lightning shivered blankly into darkness for an instant, she glimpsed a line of brightness under her door, and realized that there must be lights and perhaps windows open in the rest of the house.

She unlocked her door, flung it open, and stood listening an instant before another thunder crash came. There was no sound except the thunder, but there was a tremendous draft, pouring up the stairs. She hurried down the stairs, noting that the lights were on everywhere, and that the front door and all the windows were open just as she had left them when she went upstairs. "Aunt Blanche!" she called as she hurried down. "Corliss! Where are you all?"

But there came no answer.

Then the clock struck solemnly. "One! two! *three!*"

Dale's startled eyes went wonderingly to the clock. Was it right? Could it be three o'clock in the morning? Could she possibly have slept all this time? And where were her erstwhile guests? Asleep upstairs?

She cast a quick glance back and upward, but all the bedroom doors except Grandmother's were standing wide open. Surely they wouldn't have gone to bed and left their doors open that way, left all the lights burning and the doors and windows open.

Another gust of wind, another crashing clap of thunder, and she hurried down and shut the front door, then went from one window to another closing them quickly. In the dining room and kitchen she found a hopeless clutter of soiled dishes and half-eaten food. The big serving plate that had been piled high with delicious sandwiches was empty. Absolutely. Not a crumb left! The pie was demolished and half the bowl of custard gone. The iced coffee was gone also, and some of the milk, while half-filled milk bottles were standing about, indicating that the cream had been drunk first, and the rest left out of the refrigerator. In fact further investigation showed that the refrigerator doors were both standing wide open.

Vexedly Dale pushed them shut, gave a hopeless look about the devastated rooms, then walked on to the living room and looked around. That room was as bad as the others, for everything that could be lifted by the wind had been tossed about. Several comic newspapers and joke books were on the floor, torn and crumpled, blown hither and yon. A game of Chinese checkers was blown from the little end-table where it had been used, the chessmen all over the floor. Three or four books were lying open, face down on the floor, and two more with the pages torn and crumpled by the wind. Her guests had evidently eaten everything within sight, tried all the forms of amusement they could discover, and then gone their ways.

Dale looked about in vain for a note they might have left, but found none. If there had been one it must have blown away. Well, evidently they had repaired to the hotel for the night. A glance at the kitchen clock confirmed the hour again. And there was nothing she could do about it. It was too late to call up the hotel and waken everybody there, and what end would it serve anyway?

Dale sat down and looked around considering what she ought to do. In her indignation she would have liked to lock the house up and refuse admittance when they came back for breakfast, but she knew that would not be Grandmother's way; and, too, it would not be God's way. God who had cared for her in all that storm and wind, lying asleep and unprotected in an open house, that was lighted from top to bottom, with wide open doors and windows. Yes, God had been watching over her. Well this was what she had to meet, and she must go through with it.

"God, help me to do right, and please protect me from having to meet more than I can bear."

Then Dale got up and went to work.

She laid aside the pretty dress in which she had lain down in her weariness, and put on a cotton house dress from the hook in the kitchen. Then she went to work in the living room first, quietly, swiftly, pulling down the window shades to guard against curious puzzled neighborly eyes, if any chanced to be awake. She gathered up all the papers and scattered things from the floor, swept the checkers into a drawer of the table, piled the books and stowed them in the bookcase, taking care to lock the book-case and place the key in safety. She gathered the plates and cups that had evidently held snacks from the evening meal, and carried them to the kitchen. Then she came back and turned out the living room lights, the hall lights, closed the doors to the dining room and kitchen.

The enemy might not return very early the next morn-ing, but it was just possible that Hattie might, in case she found her sister much better, and Dale did not want Hattie to know what had been going on. For Hattie needed no more fuel added to the fury of her indignation. Hattie was already irate and she would find it difficult to restrain a bitter tongue if she once got started telling the relatives what she thought of them. So it was up to Dale to obliter-ate the traces of what had happened, and that meant doing thorough work in both kitchen and dining room.

The dishes were all marshalled into the kitchen first, then she went to work with broom, dustpan and carpet sweeper. It was too late at night, or too early in the morn-ing, to use the vacuum cleaner and startle the neighbor-hood. She must work quietly.

When the sweeping and dusting were done she gathered the tablecloth for the laundry bag. It had been shining clean when Hattie set the table for the evening meal and de-parted. But now it was smeared in several places with three different kinds of jam which had been taken from the pan-try shelves and sampled. There would have to be a clean cloth and napkins for breakfast, in case they had to serve a company-breakfast. And of course they would. There was no chance of the unwanted guests leaving for their home until they were entirely satisfied about a will, or property which they had hoped to get by coming to this funeral. Dale sighed, and wished Grandmother hadn't thought it necessary to send for these unlovely folks. But of course it was right that they should know of her death.

Dale's weariness came back upon her when she was

about half through washing that mountain of dishes that the intruders had managed to soil, but she plodded steadily on, working so quietly that even a curious neighbor who might have gotten up to look out her window would never know that dishes were being washed. She was thankful that the kitchen windows were guarded by shades that had a dark green back and therefore no light would shine through to the outside world. Thankful also for the storm which continued to thunder noisily on to cover any unavoidable noises she might make. She did not want those dear friendly neighbors to know what had happened in Grandmother's home the night after she had left it. Dear Grandmother!

The dawn was beginning to creep into the sky when at last Dale wiped and put away the last of the dishes, and washed and hung up her dish towels to dry. She was very weary, but it did her good to realize that even if her visitors should return now they would see no signs of the devastation they had wrought. It was all in order again, lovely quiet order. And if their consciences did not reproach them for what they had done, she would not be the one to do it. That was as Grandmother would have wanted it.

She cast a quick glance into the plundered refrigerator. There were eggs enough. They could be scrambled for breakfast. And there was dry bread enough to make toast. That with coffee should be enough to give them. She would make no apologies.

Wearily she turned out the lights and climbed the stairs to her own room again, undressing in the dark, and getting gratefully into bed. She would sleep just as long as she pleased. If they came back before she was up they could sit on the porch till she got up. There were plenty of porch chairs there. They might be damp from the storm, but she couldn't do anything about that now. She *must* get a little more sleep, for she felt morally certain that tomorrow was going to be a hard day. And of course she must be up and rested in time for her lawyer who was coming. She was so glad that she had called him up the night before and told him all about the situation. She knew he could be counted on to look out for everything. He had been her trusted guardian for years.

So she went to sleep again, and the day began slowly, widening into brightness after the storm.

Dale dressed rapidly. The day would be a hard one, it could not help but be, but she must not allow herself to give way to the lassitude that threatened to sweep over her now and then. She had not had enough sleep. That was true. She had been through a great strain. Yes. But she was expected to go through this. God would take care of her. How He had helped in small quiet ways all the way through these hard days. *She* must not fail Him.

She went downstairs and began to get breakfast ready. Not that her unwelcome guests deserved it, but she would not let any failure on her part be the cause of unpleasantness. Soon they would be gone—that is, she *hoped* they would—and she did not want to spend her time afterward regretting any sharp words she might speak. After all they were related to her, and her cousins' father's *first* wife had been her own mother's beloved sister. She must not let the fact that Aunt Blanche was a second wife influence her. And she had a very pleasant memory of her uncle, their father, when she was a very little girl. Once he had brought her a peach, the very first peach she had ever had of her own. And once he had sent her a funny post card. But that was so very long ago, and her thoughts faded into precious memories of her own father whom she had dearly loved.

Well, these people were all she had left, and not at all precious at present. But she would have one more try at doing her best to like them, and make them like her.

So she squeezed glasses of orange juice, and prepared delicate slices of toast, piling it in front of the toaster so it would not dry up and still keep warm. She made the coffee with the greatest of care, put as many ice cubes in the glasses as they would hold, set the table with nicety. Laid out eggs for scrambling when the relatives should come, and then having drank a glass of milk herself she hurried upstairs to put herself in battle array for the day that was going to be so filled with perplexities.

She had scarcely had time to change into a clean white dimity morning dress, and to smooth her hair, when the telephone rang. With a troubled frown she hastened to answer it. Would that be Hattie? Or Aunt Blanche?

But it was neither. Instead it was a man's voice, young, friendly, courteous.

"Good morning!" it said. "You are Miss Huntley, aren't you? I thought I recognized your voice. This is David Kenyon. I wanted to thank you again for letting me in on that wonderful service yesterday, and to ask if you are all right after the hard strain you must have had." There was such genuine friendliness in the words that just hearing his voice comforted her. He was almost a stranger of course, but somehow she felt a kinship with him. He seemed to have such an understanding of the things she had been brought up to believe.

"Oh, David Kenyon! How kind of you to call," she said in a truly welcoming voice. "This will make my day seem more friendly and pleasant. And I certainly think it was wonderful of you to go out of your way when you were on leave, and come to a funeral of someone you did not know, when you might have been enjoying yourself somewhere."

"You forget," said David Kenyon, "that you were very kind and friendly to me the last time I came to town, and I was an utter stranger to you. But now I sort of feel as if we are friends, that is if you don't mind."

"*Mind!*" said Dale happily. "Why, I'm delighted that you feel that way. And of course I'm glad to have you for a friend. Only I'm just sorry that I had to be so busy while you were here, and we had no chance to talk. But then I felt you understood."

"Of course I understood. And I was glad that you took me right into your household that way and let me be a part of things as if I had known you always. I liked that part the best. You know I haven't anyone who really belongs to me on this earth any more, that is not around here, anyway, and it was nice to get that home feeling. You see I took a great liking to you that first night I met you, and I felt I'd like to know you better. You were somehow *different* from so many of the girls I met. And I'm partly calling up now to ask you whether, in case there *is* another opportunity for me to come up to your city, you would mind if I came again to see you? I'll be going back overseas pretty soon I suppose, and I'd like to have another pleasant memory to take along with me. Do you mind if I come?"

"Mind?" said Dale again, almost breathlessly, her heart giving a little pleasant twirl, and the color dancing up into her cheeks. "Why I would just be *delighted* to see you. When can you come?"

"I don't know yet. It may not be possible at all, but if it is I'll call up and find out if it is convenient for you."

"I'll certainly *make* it convenient," said Dale joyously. "It will be something nice to look forward to. I've got a hard few days ahead of me just now, relative-guests, business to talk over and settle, some unpleasantness to face perhaps, and this will be a pleasant something to think about and look forward to in the intervals, something to be glad about."

The voice at the other end of the wire was warm and glad.

"That's nice," he said. "You've made me feel as if I would really be welcome. I shall look forward to it myself and only hope I may not be disappointed about being allowed to come. Now I won't take any more of your time.

If you have guests you are busy I know. I'll hang up now, but I'll be ringing you up pretty soon perhaps. Good-by."

She turned away from the telephone with a smile on her lips and a sudden joy in her heart. She wondered why a little thing like this should make her so exceeding glad.

Then the doorbell pealed unrighteously through the house, as if manipulated by a cross impatient soul, and she hurried to the door. She hadn't had time before to open it. This would be her guests of course.

She swung the door open and summoned the smile which she had been schooling herself all the morning to be ready to give.

But there was no answering good morning.

"Doesn't your royal princess of a maid ever sweep the front porch?" snapped Aunt Blanche. "Usually maids are very careful about front porches and sidewalks, and yours looks *scanda*lous."

"Yes?" said Dale trying to keep her cheerful manner. "It does need attention. But I just haven't been able to get to it yet. I'm afraid I overslept."

"Well," said the aunt hatefully. "I should think Hattie was the one to do that. You better send her out right away. It looks terrible here for the lawyers, and the purchaser, when they come."

"Sorry," said Dale summoning her strength, "I'll do the best I can. But I've been concentrating on getting some breakfast ready for you before the lawyers arrive. I'll get out to the sidewalk as soon as you sit down. The breakfast is all ready but the eggs. Will you come right in?"

"Why of course! That's what we came over for. I'm half starved. You must remember that we had no dinner to speak of last night. But why should *you* have to go out and sweep the porch? That doesn't look at all well to the neighbors the day after a funeral. Send Hattie. Lazy thing! She ought to have done it without telling."

"Hattie is not here," said Dale quietly.

"Not back yet? Well, the idea! I should think she was taking advantage of you. You better let me get after her, I'll soon whip her into shape. But meantime, you'll certainly have to get someone else for the time being, and if she turns out to be better than Hattie, you better dismiss Hattie and keep the new one."

Dale took another deep breath and tried to steady her voice.

"I'm sorry, Aunt Blanche. You just don't understand. Hattie is like a part of our family. I couldn't think of dismissing her. And of course *I'll* do anything in her place that has to be done until she gets back. She is having trouble herself, and has always stood by me when I was in trouble. She'll be back as soon as she possibly can come. I'm sure of that."

"Yes? You're very sure! But remember you are young. You haven't learned yet that servants are *never* dependable. They *pretend* to think a lot of you, but then when the stress comes they take time off and go and visit with their friends. You take my advice and get somebody else."

Dale gave a half smile.

"There wouldn't be anybody else to get," she said gently. "They've all gone into defense work. And anyway, your breakfast is getting cold. Won't you all come right in and eat?"

"Who said eat?" said Powelton noisily. "I'm starved and that's a fact! I hope you have beefsteak and hot cakes. I remember we used to have those when we came to see Gramma."

But Dale led the way quietly to the dining room and made no reply. She motioned to the table and went on toward the kitchen door.

"Sit down and I'll bring the cereal and eggs," she said sweetly, and vanished into the kitchen.

"I don't want eggs!" complained Corliss, shouting after her. "I just *hate* eggs. I prefer bacon, or creamed beef." But

Dale went on to take up the cereal and paid no further attention. Let her mother deal with Corliss. She had enough to do to keep other things going.

Presently she brought in the cereal and a large dish of golden scrambled eggs, piping hot and very tempting looking, and then she hurried out of the room and upstairs, as Corliss continued to wail that she didn't like eggs. What was she going to do if this kept on many days? Just ignore it, and provide what she could, and let it go at that? Well, what else could she do? And she must not carry this matter as a burden during the day either. She would just do the best she could, and then take what came of blame or faultfinding. They didn't need to stay if they didn't like it. And she wouldn't go and complain to her Heavenly Father, either. After all He had allowed these things to come into her life and He must have some good reason for it.

The doorbell interrupted her thoughts, and she glanced out of the window. Could that be Mr. Granniss already? He was ahead of the time he had said he would come. Ten minutes. That wasn't usual with him for he was a busy man. He must have something to say to her before he was ready to read the will.

She hurried downstairs and there stood her lawyer-friend.

5

"AM I too early, Dale?" he said apologetically. "There are a few questions I want to ask you. Have you a copy of the last interview we had with your grandmother?"

"Oh yes," said Dale, and turning swiftly closed the dining room door where the relatives were all agog listening for all they were worth. Dale led the lawyer into the living room and closed that door opening into the hall, which maneuver definitely hastened the tempo of the breakfast that was being eaten to the last crumb.

Aunt Blanche wasn't long in appearing, and when she found the door to the living room closed she promptly turned the knob and came in, gazed at the strange man sitting by the table leafing over a pile of papers, and then said sharply:

"Oh, excuse me! Have I interrupted a conference?"

The lawyer looked up and Dale arose and came forward:

"It's all right. Come right in. We were just about through. Aunt Blanche, this is Mr. Granniss, my former guardian and now my lawyer. This is my aunt, Mrs. Huntley, Mr. Granniss."

The lawyer arose and bowed courteously, glancing at the lady with a keen appraising look, which caused Mrs. Huntley to draw her shoulders up and stick her chin out assertively. She was not accustomed to having anyone look at her with question in their eyes, as if she might not really be all that she asserted herself to be. So in turn Aunt Blanche put more haughtiness into her own glance, a look that almost *dared* the lawyer to differ from her.

"Won't you sit down, Mrs. Huntley?" he said courteously, and brought forward a chair for her.

The lady sat down as if she were doing him a favor and kept her belligerence in evidence.

"Just how long have you been associated with my niece?" she asked arrogantly.

The lawyer did not smile. He answered in clear clipped tones.

"Well, practically ever since she was born," he said coolly. "Her father and I were intimate friends before he was married. Then after her mother died, and her father found it necessary to go abroad on confidential business for the government, he asked me to take over for him."

"Really! I never heard that my brother-in-law was connected with government work. Are you quite *sure* of that?"

Mr. Granniss looked at her with lifted eyebrows.

"I beg your pardon," he said. "It is a matter of record. If you want that verified you might write to Washington. I'll give you the address," and he took out his fountain pen and wrote an address on a small pad he took from his pocket, and tearing off the page handed it to the lady. "Of course the matter was not generally known, as it was confidential business," he added, "but I supposed his own family would be likely to know the fact. However, I suppose you may not have been interested in the matter at the time, and Mr. Huntley was not one who blazoned abroad matters of business."

Aunt Blanche was a bit taken aback by the calmness of the lawyer's statements. She had expected *him* to be awed by *her* cold manner. She was not by nature very well versed in matters of business, and was not capable of doing much logical thinking for herself. But she had always depended upon this haughty manner and her sharp tongue to overawe people in any matter of business with which she had to deal. It had been her experience that if most men were treated in her peculiar style that they would give in on any point they considered "minor" rather than to continue to deal with her longer.

But Mr. Granniss was not one of the superficial kind of businessmen, and he was not overawed by her.

"And now, Mrs. Huntley," went on the lawyer, "are we ready to read the will? Are your children here? Should we call them?" He looked toward Dale.

"Yes, yes," said Aunt Blanche rising hastily, morally certain that Powelton would never answer a summons unless she brought pressure to bear upon him. She cast a quick triumphant look toward Dale as she went out. Perhaps after all this lawyer was going to have sense enough to realize that she knew what she was talking about. The will? Yes. She had been exceedingly anxious to hear that will read. She hadn't been quite sure whether there really was a will or not, until now.

She came back into the room with a firm hand on an arm of each of her offspring, and ushered them to chairs near her own.

"Now," she said, "we're ready. And kindly get at it as quickly as possible. I have callers coming, and my own lawyer will be here soon."

Mr. Granniss looked at her with surprise, but he did not hasten with the business.

"I think there is one more to come, isn't there, Dale? Hattie Brown? Isn't that her name? Your grandmother's old servant?"

"Why the *idea!* What on earth would a *servant* have to be here for?" snapped Aunt Blanche. "I insist that you don't wait any longer. I have important business that cannot be delayed."

"I am sorry, Mrs. Huntley," said the lawyer, "but I would prefer that the servant be called. Dale, will you call Hattie Brown?"

Dale arose anxiously, about to explain that Hattie had been called away by her sister's illness, but suddenly a shadow darkened the doorway.

"I'se right here, Mr. Granniss," said Hattie comfortably as she slung off her hat and sat down in the chair by the door.

"But I don't understand!" said Aunt Blanche indignantly. "Why should a mere servant be present?"

But Mr. Granniss' calm voice rose above the indignant scream of the aunt. He went right on with the business in hand, ignoring the visiting aunt with a dignity that made Dale admire him even more than she had learned to admire and trust him during the years. An instant more, and the solemn phrases of the law broke upon their unaccustomed ears, till everybody, even the aunt, hushed down.

The reading of the will did not take long. The entire amount of the grandmother's estate was only a very few thousands. Of that she had left a thousand apiece to each of her three grandchildren, Corliss, Powelton and Dale. At that the aunt looked sharply, suspiciously at Dale, as if Dale had had something to do with this. As if she did not believe that was all Dale had got. As if she felt there was some crookedness about it somewhere and her children were being cheated out of their just rights. But she sat back with pursed lips and listened for the rest. But there wasn't much rest at all. Just a gift of five hundred dollars to the old servant Hattie, a few smaller bequests to the man who had worked in the garden, and other people who had served her in various lesser capacities, and then the lawyer folded the paper and said quietly, "And that is all."

Aunt Blanche sat up with a snap:

"Why! *Why!* I don't understand. You haven't mentioned the house."

"The house?" said the lawyer with raised eyebrows, "What house?"

"Why, *this* house. Wasn't that mentioned in the will?"

"Oh no," said the lawyer. "Why should it be? Mrs. Huntley never owned this house. She was only given a life residence in it, the privilege of living here all her life."

"But I'm sure you are mistaken!" snapped Aunt Blanche. "I am quite sure my late husband purchased this house, or at least helped *largely* to purchase it for his mother's residence during her lifetime. I was given to understand that it would come to us as next in line. I am quite sure there must be papers somewhere to that effect. Unless—of course—they have purposely been *destroyed*. But in that case, of course, there'll be some way to prove that, and to find out the criminal."

"I do not understand you, madam," said Randall Granniss with that stern authoritative manner that had won so many cases for him before famous judges of the past. And before that look even Aunt Blanche stopped astonished, startled, and her belligerence oozed out of her like gas out of a balloon.

"Well, I wasn't of course making my remarks personal. I am simply saying that if there *has* been any crooked work going on, of course *you* would be able to detect it and trace it to its source."

Mr. Granniss' steely glance became no less severe, and his voice lost its soft geniality as he answered her:

"My dear madam," he said, "there has been no crooked work in connection with anything about this house. It was bought the year that Dale's mother and father were married, the down payment was made by Dale's father, Theodore Huntley, and I myself negotiated the sale for him. His endorsed check, endorsed also by the Trust Company that was in charge of the house for the estate of M. J. Eaton the former owner, is now in the bank, in the safe-deposit box belonging to Dale Huntley, and can be examined by you at any time that you would care to come down to the bank with me. Your husband, Harold Huntley's name, does not appear anywhere in connection with this sale, and there were no checks from anyone else but Theodore Huntley in payment for this property. I have some of the original papers here with me, and if you or your lawyer would care to look further into the matter I can arrange for a meeting at the bank where you can see them. I have with me, however, the bill of sale, and several other documents, that ought to be sufficient proof to you of the truth of what I have said. Moreover, Madam, as I understand it, your marriage did not take place until after Theodore Huntley had gone abroad, for I remember he was unable to attend the ceremony because his business was very insistent, and that was two years after this property was purchased. I have here on this paper the dates relative to the matter, and shall be glad to have you examine them at your leisure. You will note that the clause concerning Dale's ownership and her grandmother's life-occupation of the house was not added until five years later, at the time of the death of Mr. Huntley's wife, when he returned to this country to make arrangements to leave his young daughter with his mother. Those are the facts, madam, and I shall be glad to substantiate any of them that you do not understand. Also if you wish to go to the city hall and look into the records of property owners, you will find that the house is now listed under the ownership of Miss Dale Huntley."

Mrs. Huntley gave a startled, almost frightened look, that merged quickly into a firm determined one as she heard footsteps coming upon the porch, and realized that it must be her own lawyer.

Then the doorbell pealed through the house and they

could hear Hattie coming to answer it. Dale sat quite still and quietly watched each person in the room as the other lawyer entered. The tense strained expression on her aunt's face, the amused grin on Powelton's disagreeable mug, the bored contempt of Corliss, and the quiet assurance of Mr. Granniss. He was not worrying about what was going to happen, because he had the facts and proofs against all the trifling claims of the pretenders.

In fact it seemed utterly absurd to Mr. Grannis that any sane woman would try to put over such an unfounded claim. He had told Dale that she need not worry.

And as for the lawyer Aunt Blanche had secured, Mr. Granniss had said that he was so notorious that he was not to be taken seriously. He was a big bluff who had a way of deceiving gullible women, and outtalking any serious questioners. Dale knew Mr. Granniss felt it would be a bore, but for Dale's sake he must listen to it, and then when it was over bring forward some convincing proof that he had with him, which would upset all the other man was planning to do. Mr. Granniss was a conscientious lawyer who went clearly to the bottom of things and left no room for clever roundabout ways.

It was at this stage of affairs that Powelton decided to take a hand in affairs:

"Oh heck!" he said yawning audibly. "I can't be bothered with all this bologny! I'm gonta beat it! See you later, mom!" and Powelton vanished with a slammed door behind him.

And next, Corliss began to wiggle and writhe and sigh audibly, and finally changed her seat until she was close to the French window that opened on the porch. It wasn't long before Corliss too was absent from the family group, though nobody but Dale actually saw her edge behind the curtain and depart.

There followed a tiresome rehash of what had gone before, listening to pompous questions asked by the newly-arrived lawyer, and Mr. Granniss' quiet brief answers. Finally Greenway Buffington arose and clearing his throat ominously said:

"Mrs. Huntley, it will be impossible for me to give you an adequate idea of what can be done in this matter until I have opportunity to go down to the city hall and verify some of these statements that have been made. Would you like to come with me now? I think we would have time to look into this before the lunch hour."

"Certainly," said Aunt Blanche rising triumphantly, and looking about at her two adversaries, as if she was already assured of the rights she had been claiming.

Aunt Blanche was not long in getting ready, and meantime her lawyer sat in imposing silence while Dale and Mr. Granniss talked in low tones about the service of the day before, and who were the singer and speakers. Nothing whatever that could possibly be connected with the matter of the property. After they were gone Dale drew a long breath.

"I'm glad that session is over. Do you think that lawyer can do anything?" she asked with a troubled look.

Mr. Granniss looked at her and smiled.

"Not possibly," he assured her pleasantly, "except to charge her a big fee, perhaps. He will probably string the matter out as long as he dares before giving her the final word that he can do nothing. Of course the property is yours entirely, and her husband never had anything to do with it. Buffington might demand some papers from her and possibly send her home to look for them, or perhaps find some way to get some papers forged, but you need not worry. Your property is as safe as property could ever be, and in the end your aunt will find that out to her sorrow I'm afraid, for Buffington has the name of never doing anything for nothing. Is your aunt intending to leave soon?"

"Oh, I don't know," said Dale with a weary smile. "She hasn't said anything about it yet. If her lawyer detains her with any hope she will probably stay indefinitely, and it just seems as if I could not stand that."

"Of course not, child," said the lawyer comfortingly. "We'll try to contrive some way to get her interested in going home. Don't worry. We'll find a way. And now, what are you planning to do, little girl? I supposed you talked that over with the grandmother?"

"Oh yes. We planned it all out together. I'm going to stay right here in the house, and Hattie is going to stay with me. I'm thinking of looking after some little children while their mothers are working in war plants. Grandmother suggested that, and I know there are several mothers around here who are greatly troubled, because they cannot find the right place for their children while they are away. In fact one mother has already asked me to take her twins, and I'm sure I'll love such work. It will be sort of a school you know."

"Splendid!" said the lawyer. "And you should be able to get a good price for such work. You know the mothers have good wages where they are working."

"Yes, so I have heard. I'm glad you approve. Grandmother heard of this through a friend of hers who came to see her, and she thought it would be a lovely way to use my home. At least for a time."

"Fine!" said the lawyer. "Are you planning to start right away?"

"I'd like to," said Dale with a troubled look, "but I can't really do anything about it while my relatives are here. In fact I wouldn't want them to know about it. They would try to talk me out of it. My aunt would like me to go home with her and do housework for my living."

"Housework! *You?* Absurd. They'd better go home and do their own work. Better hurry them off."

"I don't know how I can hurry them. I can't just *ask* them to go, can I? I don't want to be rude. Grandmother wouldn't want me to do that."

"No," said the lawyer thoughtfully, "but there might be other ways. I'll think about that. I might be able to find a way to get them started sooner. We'll see. Perhaps the result of today's investigation may be sufficient to make them see that they have got all the financial assistance they can get out of this episode. Suppose you let me know if there is any change in the status of things when your aunt returns. Better phone me from the drugstore, then there'll be no danger of your being overheard."

"Yes, of course," said Dale. "Thank you so much for your advice. It makes me feel so much safer."

"Has this aunt always been so unpleasant in her ways of talking?" asked Mr. Granniss.

"I've never had much to do with her. She came on to visit when Corliss was about five, and we had a terrible two weeks while she stayed. Then she and Grandmother had a talk and she went away in a huff, and it's been a long time since we heard from her until about three months ago when she wrote a very sweet letter, and wanted to come on for a visit. Said she heard that Grandmother wasn't so well and she got to worrying that her children didn't know her better. Grandmother didn't answer that for a long time, but finally she wrote a nice little note and said she wasn't in any shape at that time to have company, but she would send word later. That was when she told me to write the letter about her death and have it ready to send as soon as it happened, putting in the date and time of the funeral. That was why she insisted that they should be notified. For Grandmother was always courteous, although you know she had an odd sense of humor at times. She felt that she must make up for not having them visit her at the time they had asked, by inviting them to her funeral. She knew they would be interested in the will, and she had that quaint little grin when she said it. But you don't know how I have dreaded this visitation. In fact, Grandmother gave me reason to dread it in little bits of warnings. That is why I am so glad to have you here now, and why I am depending so much upon your advice."

"Poor child!" said the lawyer. "Don't worry. I'll see you through this. We'll wait till your aunt gets back from her investigations. Then we'll devise a pleasant way to get her out of the picture so you can go on with your plans. Now, I'll run down to my office for a little while and I'll be there when you get ready to phone me."

"But won't you stay to lunch? I'm sure Hattie will be glad to hurry it up so you won't lose any time."

"No, child, no. I'll get right down to the office and have a tray sent in. I often do that, you know. It saves a lot of time, and while I do always appreciate Hattie's cooking, I think this way is better for today. Tell Hattie I said so. Remember you may have your guests all here to feed in a little while, and they may even bring the other lawyer along with them again, too. But if they do, you send Hattie to the store to phone me, and I'll come up at once."

"Oh, thank you, Mr. Granniss," said Dale, her eyes full of grateful tears. "I shall never forget all that you have done for me all the years, and especially today, for I have been so tried and so disheartened."

The old friend looked at the pretty girl tenderly and patted her shoulder.

"There, there, Dale, child! Don't get that way. Don't you know your grandmother's Lord always provides some one to look after His dear children when they are tried and in need? And this time He just chose me to look after you. Now get you upstairs to your room and lie down for at least a few minutes. You certainly look all in, and you need to relax a little before the next stage will begin. So, go rest, and don't worry. Trust me, and the Lord!" he ended reverently, as he took his leave.

Dale hurried down to the kitchen and had a little talk with Hattie, who also implored her to rest. Hattie promised to get a good substantial lunch that could be served whenever the erratic guests should choose to arrive, and to make enough for Mr. Buffington too if he came back. So Dale did go and lie down with closed eyes for at least five minutes trying to pray her way through to quietness and peace. And she succeeded so well that there came a little gleam of brightness to her face. Then she remembered David Kenyon's possible coming sometime in the near future. Oh, she hoped so much that if he did come, her aunt and cousins would be gone by that time. She couldn't bear the thought of having this bit of pleasantness spoiled by their presence, for she knew just how Corliss would behave.

"Please find a way for them to go home, dear Lord, before he comes," she prayed softly in her heart.

And then there came the sound of feet flying up the front walk, stamping into the house, and Corliss' clarion voice calling loudly:

"Dale! Oh Dale! Have you got any tennis rackets? We want to play tennis. We've found a tennis court that's not in use, and we want some balls and rackets."

Dale arose with a weary little sigh. She must answer. Of course tennis was a harmless amusement. It would be a good thing if those two could get interested in something absorbing. Yes, she had a couple of rackets that she and a dear school friend, now married and gone to Africa as a missionary, used to have when they were for a year together in school. She hadn't played herself since her friend left. There hadn't been opportunity, for she had come home to stay with her grandmother who was beginning to be very feeble. But she had kept the rackets and balls, and put them away as carefully as keepsakes of her girlhood, which she recognized was about over so far as games were concerned. She hated to give them up as they were precious for old times' sake, but she didn't need those rackets, would probably never use them again. Was that right? Why should she hang on to them, when she would likely never have any use for them? Why not let these unlovely cousins get a little fun out of them? This was what Grandmother and God would likely want her to do.

"Yes," she answered pleasantly. "Yes, I have a couple of rackets. It's been some time since I had a chance to use them, but I'm sure they are in good condition. I oiled them before I put them away. I'll get them."

"Well, make it snappy! We wantta get back before anybody else snitches the court."

Dale was back in a moment, unwinding the soft tissue paper wrapping as she came down the stairs. But Corliss did not wait for her to get down. She sprang up the stairs and snatched the rackets from her, casting the wrappings in a heap on the stairs, and almost tripping herself as she tore out the door and away waving the rackets in the air, whacking the furniture and the doorframe as she passed.

"You'll be careful of them, won't you, please?" Dale called after her as she went.

"Okay, I'll be careful of the old relics," she jeered. "They don't look like they'd be able to play more'n a set or two without passing out! About the model they made before the ark, aren't they?" She yelled all this up the street at her, and several elderly women came to their front doors to look out and see what it was all about. Dale felt sure they turned away pitying her for having such ill-mannered guests.

Dale sighed and turned back into the house, almost regretting that she had loaned her precious rackets. Yet how silly that was. What difference did it make if they did spoil her rackets? It was just sentiment and that of course was silly.

So Dale put aside that burden as unworthy of her, and thought no more about it until after dinner that night when her cousin said carelessly in answer to her query of how the game went: "Oh, gee! I forgot to go back for the rackets. But it won't make any difference. They're neither of them fit to use again. They're both broken!"

In spite of herself Dale's quick indignation arose.

"Where did you leave the rackets?" she asked sternly.

"Oh, up around behind the bushes over at the end of the tennis court."

"Come with me and show me," she said authoritatively, but Corliss only laughed.

"It won't do any good to go after them. Some kids were having a fight with them when I left. They won't be any use now."

Dale gave her a withering glance and turning went out the door and down the flagging to the street, walking with swift steps toward the country club, and the banks of tennis courts that crowned the rise of the winding drive off to the left. Could she find her rackets? Well, she would try. But at least she would walk until she had her temper under control.

She went swiftly down the street and turned into the highway that led up to the country club. On, on, up the smooth wide road, up the hill, up the drive that swept about in front of the country club, around to the courts, on beyond the high stop nets at the end where the shrubs and bushes grew, down to the edge of the little winding brook that went with soft steps and glittering blue like a lovely ribbon, making pictures of itself in every nook and corner where it twinkled.

She stood for a moment letting her eyes follow the bright water down the hill, the soft sky above with white fluffy clouds floating lazily. How lovely and sweet this scene was, and how far from the ill-natured struggle of the day that had done so much to her tired nerves. She took a deep breath and let the scene creep into her senses, storing up the beauty. Just as she had so often done to carry the picture of the outside world to Grandmother.

She sighed as she turned away and thought sadly that now she had no one left to describe such things to, for she couldn't think of going home and trying to tell Aunt Blanche about the scene. Why even Hattie would be more appreciative of such talk than her relatives. She could hear her two cousins shouting with sneering laughter if she attempted any such conversation. Then her thoughts went to her new service-friend, David Kenyon. Yes, she could think of telling him about this scene. Perhaps when she met him again she would remember to tell him. But that would be foolish too, describing a scene in her local vicinity, to him a stranger. He had probably seen a lot more interesting ones. But it was lovely, and the sight of it had calmed her spirit, so that she could go back and meet her casual cousin without frowning at her, she hoped.

Then she turned to go back home again and there at her feet she saw the rackets, lying in a heap just under the edge of a great bush that reached out over the brook. And the strings were gleaming wet as if they had been plunged into the water. Some of the strings were badly broken.

She took them up, wiped the water away with her handkerchief, and tucking them under her arm went swiftly home; entering the house by the back way where she would not be seen; going upstairs, and hiding away the rackets in her own room.

Then she heard voices in the living room, a strange voice, and a loud voice. Smoothing her hair, and washing her hands she hurried down to find out what had been happening during her absence.

6

AS Dale came downstairs she could hear the pompous voice of Greenway Buffington boasting, as he stood up by the front door, in the act of departing.

"Now you don't need to worry any more, Mrs. Huntley. I'm quite sure we'll come on some definite evidence in a day or two. And if you can find those letters you spoke of, that would certainly clinch the matter. You might try long distance to your banker and have him look in your safety-deposit box. He'll have a key of course, and then he can send the letters on by air mail, and it won't take over a week to work this thing out. I'm confident I can get the judge to arrange it to come on the docket soon, and get the whole matter settled up in no time. And now, thank you for this retainer. Of course I'm accustomed to getting at least twice that for a retainer, but since it is you, and since you bring a recommendation from my friend in Chicago, why we'll call it all right for the present. And of course when you get home and your regular check comes in, you can send me on the rest. Well, good evening, Mrs. Huntley. You do that telephoning, and let me know the result. Good night." The door closed at last on the obnoxious lawyer, while Dale stood desperately on the stairs and tried to realize that there were perhaps days and days ahead of her filled with all sorts of incalculable discomforts. "Oh God, help me, all the way through," her heart prayed, as she tried to gather up her courage and go forward. "Oh, if they will only *go* before David comes," she thought to herself. And then her cheeks grew hot in the darkness of the dining room. She was thinking of him as David now. And he was coming again to see her, if only the government didn't send him away before he had opportunity to come. Well, she would have to take it all as it came of course, and surely her God could bring all things to work together for good for her, and for the rightness of everything.

To Dale's relief Hattie rang the bell for the evening meal, and they all trooped into the dining room. Dale slipped into the kitchen for a hurried whispered conference with Hattie.

The lunch had been a sketchy affair, partaken of by Powelton and Corliss while Dale was out hunting her rackets.

They were seated at the table with an air of annoyance that there was any delay in the service, when Dale came in, and they kept up a conversation among themselves, scarcely speaking to Dale except to ask her to pass the butter or order more ice water, or coffee. And once her aunt told her that she really ought to speak to Hattie about putting so little shortening in her pie crust. "It's really quite tough, you know, Dale," she said, making a great show of having to work hard to cut the crust of the delicious apple pie with which she had just been served.

But Dale smiled good naturedly.

"We're having a war, you know," she said gently. "We can't get as much fat as we might like to use."

"A good cook can make tender crust without so much shortening," said the aunt in a superior tone. "Why doesn't she use cream if she can't get lard?"

"We can't get cream," smiled Dale. "Won't you have another cup of coffee, Aunt Blanche?"

"You always have an impertinent answer ready, don't you?" said the aunt as she passed her cup for more coffee. "Well, the time is coming fast when you will sing another tune. I've found out a good many things this afternoon that will make you open your eyes in astonishment." She flung this out as she arose from the table, then she went into the living room and took up the evening paper.

Corliss and Powelton soon sauntered off to a movie, and Dale was free for a little while. Then she was called to the telephone. It was Mr. Granniss.

"Is that you, Dale?" Her voice was low, and could not be heard in the living room she was sure.

"Yes. This is Miss Huntley," she answered pleasantly in accordance with his instructions.

"Is there anyone near by to listen?"

"Possibly," she said composedly.

"All right. Just answer yes or no, or very briefly. Has anything important developed?"

"No."

"Are you worried?"

"A little."

"Well, it isn't necessary, everything is going to be all right. Forget it all and get a good night's rest. I'll be out in the morning."

"Thank you."

"Good night."

"Good night."

It was a simple conversation but somehow it lifted a load of worry from Dale's heart, and quietly she slipped from the telephone and went to the kitchen to help Hattie with the dishes and plan for the problematic morrow. Meantime she was wondering just what her aunt was planning for the night. So far the guests had taken possession of the house pretty thoroughly for whatever purposes they chose, without any by-your-leave, except at night, and so Dale was left in doubt, but she did not intend to ask any questions. This visitation would likely be at an end *some*time, and she wanted if possible to have no twinges of conscience lest she had not acted with perfect courtesy.

But there was no use in hoping that there would be any settlement of this question until the cousins came back from the movies, so she took a bit of sewing, and a book in which she was interested and went in to the living room. She would endeavor to be sociable if her aunt was so inclined, but if not then she could read.

Mrs. Huntley seemed to be doing thorough work of the evening paper, for she read on and on, studying every page as if she were deeply interested in it, and Dale sat there with her book, trying to concentrate on it, and yet continually wondering what her aunt had been doing downtown all that day.

But at last the cousins came storming up on the porch, and without further ado, and very few words, the guests took themselves away to the hotel, saying with an air of condescension that they would be back in the morning for breakfast; and rather demanding that it be an early one as their lawyer was coming again.

Then Dale, with a deep sigh of relief, locked the house and went to bed, after this long long day. But as she was drifting off to sleep her thoughts went happily to the telephone message from that officer this morning. She found herself wondering about it. Why had he taken the trouble to call her? He must have plenty of friends in camp, plenty of people who would invite him to spend a day, or a weekend, and yet he had chosen to call her. That was wonderful. Of course they had had a very pleasant hour together that first time she found him sitting alone at the U.S.O., reading a much thumbed newspaper. She had made hot tea for him and found some doughnuts, and then he had come out to the kitchen and helped her wipe dishes. She had been taking the place of three women who all had good reasons to be absent from the center that night, and it was getting late. Most of the fellows had gone away. He alone had been left. Why? Didn't he care to go to the places they chose? Or was he not feeling well? She hadn't bothered to ask him. He had just said he was a bit tired. But not too tired to wipe dishes. That was queer. Well, she had decided he was homesick and wanted to talk to some woman, so he had smiled at her and wiped dishes. They had had a nice little talk and he had walked home with her when she closed up for the night and left. Just being kind. It was nice of him. And the reason he came to the funeral, and brought the flowers? He was sort of doing that for the sake of his own grandmother whose funeral he had not known of overseas even in time to send flowers.

That the young man came because he was attracted to her never entered her head. Dale wasn't a girl who was self-centered. She had grown up in a healthy atmosphere, never realizing that she had a beautiful face and an unusually lovely expression. Never dreaming of great things that might come to her. Thinking only of love in the abstract, as a miracle that might come to anyone sometime, but not planning to go out and get it for herself. There was too much to be done for others in this world to leave much time for thoughts of self. And she had been so quiet and shy in school, and what college she had had, that she had not made many boy friends. She was just good friends with all who came her way. She didn't wear lipstick, nor paint her fingernails, nor get herself up in the latest fad of fashion to make people look at her. She was just a healthy happy girl, doing her duty as far as she knew it, and enjoying the doing of it. So, though the telephone message from the young officer that morning had pleased her mightily, and set her heart thrilling pleasantly, she did not immediately go to planning to marry him, or do anything about it except to be a pleasant friend to him, in the last hours before he should go forth to navy duty again, and perhaps to meet death. He knew the Lord. She was glad of that. They could talk more understandingly together because of that fact. And it was nice to have this pleasant prospect of meeting him in the offing to take her mind from the unpleasant memories of the day, and the threatening prospect of the morrow.

Meantime, a few miles away in the base the young officer was staring up at the moon that shone through a window of the barracks, and thinking of the immediate future and what it likely held for him. He had finished his quota of missions and been duly decorated for them. He was proud of his work in the past. He would like to go back and fight some more, but from what the commanding officer had said to him briefly the day before, he had reason to believe that something else was being shaped up for him. He didn't yet know what it was, but he didn't want changes. There was emptiness and desolation enough in his life already, and he didn't like the idea of a new background, new companions, new duties. Oh, doubtless they were honors, but somehow he had lost heart. His last two months in the hospital recovering from the raids in which he had participated prominently and now this trip home had filled him with a great desire to get back to that fighting line, and help get this war over. What he wanted was for the world to return to the old life which he had known and enjoyed before he went to war. He wanted a home and a real life. He wanted some friends, a family perhaps, a place to come home to at night and someone to welcome him. But of course that could not be until this war was over, so he was impatient to get into the active part of the fighting again and be responsible for definitely wiping out as many of the enemy as possible. They need not think they could put him on any office job and count that his due. If they tried that he would definitely protest. Such jobs might be all right for fellows who were really sick, who loathed the thought of battle, but he somehow knew that battle was his place until all this was over. He could never be content to settle down and do office work, important as that might be to the whole effort, while there was a job requiring courage and a willingness to face peril. That was what he would ask for if they let him have any choice.

But of course they might not. And he must not dwell on this. Tomorrow morning he was to meet his commanding officer and hear more about this, and he must be ready to yield his wishes to what was ordered. But if there was any chance to choose, he certainly would choose to go back and help get this job done quickly, this job of setting the world free for peace and quietness.

So he told the moon, as he turned over and sought to go to sleep.

Then came that girl's face, the face that had attracted him so much when he had first seen it, a clean, happy, peaceful face, lovely in something above the look he saw in most other girls' faces, a face without "illumination" as he jocosely called make-up. A face that had an inner illumination coming from a beautiful soul. Or would it be a beautiful spirit? A lovely inner life. That was it.

He had known from his first vision of her that it was such a girl he would like to know; and make her a part of his own life sometime when he should return to the world, if such a time was really to come for him.

So he lay now and watched her face in memory as he reviewed the few little times of contact he had had with her. Every one of them fitted. He could see her now as they had stood beside her grandmother's casket while she arranged his lilies in the white hands. There was no despair in her eyes, only a glad look as if she were preparing a loved one to go to some great festive occasion. Not getting her ready to lie in the ground. Not bidding her farewell

ever. There had been hope and trust in her eyes, in the
: of her lovely lips, and as he thought about it, his own
.ope and trust for a life hereafter seemed to strengthen.

He thought of the few minutes of hurried talk they had
had at her desk while he wrote his address for her, and the
way his hand had touched hers as she gave him the pen. It
thrilled him now to think of it. And how her voice had
sounded over the wire tonight when she recognized him,
and seemed glad. The thought of that thrilled him too.

But this was no way for a man to feel when he was going
into the thick of battle again perhaps. He should not wish a
love and a sorrow together like that on any light-hearted
girl. Had he been wrong to call her and ask for himself
these few hours of joy before he went?

There it was again! That uncertainty. He didn't even
know yet that he was going, or that going, his would be a
time of peril. He didn't know a thing about it. Suppose on
the other hand they should want him to stay here and do
something important? Suppose there was a chance he
might love and marry and have a home with a girl like
Dale? How his heart thrilled to even think of it. And yet—
and yet—. He simply must not bank on anything like this.
For if that came he knew in his heart that his inner soul
would not be satisfied unless he went out first with the rest
and faced the peril and the fire and won through. He simply must not let himself desire such home things now. He
must yield his life to God. For he had a God in whom he
believed and trusted. God had some plan for his life and it
had to be as God wanted it. That was what his inner soul
desired.

Then somehow peace came into his heart. The future
days were bringing changes. Perhaps all this problem
would be settled for him. Meantime, at least he had made
pretty sure that if he were permitted to stop over in the city
he had at least paved the way for meeting Dale again for a
little while and talking with her. And if he was able to call

her up and arrange for their meeting, wouldn't it be a
right to ask her to bring along a little snapshot of herself
that he might be able to look at her face sometimes when
he was far away again. Surely there would be no harm in
that, even if he decided that she didn't care about a friendship herself as much as he did. Surely she would not object
to having a fighter carry a snapshot of herself over the seas
with him, just in memory of the pleasant contacts they had
had. At least he would ask her, when and if he telephoned.

7

DALE awoke the next morning to the disturbing thought of planning menus for the day. The larder was getting low and she really ought to go down and order a lot of things. There would need to be vegetables of course. But everything was expensive now when one considered buying for four guests. She simply couldn't provide expensive fare if these relatives were going to stay indefinitely. If she only knew how long this was to go on! Well, perhaps she must just begin to cut down quietly on the food, and say nothing about it.

She hurried downstairs early and together she and Hattie went through the stores already on hand. They finally decided on oatmeal, toast, coffee and pears for breakfast. If the guests didn't like it, well, that was all she could do about it now. If she should go on serving fine meals she would presently be bankrupt, and they would just go on growling about her arrangements. So perhaps it was as well to do only what she could afford, and let the results be what they would. She would not apologize. She would treat her menus as if they were the best that anybody could desire. And what should she have for lunch? Perhaps some ettuce sandwiches and canned soup. If it did not please her boarders they could always go out and buy food not far away. She didn't want to seem mean, but she must not run over her budget. Perhaps they would understand without an argument. But she had little hope for that.

And what should she have for the main dish at dinner? She had no more red stamps with which to get meat. It would be two days more before others were released, and her guests had produced no ration books to help her out. Well, there was still a glass jar of tongue, and there were some lovely great flakes of codfish. What would Corliss say if they had creamed codfish for dinner that night? Well, she would try it. Of course it wouldn't be so good if Mr. Granniss had to stay to either meal. She didn't care about the lawyer Buffington. She felt almost guilty at the plans she was making. But then she knew she could depend on Hattie. Hattie would present codfish, or in fact anything, at its very best. It would be delicately flavored, delightfully attractive and appetizing, really almost interesting, on the table. There were apples, too. There could be applesauce and cookies for dessert.

Then Dale went up to her room and knelt down by her bed.

"Dear Lord, I'm doing the best I can. Is this right? Should I make some further sacrifice, sell something I want to keep, in order to buy something more expensive? If You want me to, please show me. If not, please give me courage to keep calm in the midst of any storm that arises. And please don't let us have trouble with the relatives, or about the property. Please make a way for them to go away soon."

This last sentence was like a young child's cry for help in utter despair. She went down again to meet the day with more assurance in her heart than she had felt when she awoke.

But the day did not enter smiling. At least the guest-part

of the day did not. It was almost as if the enemy understood how this child of God was beginning to rest and trust in her Heavenly Father's care, so he summoned all his wildest young demons to meet her and demolish all her defenses. They waltzed into the house along with the relatives and began to battle even before any good-mornings were said.

"I certainly hope you've got a good breakfast this morning," flung out Corliss as she slammed into the room. "I was just sick all day yesterday whenever I thought of those horrid eggs I had to eat!"

Dale tried to speak reassuringly, with a bright little wistful smile:

"No eggs today," she said. "They were all eaten up yesterday. I haven't had time to go to the store yet."

"Well, that's a good thing," said Corliss. "I don't see what eggs were made for anyway. If I had my way there never would be any."

"What would you do for floating island, and lemon meringue pies then?" smiled Dale.

"Oh, *those!* Well, I suppose it would be all right to have a few eggs for lemon meringue pie. I'm not so keen about floating island."

Dale did not go out to the dining room with them. She said she would run down to the store right away before so many others had to be waited on, as there were things they needed.

"Well, get some beefsteak," shouted Powelton.

"No, get roast beef. Prime ribs, you know," called Corliss.

"Sorry," said Dale pleasantly, "I can't get either of those. I haven't any more red ration stamps, and you can't get steak nor roasts without red stamps. We'll have to go easy on the butter, too. We have only a quarter of a pound left, and no more stamps will be released yet for two days."

"Why, that's ridiculous!" said Corliss. "I'll bet Hattie has been eating up the butter."

But Dale went on about her business, realizing that if she got out of hearing Corliss would stop talking and Hattie would not have to hear her. Poor Hattie! It was hard enough for her to keep her temper, without also being charged with eating the butter up. So Dale went on to do her shopping, hoping and praying that the breakfasters might get through without too much growling, and that Hattie would be able to carry on till her return.

But the relatives at the dining table were anything but happy. "No orange juice! Just three measly little pears!" said Corliss.

The aunt rang the bell and Hattie appeared in a leisurely manner.

"You've forgotten the orange juice," said the aunt sharply.

"There aren't any oranges," said Hattie grimly. "You'll have to make out with them pears."

"I just hate pears," said Corliss with her face all snarled up.

"Well," said the aunt, "you may bring the rest of the breakfast."

"That's all there is this morning," said Hattie, with a sort of a triumphant note in her voice, and a finality that appropriately preceded the closing of the kitchen door.

"Well, really!" said the aunt surveying the table with its neat and ample pile of toast in front of the glowing toaster where it would keep hot, the small neat portion of butter at each plate, and the glass dish of blackberry jam. "Well, what's the idea? It seems we are being put on rations. I should think it was time Dale took a little thought for running her house. She certainly can't expect that inefficient Hattie to do it all. And no cream either. That's all nonsense. They ought to take more milk then and skim the tops off all the bottles. And *oatmeal!* The idea! How could anybody possibly eat that old-fashioned stuff? And anyway without cream! Wait! I'll ring for some dry cereal. That would at least be tolerable."

But when Hattie finally decided to answer the summons she vouchsafed that all the dry cereal was finished, and that was one of the things Miss Dale had gone after.

"Well, then we'll wait till she returns. We can't possibly eat oatmeal, and certainly not without cream."

"She said she wouldn't be back in time. She said as how you were expecting some lawyer. Oatmeal ain't as bad! Even without cream. Some eats it with buttah! You better try it. It's pipin' hot, an' buttah tastes very good."

"I really couldn't endure the thought," said the lady. "Butter on oatmeal! I really think that I shall have to hunt a place to board while I am obliged to stay here on business. I wonder if you can tell me who in the neighborhood takes boarders? How about that house over across on the opposite corner? That large house with stone pillars. That looks like a pleasant place. Perhaps they could be persuaded to let us board there. You wouldn't know what they charge, would you?"

"What, that mansion over there? Not they. They's quality folks an' they'd drive you off the place ef you dared suggest such a thing. Why, they's an old family. No ma'am, there ain't anybody around these parts takes boarders. They's just private families, an' most of um's pretty well fixed for theirselves. You'd havta go down in the village ta get board. I believe there's a room or two over the drugstore an' the grocery, with mebbe a kitchenette where you could do light housekeepin', if you wanted that."

"*Mercy,* no!" said the aunt with disgust.

"I should say not!" said Corliss with contempt.

Hattie made good her retreat to the kitchen and left the unhappy breakfasters to finish everything edible within sight.

Mr. Granniss was on the front porch reading the paper when Dale got back to the house, and she drew a sigh of relief as she recognized him. Now, whatever happened, he would be there to answer her questions.

Mr. Buffington drove up in his limousine a few moments later and requested to see his client alone, so Dale ushered him into the living room and went back to talk to Mr. Grannis on the porch. But Mr. Buffington's voice was loud and penetrating, and most of his conversation came booming through the open windows, so they were well-informed about the position of the relatives before he left. The gist of the whole matter seemed to have resolved itself in lawyer Buffington's mind into the fact that there was so far nothing to prove that Mrs. Huntley's claims about the property had any foundation; and that unless she could go home at once, or at least telephone her lawyer, and get hold of letters showing that her dead husband had ever put money into the purchase of the house in question, he did not see how he could possibly undertake the case. Of course if she insisted he might undertake it, but the expense of the matter would be greater, and the retaining fee would be doubled.

Listening, Dale took heart of hope. Perhaps God was going to answer her prayer this way, but she must not think too much about it, nor get her plans made for their going away. There was no telling what her aunt would finally do.

It almost seemed as if Mr. Granniss had read her thoughts, for he began to talk about her plans for the little school she was thinking of starting, and suggested that it might be well to arrange a definite date for its opening and tell her aunt that she would need the house from that time on.

Then suddenly the talk in the living room ceased. The pompous lawyer came out and went away. With a few low-spoken words, promising to be ready to help in any need that might arise, Mr. Granniss also went away.

And now what ought she to do next? Would God show the way?

And then the future, as if in answer to her thoughts, began to open up before her.

Her aunt appeared in the doorway and looked out, saying coldly, "I should like to use your telephone. It will be a long distance call and may take some time. I thought I better ask you if you have any immediate necessary calls first, because I cannot be interrupted after I once begin."

Dale looked up pleasantly, wondering what was this coming.

"Why certainly, Aunt Blanche. Use the phone as long as necessary. I won't interrupt you," she said cordially.

Without even a thank-you the aunt turned, swept toward the telephone, and called long distance.

Dale went swiftly into the dining room and began to rearrange the setting of the table, not from any special reason, except to listen and discover if she could, what her unwanted guests were going to do next.

It was a bank that was being called up, and an official who evidently knew her aunt. There ensued a rather frantic conversation, in which it appeared that the gentleman in question would not have access to the lady's safe-deposit box, without a letter from her giving him authority, and the key, to open her box.

But the lady did not stop with one try. She insisted on getting the address of the bank president who was absent on vacation; and then did not hesitate to call him up and insist on a reply as soon as the man came in, no matter how late it was. After that, with ominous sighs, she flung herself down in a chair and snatched up a book.

Dale tried to busy herself about the house, not to seem to be listening, but occasionally her aunt would go to the phone again and sharply question long distance.

But at last there came an answer from the man she had

called, and then Dale almost felt sorry for him, for such a list of questions as were poured across the wire. Did he remember anything about her husband having bought a piece of property in the east, property in which his mother was to live? Over and over again in different phraseology she asked the question, until the man, trying to be courteous, must yet have been exasperated. The upshot of it was that he did not remember any such transaction, and that if Mrs. Huntley wanted her personal letters gone through for a matter of evidence of any kind it would be wiser if she were to come home herself and go through her own papers. He did not feel that anyone else should take that responsibility. And anyway, he was off for a time of rest and was not sure how soon he would be back. If he did as his doctor advised, it might be several months yet before his return.

At last the interview was closed, and Dale drew a long breath, for it was evident that there would be a large charge for that call, and it was most unlikely that her aunt would stop to inquire how much it was, or ever remember to ask for the bill when it came in, and pay it. Dale was not penurious, and if even a large telephone bill would open the way for her guests to go home soon, she would not begrudge it, but she was appalled at the expenses that were mounting up daily. Grandmother had warned her, but somehow she had not been able to comprehend how true it would be.

And now, noting a cessation of loud talk, Hattie opened the kitchen door and signaled that lunch was ready to be served whenever Dale desired. So she gave the signal and the boarders trooped noisily in.

"Oh, boy, but I'm empty! After that measly breakfast I could eat a whole cow," said Powelton, slamming himself into his chair.

"Yes," said his mother. "Dale, you certainly did give us

a slim meal this morning. Or was that Hattie's planning? If it was I think she ought to be dealt with about it. It was simply horrid."

"Oh, I'm sorry, Aunt Blanche," said Dale quietly. "No, it was not of Hattie's planning. I did the best I could with what was in the house. You know I was pretty well occupied yesterday and didn't get my usual shopping in."

"Well, I can't understand why you couldn't have sent Hattie down for what you needed early this morning."

"Well, that didn't just seem to be convenient either," said Dale with a quiet dignity.

Then Corliss entered, stood a moment behind her chair surveying the table with disgust.

"Sandwiches!" she sneered. "Made of lettuce too! My greatest abomination! As far as I'm concerned you can take them away. I want something real. After that sketchy breakfast we had I think we rate something better than just sandwiches."

She slumped down in her chair unhappily, and just then Hattie entered with a salad of grated carrots and pineapple.

"Oh, for Heaven's sake!" said Corliss. "You can't feed me carrots! I simply *won't* eat them, and that's all there is about it!"

"Get me some peanut butter, Hattie!" ordered Powelton.

"I'm afraid there isn't any peanut butter in the house, Powelton," said Dale apologetically. "I didn't know that you were especially fond of that. I'll get some the next time I'm in the store."

Hattie brought in the plates of hot soup, the disgruntled boarders settled down deprecatingly to eat it, and quiet was restored for the moment.

Then the pudding came in. A nicely browned bread pudding, made in Hattie's best style, with a nice little ball of hard sauce to eat with it.

"What is it?" asked Corliss with her nose in the air. "*Bread* pudding? Heavens! No! You can't get that down me, nor Pow either. We told our family long ago not to try any of that on us."

"Sorry you don't like it," said Dale. "I'm very fond of Hattie's bread puddings." But she made no further apology.

"Well," said the mother at last, after picking among the array on her plate, "I'm sure I don't know how you children are going to last till dinnertime. You haven't either of you eaten enough to keep a bird alive. Here! I'll give you some money and you can go down to the drugstore and get some ice cream."

She handed out fifty cents and the brother and sister departed. Then she sat back surveying the table dishearteningly. At last she spoke.

"It seems too bad to let your table run down this way," she said, looking sadly at Dale. "If you haven't time to go to the store, and you can't trust Hattie, would you like me to take over the ordering and running of the house while I am here?"

"No, thank you," said Dale sweetly. "I'm afraid I just wouldn't be able to pay the bills. You don't realize, Aunt Blanche, that I have only one ration book of my own to depend upon."

"Now Dale, don't begin to talk that way. You had a good dinner the night we came, and the next day. I'm sure if you understood running things right you could have good meals all the time without any more ration stamps. We didn't bring our books along of course. It never occurred to me that it would be required when we were *visit*ing."

"Well, I'm sorry you feel you are not well fed, but you know we do have to have ration stamps for meats and butter, and lots of things, and one book of stamps doesn't go so very far. You see that first day I had enough because

I had been going without meat and butter for some days, and a lot of things that took stamps, saving up for your coming. But those saved-up stamps are all gone now, and I'm really doing the best that I can. And of course I haven't a very large budget of money to go on, either, you must remember."

"Well, Grandmother left you that thousand dollars," said the aunt, almost contemptuously.

"Oh! And would you think I should use that right up for the table? And when it is gone, what would I do then?"

"Oh, I guess Grandmother gave you plenty more, if the truth were known," was the contemptuous reply. "And besides, I offered you a job which would cover your board and keep, which you turned down most ungratefully."

"Yes," said Dale gently. "I have other plans. But I am not expecting to use up my small inheritance in furnishing the table. Not at present. I'm sorry of course that my table doesn't please you, but it's the best I can do at present, and of course there is always the hotel and the drugstore if our table isn't satisfactory."

"Well, I think you are getting pretty impudent. I know of course Grandmother must have left you a large sum besides what was named in the will. I don't know how she got around the law, but she certainly must have had oodles of money, and naturally you got all you could out of her."

Dale was quiet for a moment trying to control her temper, and when she had been able to steady her voice she looked up and smiled

"I'm sorry you have any such an idea of Grandmother," she said. "I may as well tell you that she had nothing whatever of her own but her small annuity, which ceased at her death, and out of that she has through the years saved a little here and a little there, until she was able to put aside enough to cover her funeral expenses, and to give the few small bequests that were named in the will. She did not give me money other than was named. Now, shall we go in the other room and make our plans for the day?"

Dale arose with gentle dignity and led the way into the living room, and there was nothing left for her aunt to do but follow, that is if she wanted to keep up the conversation.

"Now, what are you going to do this afternoon, Aunt Blanche?" asked Dale. "Is there any way I can be of service to you? Is your lawyer coming out again today?"

Her aunt gave her a sharp look, as if she suspected she might have been listening to her telephone conversations.

"No," she said sharply, "he isn't. He's much too busy to devote so much time to one client he says, but goodness knows he's being paid enough. I think he ought to give up everything else and attend to one client until he gets things started. This is unendurable, hanging around this way. Your father certainly messed things up terribly, insisting on putting everything in his own name. I don't see what right he had to do that anyway."

Dale lifted her chin a bit haughtily.

"I would rather not discuss what my father did, Aunt Blanche. I have entire confidence in his actions of course, and I think you will find that so have all the people who had to do with him in a business way."

"Oh, of course you would feel that way," said the aunt disagreeably, "no matter *what* he did."

Dale arose and went over to pick up a book that had been dropped on the floor, and after a moment her aunt continued.

"Well, I'm certainly disgusted with everything, especially all business matters, and of course if I felt that you were willing to accept my proposition and come home with us, to help run our household, I would promise to be entirely responsible for your board and keep, and we would just forget this house and wait until a good opportunity comes later to sell it. But you are determined to be stubborn, and I feel responsible for you. I've always told dear Grandma that I would look after you when she was gone, and she needn't worry about that."

But Dale turned and spoke firmly.

"No, Aunt Blanche, you needn't feel that way any longer. I am of age and fully able to take care of myself. I have my plans all made. I discussed them with Grandmother, and she heartily approved of everything, so you can cast aside any responsibility you have been feeling on my behalf, and just make your own plans."

"But I should like to know just what your plans are. I really can't give up the burden of my responsibility for you unless I can know and approve what you are thinking of doing."

"Well, I'm sorry to disappoint you, Aunt Blanche, but my plans are not ready to be divulged yet. It is enough for me that Grandmother and my former guardian approves them, and it is better that no one else should know anything about them yet."

"Indeed!" said her aunt, "I see you are still stubborn and impudent, and I am sure the time is not far off when you will have to regret this. I think you will find that Granniss lawyer is a fraud and is pulling the wool over your eyes."

"No," said Dale, "I am sure I will never regret it. And now if I cannot do anything to help you in any way, I will ask you to excuse me. I have some errands downtown which I should do this afternoon, and I think I'll go now so that I shall not be late for dinner." Dale hurried out of the room and upstairs.

She went first to a store from which she could call up Mr. Granniss and report on the state of things without being overheard at home, and she received comfort thereby.

"Buffington is just stalling for time," he said. "He hasn't a leg to stand on and he knows it. But don't worry. This will all come out right in good time. I only wish I could find some way to send your unwelcome guests home, but that might only mean they would return again, so perhaps it is better to get it all done at once."

Dale went to see three of her grandmother's old friends, who were confined to their homes, or bed-ridden and hadn't been able to get even to the funeral. She stayed a little while with each, giving them dear little last messages from their old friend, and a few little tokens, like a hand-kerchief, a devotional book, and a small testament Grand-mother had designated for them. And when she came back to that codfish dinner, not anticipating a gay time, she was at least calm in her mind and resolved to keep sweet no matter what happened.

It was quite early the next morning, before the relatives had come over for breakfast, that the telephone rang and there was David Kenyon, her officer friend, calling her.

"Is that you Dale?" he asked, and his voice was eager.

"Yes, David." Her heart was singing that he had called her so early before there was anyone around to listen.

"Well, my orders have come. How are you fixed today? Can you meet me at the station when my train gets in, and can we have the day together?"

"To*day?*" she said joyously. "Why yes, today, of course. What time does your train get in? Eleven o'clock? Yes, I can make it. And what time do you have to leave tonight? Ten? Yes, I can do it. I'll be there by the train gate. And if by any chance you can't find me go to the Traveler's Aid desk and wait for me. But I'll be there. Good-by."

8

WITH a radiant face Dale sat down to plan her day. She must make out the best menus she possibly could for her time of absence. There was no point in making Hattie endure the grim remarks of the relatives, which would of course be directed against Hattie, in her absence, as if Hattie had perpetrated the whole idea. What could she have? An omelet for breakfast, *jelly* omelet? That was one of Hattie's great dishes. Dry cereal, orange juice and raisins. For lunch some of Hattie's delectable rice pancakes, with honey; for dinner fried chicken, mashed potatoes, and an apple pudding. That ought to be a good enough dinner for anybody, and they couldn't complain that she had run away for the day and left them without food enough.

She would start right away. She would get the chickens and anything else necessary, and hire the little Talbut boy to bring them up so that she could go on into the city and not have to return and explain where she was going or how long she was staying.

She went down and told Hattie what she was having for the meals. She told Hattie a friend who was passing through the city had called and asked her to come down and stay for lunch and maybe dinner. She would be back in the evening sometime. Would Hattie carry on?"

Hattie's face shone with willingness.

"Sure thing, Miss Dale, I carry on. And I don't know one thing about where you's goin' or what you's doin'. Don't you's tell me neither, and then those nosey people can't get nothin' outta me. I'se so glad you is gettin' a little rest up. I hopes you have a good time. Your Gramma would jest like that, and I hope you get all that's comin' to you. Them relatives, they is just too snooty and disagreeable, and no reason why you should havta dance 'tendance on them every minute. Now you jes' set down an' eat a good breakfus', and then go get yoo'se'f all prettied up, an' go off a'fore they gets here. Then they can't get up any hindrances, for I'm jes' sure they would ef they knowed about it. They is jes' folks that don' want no other folks ta hev a good time."

So with Hattie's help Dale was fed, got herself dressed up, wrote menus for the day, and departed out the back door and down the back street before her guests arrived for their breakfast.

Hattie had agreed to explain to the aunt about her sudden telephone call, so Dale went off with all her burdens laid aside for the time being, and her heart ready to take in the joy of a day's pleasant companionship.

Not until she was seated in the bus on the way to the city, with the home town in the background and the day before her, did she let herself think much about what the day was to bring forth. Then she found herself visualizing the young officer, and her heart quickening over the memory of his pleasant face. Would he look as handsome to her when she met him as he had when she had seen him first? Of course he would. How silly! But still, the other recent contacts with him had been so brief and so filled with cares and duties that she had scarcely had time to study him, or really to know how he did look. However she was sure she would know him, even if he came in company with a lot of other service men.

It was funny to her, Dale Huntley, who had never had much time to accept attention from men, to be going out to meet a young man whom she would have all to herself for the rest of the day. Would she be able to make it interesting for him all that time? Wouldn't he presently get bored and wish he hadn't asked her to meet him? Wish he had merely called, so he could go away at any time if his interest flagged? Well, he *hadn't* and so it was up to her to make the day interesting for him. And how should she do that?

Should she plan to take him to see the notable places in the city? Would he like that? The museums, the historic buildings?

But it was silly to try to plan until he came. He would likely know what he wanted to do, and he should be the one to choose.

Dale looked very pretty that morning. The cares and annoyances that had been with her ever since her grandmother's death, were lifted from her for the time being, and she was going forth to be a real girl and just have a nice time. Grandmother would have loved that for her. She wondered briefly if Grandmother was where she could see her, and be pleased about her day.

She was wearing a simple little cotton frock of blue, with white printed flowers in delicate design, and a plain little white sailor hat, not recent enough to be exactly stylish, but it was very becoming. She had always liked it and felt at home in it. Its band was a simple black velvet ribbon tied in a neat bow a little to one side of the front. There was a soft pink flush of excitement on her cheeks and her eyes were starry, a sweet smile on her lovely lips. More than one fellow-traveler in the bus looked at her with admiration, and looked again because she made a pleasant picture and was very lovely. Dale would have been amazed if anyone had told her that she was. Perhaps that was what gave the perfect touch to her loveliness, that she was utterly unaware of her own beauty. But with that bright anticipation in her eyes she was really very beautiful.

Then suddenly they were at the station, and she saw by the clock on the tower of the station that it was almost time for her navy friend's train to arrive.

She got out and hurried up to the train floor, searching out the right gate, making sure by reading the sign over the gate, asking a question of the gateman. She found that the train was on time, and though the clock on the wall said it would be there in just two minutes, yet those two minutes seemed each an hour long.

It was coming! She could see it down the track, a mere speck in the distance, rushing toward her. Then it had arrived, and she stood behind the gate watching as the passengers poured from the train and crowded up to the gates.

Dale studied each face as the uniformed men came up, but none of them was the right one, and her heart began to sink. Now the crowd was thinning, most of the passengers had entered the gates, met their friends and gone on into the city. There was just one man down the length of the train, talking to a redcap, handing over some baggage, and paying some money. Could that be David? And if it was, what was he doing? And now the redcap was running toward the gate, bearing some bags, and dashing over to the checking room. Her quick mind caught the idea at once, and she looked back at the man. Yes, that was David. Her heart thrilled at his fine bearing, his brisk military walk. He was coming to her? He had gotten rid of his baggage for the day so that he would be free to go with her!

Her face was beaming, radiant, there was a banner of welcome in her eyes, as she stood there behind those bars and looked out, and David saw her and came on. How beautiful she was! How had he dared call her up and make a date with her?

He came on quickly and swung inside the gate, came and took both the hands she held out to him, in both his own, warmly clasped, and drew her aside from the gate entrance where a few stragglers were still coming through. He held the hands an instant and looked down into her eyes, and the look he gave her set her heart to thrilling and brought the color sweetly into her cheeks.

They almost forgot that there were other people around and that some of them might be watching, for each was so engaged in reading the look in the other's eyes. But just then a group of people rushing to catch another train came bumping and elbowing by, till they had to draw further aside. But David did not let go of the hands he was holding. He drew one of them up through his arm, and laid his other hand on the soft little hand that almost seemed to nestle on his arm. Was he imagining all this, or did she really feel as he did? He looked down at her sweet shy face, but it was a glad look she wore. She was not annoyed, nor yet embarrassed. Just a great gladness seemed to envelope her, and he knew he mustn't let her know what he was reading in her eyes, not yet, anyway. Perhaps she wasn't conscious yet of her own reaction to his touch. Bless her! And he mustn't startle her with it. He mustn't run any risk of losing even a fraction of this wonderful thing that had come to be between them.

But both these young people were trained to be ready to meet emergencies, and so it was scarcely a minute before they came to themselves, and realized that they were in the way of a lot of hurrying people and must get out of it.

David smiled down into her eyes, and kept his hand close over the hand on his arm.

"Come!" he said, and led her across into the main station room, and to the elevators. As they went slowly down his eyes were upon hers, their glances locked in a look of delight, as if each glance were a new discovery to the other.

The elevator came to a stop and they went out with the other passengers.

"This way," said David.

Dale smiled and turned her footsteps as he led.

"Where are we going?" she asked, like a pleased child in a dream.

"Do you care?" he asked smiling. "Had you some place you wanted to go?"

"Oh no," said Dale. "I wasn't sure just what you were planning to do, or where you would want to go."

"Then that's all right," said the young man. "The last time I was in this city I picked out a place where I would like to take you if I ever got the opportunity, and now we'll have a try at it. If you don't like it we needn't stay there. We can easily go somewhere else later. In fact, we probably will, *later*. But—do you like the woods?"

"Oh, I *do!*" said Dale with happy eyes. "I used to think a day in the woods was the next thing to Heaven, when I was a little girl. And after all I've been through this is going to be wonderful!"

"I'm glad of that," he said, pressing the fingers under his hand. "Here! Here is a taxi." He handed her in, explained to the driver where he wished to go, sat down beside her, and they were soon on their way. But the young man lost no time in quietly possessing himself of her hand again.

It seemed amazing to Dale that just a quiet little hand-clasp could become such a wonderful thing, going to the heart of her being and bringing her closer to this almost stranger than she had ever imagined anyone could be to another.

She found her own fingers clinging to his hand, and caught her breath at herself. And yet it seemed so right. Was she in a dream and would she presently wake up and find it all had not happened? Could she be losing her head?

They whirled through the soft greenness of the park, tall trees arching overhead, wide drives, and banks of shrubbery on every hand. Breath of the great sweet out-of-doors wafting in at the open window, here and there a little cottage with some historical legend painted on a board at the side, beds of fall flowers, glimpses of the sky above, arches of a great bridge spanning overhead. It was like going into a new world. And David knew a lot about all these places. He had purposely come here on his last trip to find out about it, so that it might be of interest to them both. He was telling her now what he knew, with animated words, but his hand was yet warm about her own, and his eyes were telling pleasant friendly happy thoughts to her heart. She couldn't quite place herself in all this delight. It wasn't anything she could well withdraw herself from, as her dignified life training would have admonished her at another time to do. This was a real friend, telling her good things, in a gentle friendly way. A Christian young man. Couldn't she trust herself to be happy over it?

They climbed a hill presently, and dismissed the taxi, and then turned into the deeper, higher woods, till they came to a pleasant sheltered clearing where they could look out over the far world that seemed so distant, and yet was so near that she drew her breath in ecstasy.

They stood together for a moment, looking out across the world, David still holding Dale's hand, quietly, warmly, as if it belonged there, and then he turned and looked down at her, straight into her beautiful eyes that were looking so earnestly, so questioningly up into his, and it suddenly seemed as if their whole brief acquaintance was climaxed in that wonderful moment. David's other hand stole out almost reverently toward her, as he bent his head and drew her close within his arms.

"Dale!" he breathed softly, in almost a whisper. "Dale!

My darling! I *love* you! I love you with my whole heart! I've loved you since I first saw you. And because we've had so little time to get acquainted, and I have to go away so soon, I've brought you here to this lovely spot so near to Heaven to tell you about it. I pray that God will help you to forgive me for being so abrupt about this. But Dale, darling, I love you."

Then he drew her reverently closer, and bent and laid his lips upon her own.

There swept over Dale such joy as she had never dreamed could come to a girl on this earth as she surrendered herself to his embrace, and her soft lips answered his caress.

They came to themselves presently, and he drew her down to sit beside him on the broad pleasant bench that was placed comfortably with a background of young hemlocks. His arms were about her and he gently put her dear head down on his shoulder.

"Have I rushed you too much, my dear?" he asked tenderly. "I know it's a very short time to get you used to such a great love as I want to give to you before I go away, but this was all the time I had, and there hasn't seemed any other way. I love you and when I come back I want to make you my wife,—that is if you're willing to wait for me. To take a chance that I will live to come back. Am I being too presumptuous to dare to hope you could love me?"

Dale nestled her head closer on his shoulder, and her hands in his clasp.

"Oh, I do love you," she murmured. "It does not take time to love."

"Dearest," he breathed, "perhaps that is true. As soon as I saw you I loved you. The first time I looked at you I said to myself, 'That is the kind of girl I would like to marry. How can I get to know her? When will there be time to win her? If I go back overseas will there ever come a time for me to be with her? How can she be willing to trust me?'"

"Trust you?" said Dale. "Oh, I trusted you the minute I saw you. But I never dreamed that you would ever love me."

"And I haven't even asked you the question that I have been so afraid to ask. Is there someone else in your life that you love? Someone who loves you and has a right to your love? I should have asked you that first."

"Someone *else!*" laughed Dale, with a sweet little ripple of amusement, as she looked up into his face. "Why no! Don't you know I've never had time to love anybody? I've never had much time to know boys and go out very often. I was in school of course, and of course I went out occasionally, and then came college, and then there was Grandmother. She began to fail and I had to be with her whenever I could. I was in love with Grandmother you know. But oh, she would have loved you, and she would be so glad to have me love you, glad to know you love me. I think perhaps God will let her know about us."

He drew her then close within his arms again, and they sat quietly, listening to the sweet fall sounds of nature. A few birds calling, some purple grackles crying to one another, a rusty-throated cricket rasping sharply in the thicket below them. And every sound seemed to be counting out the moments that were so precious, the moments that they still had together.

But they lived hours during those carefully dealt out minutes. They touched on many things in their past lives, just sketchily, as they heard the minutes grow into hours, and the hours chimed dimly from some distant city tower. And at each hour realization would come, their hands would clasp closer and their glances would clash sadly, as the sharp thought came to each that they had just so little time together, and now had so little time ahead in which to make this up.

And then when the distant clock struck a solemn

"ONE," David looked up suddenly and grinned at her.

"It's time for mess," he said brightly. "Aren't you hungry?"

"Oh, I never realized," said Dale. "It's been so wonderful to be with you!"

"You sweetheart!" said David with one of his gentle looks that made Dale feel so protected and beloved.

"But I should have brought a lunch along," she said, appalled. "I never thought. I lost my head. I was so engaged in getting menus for my relative guests, so I could get away before they came to breakfast. So they wouldn't know where I had gone. And it never occurred to me I had a social obligation to us. If I had only known you were coming to a wonderful place like this!"

"Ah, but this was *my* party," said David. "You see I invited you, so the social part was entirely up to me."

"But you had no way to get ready a lunch," said Dale. "A base wouldn't have facilities."

"Wouldn't they?" grinned David. "But you see I had other facilities besides. Wait till you see." He reached over to the end of the bench where he had parked his overcoat and drew forth packages from its ample pockets. "What do you think of that? I got those sandwiches on the diner of the train coming up. I found the fruit at a station where we stopped five minutes. And this box of candy I bought in the Washington station. I found these little paper cups there too and I discovered the other day that there is a neat little spring just around the knoll below us here. Wait, I'll bring the water while you spread out the eats."

He was gone only a minute or two, and Dale arranged the food on the bench between them as attractively as she could. The sandwiches were in neat paper wrappings. She opened the fruit bag and there were peaches, pears, two red apples and two bananas. He seemed to have thought of everything. She smiled to herself in admiration of his cleverness.

Then he appeared between the trees, walking cautiously, two brimming cups of water in each hand, intense attention on his face.

"There!" he said with a relieved sigh. "I didn't upset any of them. And now, would you like to have some lemonade?"

Reaching into his pocket he produced a lemon and an envelope of sugar in triumph. "I saved that sugar from my coffee at the base for a week," he said.

"Oh, how lovely!" cried Dale. "You have thought of everything! This is a real picnic lunch."

"Yes?" he said comically. "But not as good as the lunch you would have prepared, I know."

"Oh, but you don't really know. You've never eaten any of my lunches."

"You're wrong," said the soldier positively, with a twinkling grin. "Have you forgotten the cup of hot tea you made and the doughnuts you wrestled for me at the U.S.O.?"

"Oh," said Dale, a lovely flush flaming over her sweet face. "No. I haven't forgotten. I—loved—doing that."

"And you didn't know me at all then," said the officer with satisfaction.

David went and stood over her and stooping kissed her forehead.

"And you're mine, now. And we feel as if we'd known each other for years."

"Oh, yes!" said Dale softly.

Eventually they got down to earth and managed to eat all the sandwiches and a great deal of the fruit, and to drink cups of lemonade.

And then shadows on the grass in front of the bench began to grow long, while they talked, and laughed and loved each other with stars in their eyes. And finally they picked up their cups and their paper bags, and the banana peels, and left the lovely hidden bench behind the hemlocks. They went slowly down the hill hand in hand, knowing that they were going into the world again where there would be no cool green retreat, and where they could not stop and kiss each other every other minute. But still as they loitered their fingers linked together, David's arm now and again about Dale's waist, he would stoop in the shadow of some foliage and touch his lips to hers.

At the broad winding road they stopped a moment and turned back, looking up to the sheltered nook where they had been, as if it were somehow a hallowed place.

"It's been a wonderful day," said Dale wistfully, almost sorrowfully. "I wish it were just beginning!" and a bit of a sigh escaped from her lips.

"Yes," said David. "It has. And it's going to be a wonderful time to remember—when I—that is when we—are—" he hesitated.

"Yes, I know," said Dale bravely. "I know. Don't put it into words. We'll just put the memory of this day into the place where words come that we cannot bear to speak."

They walked slowly on, keeping to the grassy side of the road where cars would not come too near.

But all too soon the walk was over and they were come to the highway and a taxi.

Seated in the taxi Dale came to herself enough to ask a few questions. When did his train go? How much did he know of his destination, and could he tell her anything, or must she just wait and trust? How soon, how often could he write? Oh, there were so many questions, and the afternoon was gone. She ought to have asked them before. There would come a long lonely time when her heart would be all questions, and no way to ask them.

For answer he smiled.

"It's all right, dearest," he said. "My train is supposed to leave the station at ten. Shall I take you home first or can you find your way back alone safely after I leave? Ten o'clock is not late, and I thought I could put you in a taxi before my train comes in."

"Oh, no," said Dale. "I'm used to going around alone, and ten o'clock is early. Besides there is a bus that passes the station that comes right up to our street corner. I'm staying, please, until you leave if you don't mind."

"That's what I hoped you would do. I want to be able to watch you out the car window as we start off. And now here—" He handed her an envelope filled with papers.

"Inside that envelope you will find all the addresses, and the answers to as many questions as I am permitted to answer. It isn't very much, but I knew you would understand. And I'll be writing you almost at once after leaving. I couldn't do otherwise. There are so many other things we haven't had time to say. After I got my bags packed yesterday I spent the most of the time getting these things together and trying to think of everything that might come up to trouble you after I am gone. I hope I haven't forgotten anything. But if I have, we'll be able to write, and you can trust God with it. It's such a comfort that you know God, and are not frivolous like so many girls I've met! I'm so glad you're the kind of girl you are. How I love you for it."

There were thrilling glances between them, even when they were where they could be overheard, and could not talk intimately. Dale was conscious of storing the glances away in improvised corners of her memory where she could take them out and exult in them afterward. Perhaps David, too, had visions of a time ahead when he would be needing such memories to help him through hard days.

He took her to a quiet dignified hotel where they could talk without interruption, and where the food and service were of the best. He had not been idle during his days in the city and had carefully selected this place because he felt that it was to be a memorable night. He wanted everything to be of the best for the sake of its memory. After all it just might happen that it would be the only festive supper they could ever have, at least for a long long time, and he wanted it to be happy all the way through.

They were not either of them in a mood to be very hungry, and at first began to eat indifferently, but after all they had spent the greater part of the day in the open air in the woods, and that made for good appetites. So they presently began to enjoy the wonderful dinner.

"Oh, David, this is going to cost a lot," protested Dale, as he kept on with his ordering. "A service man's pay doesn't rate all this."

"I hope it does," said David with a stubborn grin. "After all, it's got to stand for all the times I'll be *wanting* to take you out and can't, in the next weeks, or months, or whatever it is."

"But you are ordering as if I were a princess."

"Aren't you my princess?"

"Oh," said Dale, putting shy hands up to her crimson cheeks, "I never thought anyone would call me that!"

"But why not?" asked the smiling lover, watching her with happy eyes. "You are very lovely you know."

The dinner was good, and the room was fairly quiet. They could sit there and talk. They searched out each other's innermost thoughts and rejoiced in one another. And so at last the hours sped on till it was time to hurry to the station, time for David to retrieve his checked baggage, and answer the call of the train.

There were other service men standing there with friends, mothers, and girls, and some fathers. Tears on averted faces, earnest last words. But Dale and David had no eyes for others. They were taking those last looks at each other.

And then the final call. David stooped and kissed her now, as if he had the right before all the world to own her as his, and she dared to put her arms about his neck for one brief instant.

"It is night now," he whispered as he held her close, "but it will be day, by and by. And 'All through the night, my Saviour will be watching over you,' my darling!"

One more kiss and he was gone, flying down the platform with other last ones, swinging on the train and waving from the step with a real smile on his lips, forced there in answer to the bright teary smile with which she was waving him farewell. And then the train passed out of the car shed and into the darkness of the night. He was gone!

Dale turned and went back into the great empty station, her heart suddenly crying out for him. Then she heard his whispered song-words: "All through the night, my Saviour will be watching over you," and she passed on, her heart comforted with the thought.

9

ALL the way home Dale was reveling in the things that had come to her, and thrilling with joy over them. Life could never again be the same to her. Someone loved her! Someone wanted her, needed her. Come life or death that would always be something to rejoice over. And she did not once think what else was before her save the great empty space until her lover's return, nor once remember the problems she had left behind her in her own home, problems that had loomed so large last night. Not until she got out of the bus and saw her house standing in its usual place up the hill a little way, and remembered that there were other people in the world besides her lover. There were other things to think of besides loving and being loved. There were people perhaps waiting for her in her house who felt anything but love for her, and who could well engender hate if one wasn't on guard continually. But all through the night her Saviour would be watching over her. And He would also be there in the day, too, when problems thickened and storms arose.

Then she turned into her own street and walked up the hill, and was surprised to find her home ablaze with light.

Lights in every window, even up to the third story. Someone must have been rummaging. Of course Hattie hadn't discovered that yet or the lights would have been promptly turned out. But what could be the occasion of the other lights? Every room visible from the front and one side had a light in every window. Only the windows in Grandmother's locked room were dark. She was thankful for that. She had worried a little about Corliss. There was no telling if she would not even get the ax and break the door if she took the notion. She was that way, and she was so determined to take possession of that particular room, just because it was forbidden, perhaps. But Dale was greatly anxious to protect the room from desecrating, prying hands, and to keep it, as far as possible, just as Grandmother had left it. She could not bear to have it disturbed, not yet.

But what was going on in the house? Surely the neighbors had not all decided to call in a body! That was not like them. Also she had felt intuitively that they had not liked her relatives. They would not be likely to call on them at present, not without being especially invited. And Dale had not felt sure enough of her unwelcome guests to do that. Not yet. She doubted if she ever would. Aunt Blanche would not like any of them either. She had plenty shown that the day she arrived.

But now Dale hurried on, for the sounds that reached her were a bit hilarious, as if a gay crowd were together. But who were the gay crowd?

As she reached the gate it became apparent that the crowd in the house were not only gay but decidedly boisterous, and one voice sounded actually *drunk!* Oh dear! Now what could be going on?

There were two men on the front porch smoking long cigars. There was a noisy bunch of youngsters on the side porch, glasses and plates in their hands, talking in loud screaming voices, and beside themselves with laughter.

Unholy laughter it sounded like. But of course she must not judge them. They were young. That was Corliss' style. But oh, it didn't sound like Grandmother's house! What should she do? Did she have to stand this?

A glance toward the living room showed her several tables set around the room, and two separate groups were sitting about the tables playing some kind of a card game, between times taking sips from glasses that contained some dark liquid. Well, it looked like a gay party all right, whoever the people might be, and the sounds of hilarity that boomed forth from the simple old house did not seem in keeping with the atmosphere that Grandmother had always had there. Somehow it shocked Dale. Not that she disapproved of laughter and merrymaking, of course not, and neither had Grandmother. But this was not just simple-hearted merrymaking. This was more hilarious merrymaking than seemed in keeping with a beloved place where death had just been to take a dear one away.

With distress in her eyes Dale stole softly around to the back of the house to find Hattie if possible, and discover just what was going on.

She did not have far to search for Hattie, for she stood in the deepest shadow just around the corner by the kitchen door, evidently watching for her.

"What is it, Hattie?" she whispered.

"Oh Miss Dale. I'm certainly thankful you've come at last. Such goings on! I did my best to stop it, but she allowed it was none of my business, so I took myself off where I could watch an' not be seen. They think I've gone to bed, but I couldn't sleep with the likes of this goin' on, and I'm jes' morally certain they've broke in to the sideboard drawer and took the best napkins, an' they're usin' the Spode plates Grandma liked so much, an' only got out fer her lovingest company," wailed the woman in a subdued whisper.

"Never mind, Hattie, don't let them hear you. Who are

they, do you know? People who called to see Aunt Blanche?"

"Naw. They's jes' a pick-up crowd. Some that old Buffington brang along, an' some she brang over from the *ho*-tel! She come out inta the kitchen an' says they was goin' ta have a party, an' ef I wanted ta make some cakes an' wait on her comp'ny she'd give me a whole dollar fer the evenin.' I said no, I worruked fer *you,* an' I couldn't do nothin' you hadn't tole me to do, an' anyhow I was tired, an' half sick, an' I was goin' ta bed. So I went off an' tended like I was goin' up ta my room. But I come right down soon an' heard tell what she was doin'. She went to the telephome, an' she called up a lotta numbers, an' she got a case of liquor sent over from de *hotel,* an' a lotta cakes and ice creams and things, and then she rafted round the furniture till you wouldn't never know the place. An' Miss Corliss, she went out and searched up a couppla sojers, an' a drunkem sailor; and that brother of hers brought three of the toughest girls I've seen in this town, besides one boy, Greek Lufty, who has just come home fum reform school! Listen at 'em sing them sickenin' songs. It worse'n ever anythin' comes over the radio. Now, Miss Dale, watcha goin' ta do? We can't hav' no goin's on like this is Gramma's place, now she's gone."

Dale had been thinking rapidly as Hattie talked.

"No," said Dale thoughtfully. "Wait. Let me think! I'll tell you, Hattie. Suppose you run over to Mrs. Relyea's back door—I see there's a light in the kitchen there yet, and ask her if you may call up somebody on her telephone. Tell her there's so much noise over here with my aunt's friends that we couldn't phone without their all hearing. And then you go in and call up Mr. Granniss' number, and ask him can he and Mrs. Grannis come over here quickly, that I need them both in a hurry."

"Yes, ma'am! That's a good idea."

"If he wants to know what it's all about, tell him my

aunt has a very noisy party here, and I don't know how I can quiet it down. He'll understand, and he promised to help any time."

Dale stood still in the darkness of the back yard and tried to think how this thing was going to work out. Suppose Mr. Grannis was not at home? Suppose Hattie came back having failed to make a contact? What should she do? There wasn't a neighbor she cared to bother to help her. Indeed they were mostly quiet women, or shy men. They wouldn't be able to get anywhere with that crowd in there. It would take a person with some degree of sophistication to deal with a problem like this. In fact there were only a few lights downstairs in any house along the street, indicating that her neighbors were going to bed at this hour. There were early risers, most of them war-workers in some way. Poor things! They must have been annoyed at the unusual tumult on their quiet street. Her cheeks burned with mortification as she thought of explanations she would have to give to a few who were always wondering about anything unusual.

Then suddenly Hattie was beside her, looming out of the darkness, all out of breath from hurrying over the rough grass lest her footsteps would be heard on the walk by the gay party.

"He's comin'," panted Hattie, "right away off, he said, and he said to tell you not to worry. It'll be all right. He's bringin' somebody with him, an' he'll see that they understand the situation. Miss Granniss is a' comin' too. Now, what all you want I should do?"

"Well, I think I'll have to go in and do something," said Dale with a troubled glance toward the house. "Suppose you slip in and stay where you can hear if I need you. Is there anything around in the kitchen that needs clearing up? Just seem to be busy you know."

"There's plenty," said Hattie grimly. "There's a whole lot of bottles in some kind of a contraption, right in the middle of my kitchen floor. They come out as big as you please and open up their bottles, and cut their cake, an' they took our best dishes, and broke one right before my face, when they first asked me to serve, an' they was mad 'cause I said I worked only for you, an' under your orders. They was hoppin' mad."

"Well," said Dale, "I'll go in and see what I can do. Perhaps they will go home of their own accord, and we can phone Mr. Grannis not to come."

"Not them, they won't. They ain't that kind! You'll see!"

So Dale went into the house the front way, and paused in the living room door.

"Oh," she said with a well-feigned surprise, "you have guests, Aunt Blanche. It is nice that you were not lonely. I didn't know that you had friends living near."

She looked around with her sweet engaging smile, and hoped her hands were not trembling. She did not know how very sweet and young and beautiful she looked, with the quick color in her cheeks, and her eyes so starry bright. The guests looked up in amazement, and one sophisticated woman from the hotel asked: "Why, who is this, Mrs. Huntley? I did not know you had a young niece. Won't she come and play with us? That will just make up for Buff, if he really has to go."

Aunt Blanche froze into haughtiness and performed a few reluctant introductions, beginning with, "Oh, Dale, is that you? I understood you were to be quite late tonight."

Then the men drew near, including the lawyer Buffington, quite openly admiring the pretty newcomer. There arose a clamor for Dale to take off her hat and join them in their game, and one of the men hurried to her with a glass of wine.

"You'll have a glass of wine, first, won't you Miss Huntley? And shall I get you a piece of cake?"

Looking up Dale caught a glimpse of an angry jealous

Corliss scowling in the front door, but somehow she was enabled to keep on smiling as she shook her head courteously.

"No thank you. Nothing to eat or drink. And I don't play cards, so I'm sure I wouldn't be any addition to your number. But now, if you've all quite finished your refreshments I'll have Hattie remove the plates and glasses if you don't mind. You see I have some friends coming to see me shortly. So I thought it would look a bit tidier if we just got rid of the soiled dishes."

"Oh, for Heaven's sake!" said the aunt, arising in anger. "You have people coming here at this hour? You have no right to do that, right in the midst of my party!"

"Sorry, Aunt Blanche. But you didn't tell me you were having a party," smiled Dale.

"Oh, for Pete's sake!" ejaculated Corliss furiously. "Can you beat that?"

"Well, Dale, you know now, so go to the phone at once and call them. Tell them they can come tomorrow night or some other time, but you find it isn't convenient now."

"I can't very well do that Aunt Blanche, for they are just arriving at the door now."

"Oh, certainly you can! I'll send Corliss or Powelton out to inform them the house is occupied, and they'll have to come again."

Powelton quickly dodged around the corner of the porch out of sight and remarked aloud to himself, or to Corliss, who had also dodged out of sight, "Well for crying out loud! Can you beat it?"

But Dale paid no heed to her aunt's admonition. She was at the door now, her hands extended cordially, and a little lilt in her voice as she said clearly: "Oh, Mrs. Grannis! I'm so glad you were able to come! And how lovely that you brought the Bonniwells with you. This makes it just perfect!"

But behind Dale the former guests sprang to their feet in

consternation, with a shower of playing cards all over the floor at their feet, where they had fallen from the hand of the one who was dealing.

So the guests entered, five of them. The Grannisses and the Bonniwells and their charming daughter, the latter in gorgeous evening dress.

"You must excuse our formal dress," said Mrs. Bonniwell, entering cordially into the room and not seeming to notice what was going on. "We are just from the Newell wedding you know, and the Grannisses simply insisted that we come along with them. I do hope we're not intruding."

But Dale turned graciously, looked at the dismayed group behind her, and began her introductions with pleasant poise, more than she likely would have had if there had not been the interval out in the darkness of the back yard to prepare herself, and gather strength from above.

"This is my aunt Mrs. Huntley, Mr. Bonniwell. I think you, Mrs. Granniss, have met her before, haven't you?"

The incoming guests were full of courtesy and graciousness and appeared not to notice the distraught look of the erstwhile gay crowd. Of course they couldn't know how funny they were, caught all unaware, with that ridiculous shower of cards at their feet and that guilty look over them all. The strangers from the hotel were impressed with the callers. The Grannisses were always distinguished looking people, and the elegant simplicity of the Bonniwells in evening dress was certainly impressive. There was always something about the appearance of the Bonniwells, even the young daughter that was attention-compelling, and they looked the Bonniwells over thoroughly and realized that these were people from another world.

But it was Greenway Buffington who seemed the most uncomfortable and made the first move, with a troubled glance at his watch.

"I'm afraid I must be moving on, Mrs. Huntley. You

know I told you my time was limited." And with a hurried bow toward that embattled lady, he turned to slide out by the dining room door, thus side-stepping any contact whatever with that Granniss man, of whom he was not at all enamored, was in fact at present almost afraid. At least afraid that here was one who would upset his own plans for personal aggrandizement, with this rather promising client.

Now Hattie had been quietly, deftly stepping about the living room, picking up and removing, first the precious Spode plates, which she had placed safely on the dining room table, then the glasses, and she had just gone through the dining room door, and was carefully turning around to avoid hitting a chair in her way, when lawyer Buffington barged through the door, coming full tilt against her tray which was more than overloaded, some of the glasses having just been refilled, and Hattie had been trying to keep them from slopping over.

But lawyer Buffington was coming full sail with plenty of power behind him, and he hit the loaded tray squarely and knocked the glasses hither and yon, not only making a great crash, but also a widespread splash, for the wine sloshed all over his immaculate white suit, streaming down in ugly dark rivulets, and up into his face, even in his eyes, utterly putting him out of commission for the moment as far as sight was concerned.

Meanwhile the whole tray of glasses went down on the dining room hardwood floor with a mighty crash, and Hattie could do nothing about it. But before she tried to pick anything up or even to exclaim over what had happened, she did have presence of mind enough to reach out and close that dining room door, thus shutting the other guests out of the scene of disaster, but shutting them in to their own utter undoing.

The first impulse of the strangers caught in the general melee was flight.

"I really think we should be going, too," spoke up the woman from the hotel who had suggested the way to get the wine, and had drunk deeply of it already. "You know my dear, we are greatly indebted to you for this delightful party," she turned to Aunt Blanche hastily and gave her a hurried little pat on the shoulder, "and you have made it so delightful for us that the time has passed for us before we knew it. Do you realize how late it is? I am afraid the band has finished my piece that I especially requested for tonight and I promised I would be there to applaud. Come friends, we must 'scram' quickly, isn't that what the children say? Good night! See you in the morning!" and the visitor "scrammed."

It was really very funny when one was looking on. The guests that Aunt Blanche had brought in through lawyer Buffington made brisk adieus and vanished. Aunt Blanche and her two guests from the hotel decided they too must leave. The young people had disappeared.

And when the sound of the hurrying cars that they had come in was dying out in the distance, the Granisses and the Bonniwells and Dale by common consent sat down and laughed.

"Well," said Mr. Grannis, taking off his glasses and wiping them on his immaculate handkerchief, "that was about the easiest job of ejection I ever was called upon to do."

And then they all laughed again.

In the sudden silence that followed the second laughter they could hear a broom plying in the dining room, and the tinkle of broken glass, as Hattie hastened to clear away the traces of the disaster.

Then Dale arose and opened the door.

"Don't you want more light, Hattie?" she asked. "There are bits of glass on this side of the door, too. I saw them fly under through the crack."

"Yes ma'am, Miss Dale," said Hattie in almost a sob, "I

spec's somehow this whole thing was somehow my fault, but there didn't seem no way I could uv pervented it. There's only just one thing to be thankful for. There ain't none o' them Spode cups yor gramma laid such store by broke, notta one. An' I got money enough to buy new glasses, so yoh needn't ta worry none, Miss Dale, only I'm that 'shamed it shouldda happened on me. I was only tryin' ta get outta that old galoot's way, and he come bargin' right in on me."

That started the crowd laughing again and Dale had to go right up to Hattie and tell her she was proud of her, and she didn't mind it happening, and it would be all right, and she needn't pay for the glasses, they were only cheap ones any way, and they all knew it wasn't her fault. And presently Hattie so far recovered that she was able to come into the living room and laugh with the rest. It might be that if Aunt Blanche had seen that, Hattie in the best room laughing at her crowd and hob-nobbing along with the elegant Mrs. Bonniwell, she would have passed right out. Dale was thankful she wasn't there and need never know it.

"I can never thank you enough for coming to my rescue, Mr. Grannis," said Dale. "I was perfectly appalled when I got back here and found what was going on. And I don't know what the neighbors are thinking of it yet. They are such quiet respectable people, and such dear friends of Grandmother's. It would seem to them such a desecration."

"I don't wonder, my dear," said the old guardian. "And I'm glad you called on us. Do it again as often as there is need. Of course you understood that I would tell the Bonniwells all about the circumstances and they were delighted to help."

"Well, it was wonderful. And it was all the better that they were wearing such lovely garments. I could see the evening dresses went over big. One diamond speaks volumes to my aunt and cousins."

"You dear child! Well, it's good the diamonds can be of real use somewhere," said Mrs. Bonniwell smiling. "And I'm sorry dear that you are having such an uncomfortable time—just after your recent sorrow. But don't worry. This sort of thing doesn't last forever, and someday it will pass. I'm so glad to have had an opportunity to help in a small way, and of course you understand I'll say nothing about all this to anyone."

When they were gone, Dale felt a surge of relief, and a return of her joyous thrills as she remembered David Kenyon, and the day they had spent together.

She turned out the porch light, gave a quick comprehensive glance about the disheveled living room, and then turned toward the opening dining room door where Hattie stood, her face drawn into the most disapproving expression she knew how to wear.

"Well," she said with a tone like a punishment, "now will you do something about her? *Now* will you see what I mean and send her off?"

"Listen, Hattie," said Dale, still with that lilt in her voice, for somehow she was sensing that there was a new joy to revel in, in spite of all her annoyances.

"What would you think I should do?" smiled Dale. "You know after all Grandmother wouldn't want me to be rude to her. But I think there will be a way, somehow. I think God will do something about it."

"*Rude!*" sniffed Hattie, "I should say *she* was being rude to you."

"Well, perhaps that doesn't matter, Hattie. I'm a Christian, and I must be sure not to do anything the Lord would not approve."

"Now, Miss Dale!" sniffed Hattie indignantly. "You *know* the Lord couldn't never like such actions as was goin' on here tonight. Drinkin' and shoutin' crazy things so all the neighborhood could hear. Desecrating the home of one of the holiest women that ever lived on this earth."

Dale drew a trembling troubled breath.

"I know, Hattie. It was rather dreadful, wasn't it? I'm sure we shall hear from the neighbors tomorrow in some way. I think they must have been shocked. No, I'm sure it wouldn't have pleased the Lord, but the Lord never set me to judge other people's wrong actions."

"Well, I ain't so sure," said Hattie. "This here is *your* house, ain't it? Nobody else can't say what shall go on here, but *you* can. An' shorely you don't think the Lord wants such doin's in a Christum home. You don't think that's honorin' Him, do you?"

"No, I suppose not," said Dale thoughtfully. "But I'm not just sure yet what *I* should do. I'll think it over, and I'll pray it over, and I'll ask the Lord to take charge. Of course if it's only a matter of annoyance to *us*, or even embarrassment, maybe we are supposed to be gentle and forgive and stand it."

"No *sir*, Miss Dale, not in yer own house! Effen you was a man you'd jes' tell her it couldn't go on. Of course I know you be young an' it ain't easy to speak up to a humbugger like that aunt, but I guess somehow you gotta do it."

"I'll pray about it," said Dale smiling, and patting Hattie's shoulder. "But now come on and let's go to bed. You lock up the kitchen and I'll lock up the front."

So the two went to work, and presently were up in their rooms preparing for rest.

As Dale turned out her light, she paused a moment by her window in the darkness and looked at the sky. Dark dark blue, set out with stars, many of them. And off somewhere under those stars David was in a train hastening away from her into another world. He hadn't said which way after New York, but she had a feeling it might be west. But she knew in her heart he was thinking of her wherever he was. And she stood there thanking her Heavenly Father for the wonderful love that had come so unexpectedly into her lonely young life.

A little later she lay down on her bed, her heart at rest. All through the night her Saviour would be watching over her. She was content to trust the annoyances and necessities to Him. He would know how to control this thing, and she would leave it to her Heavenly Father.

10

THE morning mail brought a brief letter for Dale, sent special delivery, mailed on the train. How had he managed to get it started in time to reach here so soon?

My precious Dale:

It seems incredible that I have the right to call you mine. Only just this morning I didn't, you know, and my heart is full of rejoicing that you have given me this right.

Oh, my darling, I thank my God that as I go out into the unknown, I may carry the knowledge of your love with me, and leave my love with you. You don't know how very much this means to me.

And I am deeply grateful for the lovely little picture of yourself you gave to me. I shall carry it close to my heart, all the way, wherever I go.

And there is another picture of you that I shall carry in my memory. The lovely vision that you were as I met you this morning. It is fixed in my thoughts indelibly. Did I tell you how beautiful you looked to me? But perhaps there were too many

other things to say, and the time was too short. So I
will save it up in my mind, for every detail of the
blue frock, the charming little hat that seemed so
fitting for you, is stored away in my heart so that I
can take it out and look at it, and I shall be writing
you from time to time and telling you about it.
There isn't time now, for I want to go back to the
mail car and see if I can wangle this into the mailbag
that is thrown off when we meet the Express pretty
soon.

I love you, my sweet, and I had to tell you again
before I slept. And may the dear Lord be close beside
you continually to comfort and guide you all the
way, till we meet again.

> Yours,
> DAVID

Dale went hurriedly up to her room, hugging the
thought to her heart that this letter had reached her before
Corliss arrived, for if she had been here she would have
been sure to meet the postman and sign for the letter, and
examine it thoroughly before she brought it to her. Perhaps she wouldn't even have brought it. That was a
thought. She must do something about her mail. There
would be other letters she hoped. She could not have them
at the mercy of Corliss. Of course she could take a box at
the postoffice and have all her personal mail held there. It
would be well if she did that at once. Meantime, she must
meet the postman herself until she was sure this had been
done. Corliss was a little vandal. She wouldn't hesitate to
destroy mail before it had been read if she got the chance,
or if she thought it would annoy her cousin. Besides, she
would delight to try and find out personal matters and
annoy her by speaking of them at most inopportune moments. She must lose no time. With a quick glance at the
clock Dale hurried down to the postoffice and arranged for

a box. This wasn't going to be a bit convenient, but it was going to be necessary as long as her relatives were with her. With a sigh she wondered if she would find out anything that morning about their plans.

But when she reached home again they had not as yet come over to breakfast.

"Mebbe they had too much last night," said Hattie with a grin. "Mebbe they decided to leave today."

Dale shook her head.

"No such good luck, Hattie," she said with a smile. "There are a couple of suitcases upstairs in the room where Aunt Blanche takes her naps, and a lot of their other belongings."

"Well, I wouldn't put it past 'em to telephone you to pack 'em up and send 'em on," said Hattie. "Want I should tell you what I think? *I* think they're ashamed to come back after the way they acted last night. The know the whole neighborhood would be roused up against 'em, after yelling and screaming the way they did in Gramma's house just after she's gone."

"No, I'm afraid not, Hattie. They have no such shame. In fact I don't believe they were ashamed. I think they were only angry because I brought Mr. Granniss here when that other lawyer had brought his friends. They are staying away now to punish me, perhaps. Or else they stayed up so late last night that they haven't got up yet."

"Well, whatever it is," said Hattie grimly, "I s'pose you'll forgive 'em, and be as sweet as a peach to 'em What you goin' to give 'em to eat today? Roast turkey, or pheasants' breasts? Me, I'd give 'em another dose of codfish, and even that's too good for 'em."

"Was there enough chicken left to make a few sandwiches?" asked Dale.

"Coupla wings an' a few scraps. But you ferget. The princess don't care fer sandwiches."

"Well, that doesn't matter, I suppose. But perhaps you

better cream it and put it on toast. It will go farther that way."

"Okay," said Hattie affably, "and we'll have a gelatine pudding. There's some extra milk oughtta be used up."

"That's all right, Hattie. And fix a little salad of some kind, too."

"Oh, all right. It'll piece out. But you just baby those folks I say. After they acted like they did I should say it didn't matter if they had anything to eat or not. But I'll make it."

Hattie went away with a chastened look on her grim face, and Dale smiled after her and went upstairs to write an answer to her letter, and send it immediately so it would get to her beloved at the first possible moment.

So she sat joyously down and began to write.

It was quite a good deal later that Dale heard a sputtering of angry voices, mounting to a perfect tornado of sound that bore the accents of Hattie in her most indignant mood. And then haughty indignation from her aunt, interspersed by screaming denunciations from both Corliss and Powelton.

Dale smiled half amusedly, and went on with her writing, but she drew a sad little sigh. It was scarcely possible to continue writing loving words when vituperations were going on so near her. She folded her letter, locked it away in the little secret drawer of her desk, and took out fresh paper. There were other notes she must write. She would get those done now while her mind was likely to be distracted. She could not bear to write to David out of the midst of annoyances. He would presently have battles enough to think about without getting even a hint of her own home front battles. He must not even get the subconscious atmosphere of distress.

So she began to write "thank-you" notes to people who had sent flowers to Grandmother's funeral, and to some who had written beautiful letters of condolence. She presently grew interested in getting as many as possible ready for the mail. She had no wish to go down into the atmosphere she was sure she would find in the dining room. So she wrote on.

But after a little she heard footsteps coming up the stairs, and then became aware of someone standing in her open door looking severely at her. But even then she did not stop writing nor look up.

"Oh, so you *pretend* to be *very busy!*" said the sharp querulous voice of the aunt. "You have no apologies to offer for the outrageous way in which I was treated last night."

Quietly Dale looked up, her pen poised for the next words she was about to write.

"Apologies?" said Dale with a surprised lifting of her brows. "Apologies for what? Or—did you mean *you* came to apologize?"

"*I? Apologize?*" screamed the aunt. "Why should *I* apologize?"

"Well, I'm afraid I wouldn't just know what you would consider a sufficient reason for apology," said Dale, speaking gently almost as one would speak to a child who had misbehaved. "Perhaps you did not realize that the whole street, who are all very dear friends of Grandmother's, were greatly scandalized at the sounds of hilarity that proceeded from the home where she had lived, so soon after her death. You see the people around this neighborhood are quiet respectable people who are not in the habit of attending night clubs, and getting even slightly tipsy, and to hear such sounds coming from Grandmother's home shocked them. But you are a comparative stranger here of course, and did not know those people who came here, and probably thought you could not help what your guests did. I felt rather mortified for you."

"*What?*" screamed the aunt. "*You* felt mortified for *me?* You outrageous little baggage you! And what did you think of yourself, coming in to *my party* and bringing a lot of old fogies, and practically sending my guests all home? Have *you* any apologies? Oh no! You turn on us, your guests. It is a pity that Grandma couldn't have lived long enough to know just how rude you were to her nearest relatives."

Dale looked at her aunt steadily.

"Aunt Blanche, what did I do but come to my own home, where I had a perfect right to come, and expect quietness and respectability, and introduce my friends who are among the finest in our city? I am afraid I do not see any reason for apology in anything I did. And now Aunt Blanche, since we are coming to some understanding I think I should go on and explain that I am starting a school for the children of defense workers here in the house, and that after next week I shall not be free any longer to entertain guests. I am sorry to have to seem inhospitable, but the matter has been all arranged, and I have promised to undertake it without any further delay. I don't know what your plans are, or whether you were arranging to stay in this region longer than next week or not, but if you feel that you would like to stay I think I can suggest several nice places down further toward the city where you might secure board."

"Well, *really!*" said Aunt Blanche rising and snapping her furious eyes, "so we are being turned out of the house are we? Well I shall certainly remember that."

"But I haven't meant it that way, Aunt Blanche. You see I have a regular job, at least for the duration. Grandmother helped me plan it. Besides Hattie is going to the hospital for an operation pretty soon, and I can't possibly look after twenty children, and cook meals for a family besides. I'm sure you must see how it is."

"No, I don't see how it is at all," snapped her aunt. "In the first place you never had to take a job like that. And certainly you don't need to begin it while we are here. As for Hattie, she isn't the only working woman left in the world, and I'll engage to get you another as good or better than she is. Certainly I'm not going to leave here to accommodate Hattie. Not until my business is finished, anyway."

"I'm sorry, Aunt Blanche, but you can't run my life for me. I'm of age, and this is my house. I'll do all I can to find a pleasant place for you to board. I'm sure there must be one that wouldn't cost you as much as you are paying now at the hotel."

"*I* am paying!" screamed the angry woman. "It was not *my* idea going to the hotel, in the first place. It was *you* who suggested it, and therefore the paying was *your responsibility*. I told the hotel manager when I went there that they might send the bill to you, and it will probably be here in a day or two. I understand they send bills at the end of the week, or perhaps month. I don't know which. But you'll find out."

"Aunt Blanche, I'm not going to argue with you, but certainly I am not responsible for your bills at the hotel, and I shall not pay any of them! You had no right to tell them I would. I shall certainly make that plain to their management. But I'm sorry you do not understand. I am not doing this to be disagreeable. I am only telling you what my present obligations and plans are. And inasmuch as you are not staying here nights anyway I didn't think it would make so much difference to you where you ate. Besides you haven't seemed satisfied at all with our food. Certainly you wouldn't want to be coming to meals with twenty children running all over the place, would you?"

"*Twenty* children! That's ridiculous! What right did you have to take twenty children into the house, especially when you had relatives visiting you? This is the most absurd thing I ever heard of, and you might as well understand *now* as any time that *I am not* going anywhere else. I am staying *right here!* We are the wife and children of

Grandma's son, and that at least gives us the right to stay in her house, even if she did see fit to leave it to you. And while we are talking about it you may as well understand that Corliss is going to have Grandma's room from now on. If you don't unlock that door I shall get a carpenter this morning to do so, and you can't do anything about it. I'll see if I have to stay in a hotel because a little upstart of a girl like you takes a notion to be disagreeable. Now, I hope you understand. I'm going out for an hour, over to the hotel to get our suitcases, and when I get back if Grandma's room isn't open I shall phone for a carpenter at once to knock down the door!"

Then Aunt Blanche arose with a grand gesture and left the room. Dale's heart went down with a thud. What was she going to do about this?

Suddenly she got up, locked her door, and knelt beside her bed.

"Dear Lord, I'll just put this all in your hands. Will you please help me and show me what to do. Please don't let me have to fight for my rights."

For some little time after she arose from her knees she stood by her window looking out. Was she wrong? Could it possibly be required of her to let these vandal relatives into Grandmother's precious room? Was she making too much of this? She did not worship that room in any sense, but it was a dear place to her with precious memories. Even now in her mind she could see Corliss jeering at the little framed sampler hanging on the wall, that Grandmother's little-girl hands had wrought. "The Lord is my light and my salvation; whom shall I fear? the Lord is the strength of my life; of whom shall I be afraid?"

She could see the sneer that would curl Corliss' lips, the ugly antipathy that would register in her expression as she read that. She could see Corliss' hands snatching the poor old sampler down and stamping on it, smashing the glass that protected it, if she were ever allowed the freedom of that room. She could see the derision that would greet the quaint old picture of Grandfather, with his antique haircut, and the stock around his neck. Corliss simply wouldn't be able to comprehend how anybody who looked like that picture could possibly be dear to anyone and Corliss would never stop her vandalism because somebody else reverenced the object of her scorn.

The quaint little vases on Grandmother's bureau, with their gilt edges, and their hoop-skirted maidens and old-time swains. They would all come in for her contempt.

Grandmother's old rocking chair with its patchwork cushions, made of the pieces of family dresses of bygone days. Grandmother's pretty little desk that Grandfather had bought for her, with its small bundles of precious letters and papers, everyone of them heirlooms that under Grandmother's direction had been left there for Dale to read over and put away among the other heirlooms. There hadn't been time for her to go over everything since Grandmother's last attack that brought her death. And she must do it quietly, without alien eyes looking on. There was no use. She simply couldn't let Corliss into that room. Not unless everything was first moved out, and there wasn't any place to put the things if she were to try to do that.

She thought of the neat piles of Grandmother's garments, and the little gray dresses hanging in the closet, including the shining gray silk to be worn with the lovely white lace kerchiefs in the top drawer of the bureau. She thought of the fine silk shawl with long handsome fringe, that Grandfather had bought for Grandmother on their first wedding anniversary. She imagined how Corliss might stretch it about her, and sail out even into the street dragging it behind her as if it were an evening dress. Corliss was capable of all sorts of things like that. She remembered the groups of much loved photographs of Grandmother's old-fashioned family, even the daguerreotypes of her two boys, now dead. Oh, she couldn't have Corliss laughing at their queer clothes, their little copper-toed shoes as they stood sturdily beside the photographer's chair, one hand stiffly outstretched to grip the plush arm. Oh, surely, it wouldn't be right to let the relatives in there, to destroy all that belovedness that Grandmother had meant to leave for her memory. They had often talked about it. So she wasn't being just selfish. And it wasn't as if it would have done Corliss any definite good to sleep in that room. It was just a notion she had taken, which would probably pass. Probably the only reason she wanted the room was because she knew that Dale treasured it, and she had always enjoyed being unpleasant to Dale.

However, of course she was not going to allow any carpenter to knock the door down. That was absurd. She would do her best to settle this matter peaceably, but if not, she would have to resort to—well, what could she resort to? Of course she might appeal again to Mr. Granniss, but she couldn't bear to trouble him with such trifling matters of bickering. Well, she had told the Lord about it, now what was there else for her to do?

But down in the kitchen Hattie, who had hung around at the foot of the backstairs listening, and had heard the whole conversation between Dale and her aunt, decided to take matters in her own hands. So she called up the backstairs to Dale:

"I'm just goin' down to the drugstore to get some more pills. I took the last one last night and I need some more. Is there anythin' you want Miss Dale?"

"No, Hattie, not unless—why yes, we need some peanut butter and some cinnamon. You might get a yeast cake too and make a few cinnamon buns."

"Yas'm," said Hattie. "Okay by me," and then under her breath, "though what you wantta pamper that old battleaxe and her brats for I don't see!" So Hattie took a hurried way to the drugstore and called up Mr. Granniss. She felt that he was a tower of strength at all times.

"Mistah Granniss, sir, I hope I'se not interruptin' your worruk, but there's a question I like ta ask. Is there any way you can stop a relative frum tearin' down a door when she wants ta get in a room where you don't want her? 'Cause that ole battleaxe of an aunt has gone after a carpenter to break down the door of Gramma's room so her girl can have that fer her room. An' is there any way to stop her?"

"Why yes, I think there is Hattie. Does Miss Dale know you are calling me? Did she ask you to?"

"Oh, no sir, Mistah Granniss. An' don't you go tell her, neither. I just overheard a conversation, and I thought mebbe I oughtta do somepin' about it."

"Well, don't you worry, Hattie, I'll look into things. I don't think she'd dare go that far anyway."

"Oh yes, she would. You doan know dat woman."

"All right, Hattie. I'll look after it."

"Okay, thanks Mistah Grannis!" and Hattie hung up and went for her pills and cinnamon.

What Mr. Granniss did was to call up the police headquarters that wasn't far from the Huntley home.

"Is that you, Mike? Well, glad I caught you. This is Granniss. I think I want your help in something. It's rather a difficult matter and as usual I'm butting into affairs that don't perhaps rightly concern me. So I thought I better rope you into it. You remember Dale Huntley, the little girl you used to look out for when she went to school."

"Sure thing I do," said Mike heartily. "Her Gramma died the other day, didn't she?"

"Yes, she did, and she's having a stiff time of it just now. Some in-laws came to the funeral, and don't seem to know enough to go home. The woman is the widow of Dale's Uncle Harold, and she's a tartar. She's trying to make it appear that she ought to inherit at least a part of that house, and she's making life miserable for Dale. She hasn't of course a leg to stand on, for the house is Dale's out and out, but while she's here trying to see what she can work, she's doing everything she can to make herself unpleasant. Just now I hear she's taken a notion she wants her daughter to have Grandmother's room, and because Dale has locked the door, and doesn't want it opened—wants to keep it just as her grandmother left it—the aunt has gone off to get a carpenter to break down the door. Can you manage to stop that, Mike? You see Dale doesn't know I know. Hattie, the maid, phoned me. I wonder if you can't invent a reason for hanging around and helping out if it really comes to a showdown?"

"Sure thing, Mr. Granniss. I'll find a way. Dale used to be a little pal of mine in her little-girl school days."

The big policeman asked a few more questions, and promised to do what he could and keep an eye on the house, and when he had hung up he gave a few terse directions to some of his men, and then went out walking in the vicinity of the Huntley house, first encircling it at a distance, until he had pretty well taken in everything that was going on. From different points he did some watching of the house, and it was so that he finally saw Aunt Blanche approaching purposefully up the street, with a shambling, ancient carpenter, carrying a small chest of tools, in her wake. She had the appearance of towing him, like a truck and a trailer. Mike smiled grimly behind his hand, and changed his position somewhat so that he could take in the whole situation.

Aunt Blanche came briskly up the steps of the house, and let herself and her workman into the living room, not pausing to look for anybody, but mounting the stairs determinedly, the carpenter obediently following her.

Mike by this time had crossed the road and put himself within hearing distance, for just then Aunt Blanche had her hands full and was not listening for rubber-shod footsteps behind her.

Dale stood at the head of the stairs, blocking the way to Grandmother's room effectually.

But the aunt's voice was determined and clear, as she pointed to the closed door down the hall.

"That is the door we want opened,"she said forcefully. "Someone has locked it, and we need to get in."

But Dale stepped up in front of the carpenter.

"No," she said firmly, "we do *not* want that door open, Mr. Moxey. My aunt is mistaken. This house is mine and I definitely do not want the door open. I locked it myself, and do not wish it interfered with."

"But lady, you said the *owner* wanted it open—" said the old man turning puzzled eyes to Aunt Blanche's angry face.

"You don't understand, carpenter, I am really the owner of the house, though there are some legal matters to be attended to before I take possession, but I *must* have the door open at once, and I'll pay you double what you asked if you do it at once without further discussion. Step aside, Dale, and let him pass. I simply won't be interfered with."

But it was not Dale, but the policeman who did the stepping. He strode up the two remaining steps of the stairs and planted himself right in the way between Aunt Blanche and the closed door.

"Sorry, madam, I'll have to interfere. This house belongs to Miss Dale, and she's the only one who has a right to say whether her doors shall be open or not, so, Moxey, you better scram! You don't do any carpentry work on this home unless Miss Dale Huntley hires you to do it. So scram! And do it quick if you don't want I should take you to the station house."

"Now look here!" said Aunt Blanche. "Who are you, I should like to know, and what business have you butting in on my affairs?"

"I'm the Chief of Police, ma'am, and this doesn't happen to be your affair. It is entirely Miss Dale's affair, and she says she doesn't want her grandmother's door open, so it doesn't get opened. I been asked to look after Miss Dale's affairs, and keep an eye on her house, and I'm doing it. I've known Miss Dale since she was a baby, and I don't intend she shall be put upon. I don't know who you are, nor what right you have in this house, but if you don't belong here, *you* better scram, too."

"The idea! The very idea! I'm Dale's aunt, and I've come here to look after her affairs for her since her grandmother died. So you see she doesn't need your care any longer. *I'm* here to do that."

"No ma'am. You made a mistake., You ain't Miss Dale's guardian, and I happen to know she's of age and don't need no guardian no more. I'm just here to look out she ain't bothered, not even by a so-called relative."

"Oh! So that's the idea," said the irate aunt, "Dale sent for you, did she? And she asked you to protect what she chooses to think is her own. Well, Dale, I didn't think you'd descend to sending for the police, but since you have, I shall have to send for my lawyer."

"Send for all the lawyers you want, lady," said the imposing policeman, "but you'll still find you're up against something bigger than lawyers, and that's the law. But you're wrong about Miss Dale. She didn't send for me, and I didn't know just how she felt about this door till I come up the stairs and heard her say she didn't want it tore down, so I thought it was time for me to get to work. And now lady, I'll thank you to walk downstairs and to look out that you don't make any more attempts to tear down this door or else I'll have to take you a trip in my car to the station house."

"Why, you—*you*—out*rage*ous creature. To talk to a lady like that! I shall certainly report you, and have you ousted from your job!"

Mike grinned.

"Sorry, ma'am, I jus' made one mistake in this here

transaction. I shouldn't have called you a lady I see, but we'll let it go this time. Would you like me to help you down the stairs?"

"You let me alone. You take your hand off my shoulder this instant!"

"Okay, ma'am, just as soon as you scram!"

Aunt Blanche, as she felt the iron hand of the law tighten on her shoulder, "scrammed" rapidly, so that she almost fell full length down the stairs, except for the firm hold of the policeman, which steadied her safely to the hall below.

Mike steered his lady to a comfortable chair, sat her down and stood ominously before her.

"Now, ma'am," he said grimly, "if I hear of any more doings like this you may expect me around to escort you to the station house. I hope you understand!"

Then getting no answer from the frightened woman he turned and went out into the hall, where he addressed the anxious Dale who was coming down the stairs.

"Now, Miss Dale, if this so-called lady cuts up any more didoes like this, just you send word ta me. You still got Hattie, haven't you? Well, you can have her call me on the phone if anything like this happens again, and I'll be here before you can count ten. I guess mebbe it wouldn't be a bad idea to have your lawyer tell this person that you own the house, and if that doesn't do the trick I'll take her myself down to the city hall and show her who owns this house. And now, is there anything more I can do for you before I go? I just stopped around to get a line on how many folks you had here. We had a report on some very noisy doings around here couppla nights ago, with some drunks makin' a lotta whoopee! I thought I better understand what to count on. Grandma never had such doings here, and I couldn't rightly understand it. Thought I better come and ask you."

Dale's cheeks flamed scarlet with embarrassment.

"Why—it was just some callers, strangers to me, who

came to see my relatives. They brought some liquor with them. But they soon went away."

"Well, Miss Dale, if anything like that happens again you better call me up as soon as it begins. We're tryin' to put a stop to such doin's in this township you know. Well, thanks for the information, and call me again if you need me. Good morning!" and Mike tramped out the door and down the walk in his rubber soles, making a vague sound of law and order.

Dale did not go into the living room, where she saw Aunt Blanche getting ready for a showdown of words. Instead she went quickly into the kitchen and almost fell over Hattie who was well placed by the crack of the partly open door in a position to hear all that went on in the front part of the house.

Quietly Dale steadied Hattie to a firm stand, and closing the door softly behind her, she then came near Hattie and whispered:

"Hattie, did you telephone to the Police Headquarters for Mike?"

Hattie opened wide innocent eyes.

"Oh, no ma'am, Miss Dale. I never telephoned to no P'lice Headquarters. I'd be scared to death to do that."

"Well, I wonder whatever started him here," she murmured more to herself than to Hattie, but Hattie hurried over to turn the burner down under the stew she was concocting, to hide a knowing glint in her innocent eyes. Was this the way Mr. Granniss had taken care of the message she had confided to him?

A few minutes later Dale heard the front door open and close, and footsteps going down the walk to the gate. She hurried over to the door and called:

"Are you going far, Aunt Blanche? Because lunch is almost ready and I know you like it really hot. And are the young people coming soon?"

Aunt Blanche's voice came back coldly.

"I don't know I'm sure when they will be here. Whenever they please, I suppose. As for me, I'm going down to see my lawyer! I'll see if this kind of thing can go on any longer."

Dale closed the door softly and leaning back against it drew a deep breath, and lifted her heart in thankfulness. Whatever was coming next Aunt Blanche wouldn't be likely to be here for lunch, and it would be good to have a little interval for anger to subside before there had to be any more family conversation.

But if Dale had known what was coming next she might not have felt so relieved.

POWELTON and Corliss came rushing in an hour later, shouting to know if lunch was ready, and Hattie appeared quietly in the kitchen door and said that it was if they would sit down right away. She didn't know that Dale was coming downstairs. She knew that she must be very much upset by what had gone on that morning, and of course these two young people had not likely heard of it all, unless they had met their mother, which didn't seem likely. They were talking eagerly about the golf course where they had been playing that morning, and it didn't sound as if they had been with their mother. They must have all taken whatever breakfast they took, at the hotel. Perhaps only coffee. They were like that. And they had been at the party the night before, so they might have felt shy about coming to the house, not quite knowing how they would be received.

But the two youngsters were not shy, not they. They swarmed into the house as if they owned it and shouted out their wants. They chattered and they clattered and Dale, hurrying downstairs to prevent any new kind of an outbreak, marveled at them, how easily the night before might have embarrassed them if they had any fine feelings at all. Apparently they had none for they greeted Dale quite hostilely and demanded strong coffee and pie.

Dale had determined to try out a new system with them and see if she could not possibly win them to some kind of friendliness, just because she could not bear to have them go away with a feeling that she was their enemy. So she sat down smiling, and asked them gaily where they had been that morning, what they had been doing, and did they make good scores in golf? Asked about their home grounds, what sports they liked best, where they went to school, and what studies they enjoyed the most, at which last question they hooted. Imagine anybody enjoying anything by the name of studies!

She did not attempt to enter into an argument on the subject, just skated on gaily to other topics, until finally she was rewarded by actually making them laugh at a story she told, and they looked at her with surprise that she could possibly be interesting when she talked. The haze of hostility with which they had up to this time surrounded their personalities, began slowly to melt, and the brother and sister grew almost voluble in telling their cousin several jokes and funny stories about their pranks in their home school, and they laughed immoderately.

Dale did her best to laugh with them, though there were a number of somewhat questionable pranks that really deserved a severe rebuke. But this was not the time, and she was not the person to administer it. Her object just now was to gain their friendship, and find some congenial point of contact.

The climax was reached when the lemon meringue pie came in, a really dressy pie it was with piles of meringue in fancy forms, and the two young people received it with whoops of joy and almost seemed to be having a good time, and to be glad they were there. They did their duty by the pie, each demolishing two more than normally large pieces, and sighing that they were unable to hold a third. Then they sat back and discoursed some more on school themes, and the things they were and were not going to do next winter, definitely, when they went back.

It was while they were laughing and talking and Dale was taking a deep relieved breath that they had gotten through one meal without a single combat, that the telephone rang.

It was Corliss who jumped to her feet and demanded to be allowed to answer it. But when the message began to come through she grew panicky.

"What? Where are you speaking from? The Mercy Hospital? *Where?* Who *are* you anyway? A *nurse?* Well, why are *you* calling *us* up? What? Yes, I'm Corliss Huntley. What do you want of me? Why should a nurse in a hospital want to speak to me? I guess it's my cousin Dale Huntley you want, isn't it? What? You say some one is hurt? Some one who knows me. Who is it? You say she was hit by an automobile? But *who* was it? My *mother?* But that can't be so. She just went out a little while ago. She went down to her lawyer's they say. No, I don't think she was in the neighborhood of that hospital. I don't think she ever heard of it. You're haywire. You've got your numbers crossed. *What?* You say it was Mrs. Huntley? Yes, Mrs. Blanche Huntley. Yes, that's my mother's name. Won't you ask her when she is coming home? Tell her we are all through lunch! *What?* You say she is badly *hurt?* She isn't *dead* is she? Oh, she *couldn't* have been run over by a car. She's very careful crossing streets. What? You say she wants *me?* She wants *us both,* me and my brother? Yes, he's here. But wouldn't it be better for her to take a taxi and come back home? Oh, you say she is too badly hurt. You say she's unconscious. Oh, *Powelton,* what shall we *do?*" and with a shriek that for once wasn't planned for effect, Corliss flung the telephone from her and threw herself on the floor in a spasm of frenzied tears and screaming.

"Oh, my mother, my *mother!* I just know she'll *die,* and what shall we *do?* We shouldn't have come to Grandma's funeral. I knew it was bad luck when we started, and now Mother's going to die, and what'll become of *us?* Oh, they say there are always three deaths in a family after one has come, so one of *us* will have to die, and it *can't* be *me,* for I'm *scared!"*

Wildly Corliss was carrying on, screaming so that the sound could be heard all up and down the street.

Dale reached over to her aunt's place where a clean napkin was set by the plate, and unfolding it she dipped it quietly into the glass of ice water, and then went over and knelt beside the frantic Corliss. Talking gently she put the cold wet napkin on the girl's hot forehead and eyes. Quickly she washed her face till the girl gasped and finally ceased to scream so wildly.

"There, there, dear," she was saying, "quiet down, little girl. We'll call up and find out just how your mother is. Maybe it isn't as bad as you think. It's always hard to understand anything over the phone, especially when you're excited. But you'll have to stop crying before I try to call, or I can't hear what they say."

"Aw, shut up, Corrie," said Powelton suddenly rousing to the fact that he was the man of the family and ought to do something about it. "Shut up, Corrie. Shut up till we find out!"

And at last the screaming ceased entirely and Dale went to retrieve the receiver and discover if she could what nurse had been talking to Corliss. For by the time of course the hospital had hung up and the operator was calling: "Operator! Operator! Won't you please hang up your receiver?"

But at last Dale got the right nurse, and a small amount of information, enough to know that they could not tell yet how badly Aunt Blanche had been injured. They had just taken her to the operating room, and wouldn't be able to give more definite information until the doctor came back from the operation. And anyway the woman's relatives had better come to the hospital as soon as possible, as they might be needed. If she rallied she might want to talk to them by and by.

At the word about her mother having gone to the operating room Corliss went into another fit of terrible weeping, and Dale had to put more ice water on her face, and pet her like a child to bring her back to normal again.

"Aw, shut up, can'tcha!" wailed the boy, almost as overwrought as his sister.

"Come on," said Dale. "We'll have to go right down to the hospital and see if she wants us for anything, and you two mustn't be weeping when you go in or they'll put you right out of the place. And you know your mother might need you very badly for some reason. Come, grow up and be a man and a woman for this emergency."

So she coaxed them along till she got them to go upstairs and prepare for going to the hospital.

"Corliss," she said, "I've got a pretty pink bedjacket. Come over to my room and see if you think your mother would like you to bring it over for her. And wouldn't she want some pretty nightrobes? Go to her bureau and pick out a couple. I know she won't like wearing those hospital gowns they have, not after she begins to get better."

So she distracted the child from her horror and fear over her mother's possible fate, and got her interested in preparing to please her mother, a thing she had hardly ever got her interest off herself long enough to even think of. Then presently she talked in a soothing way.

"Come, cheer up. You don't want to go weepy when you get there. Your part will be to act cheerful. That will help her to get well quicker."

"Oh, do you think she'll ever get well?" It was Corliss who cried out again.

"Why yes, of course," said Dale with more hope in her

voice than she actually felt sure of herself. And in her heart she began to pray that the Lord would overrule this happening, and help them all. Then, finally, with the aid of Hattie, who appeared helpfully at the right minute, they finally got started to the hospital.

Out in the street Corliss seemed to put aside her fears, and became interested in the people she was passing, but the boy walked gravely along, scarcely speaking at all. Dale wondered if he really was touched by his mother's condition. And what kind of a scene would they make when they reached the hospital? Corliss, who was used to letting her feelings govern her actions. Would she realize that they wouldn't stand for her tantrums in a hospital? Once she tried to explain to them that they must remember they would have to be very quiet when they got there, because there were a great many sick people there, some of whom were in a most critical condition.

"Well, I guess my mother's as sick as anybody, and why should I think about other people when I'm feeling bad about my mother?" put in Corliss.

"But why would you want to make other people suffer? It won't hurt your mother any for you to be kind and thoughtful for others."

"I should worry about other people. I'll feel bad about my mother if I want to. And you can't stop me. I'll scream if I like, no matter what you say." This from Corliss.

"I'm afraid you would have somebody more unpleasant to deal with than myself," said Dale quietly. "The hospital authorities would not allow you to stay there if you should make an outcry. They would have the orderly put you out."

"Put me out! They wouldn't *dare.*"

"Oh, yes, they would. It is their business to keep the hospital quiet for the sick people for whom they are responsible. Your mother is one of their patients, and for *her* sake, at least, you would not want to make a disturbance.

Your mother might hear it, and it would make her worse."

"Oh, she knows me. She wouldn't mind what I did," said Corliss.

"Well, I don't believe you would enjoy being put out of the hospital because you wouldn't keep the rules, and not be allowed to enter it again while your mother was there."

"They wouldn't *dare!*" said Corliss indignantly. "I never heard of such a thing. I would certainly tell them where to get off. I would get my mother's lawyer to go and tell them. I guess they would be afraid of a lawyer, wouldn't they?"

"I'm afraid not, Corliss," said Dale sadly. "You see they have their patients to look out for. You wouldn't want them to let any harm come to your mother, would you?"

"Oh, there couldn't any harm come to her that way. She knows me!"

"Aw, shut up, you little fool you," said Powelton, "and if you dare put on one of your acts at that hospital I'll wallop you, and I don't mean mebbe."

Corliss gave a half-frightened gasp and glanced at him sideways. It was evident she had experienced one of her loving brother's wallopings in the past, and had no desire to have another. Not this time. So they passed on their way in silence, and Dale felt almost sorry for the naughty girl who kept giving her brother speculative glances from time to time. When they reached the hospital Corliss paused at the steps of the great building.

"I'll just wait out here," she said, "while you go in Dale. I'm scared to go in until you find out how mother is."

"No," said Dale firmly, "you'll have to go in now with me. You might be needed at once, and there might not be time for me to come out and hunt for you."

"Whaddaya mean?" she asked with bated breath, a gray look coming over her face. "You don't think she's dead, do you?"

"No, no, Corliss," said Dale quietly. "I trust not. They told us to come at once, so we must go in."

"Oh-h-h-!" began Corliss with every evidence of a tantrum in the offing. Dale cast a hopeless troubled look at her, and wondered desperately what she should do next to prevent an outbreak, but to her astonishment Powelton stepped before his sister and looked into her eyes.

"Now, Corrie, you just pipe down and behave yourself. Understand?"

Corliss dropped her glance and ducked her head, and went beaten, up the steps. She dropped gratefully into the seat where Dale placed her, while Dale went up to the desk and found out where they were to go.

They had to wait a little while to get any information at all about the invalid.

"She's still in the operating room," was all the information they could get at first. But after a long long wait a white starched nurse came rattling down the corridor and told them they could come up and look at her for a moment, but that she was not yet out of the ether and they could not stay.

They followed the nurse, filled with awe and horror as they passed open doors with glimpses of white beds and white faces on the pillows. And then they arrived at the ward with rows of beds and more white faces on pillows.

As they entered the doorway Corliss stopped stock still.

"But that is the *ward*," she said to the nurse. "You can't put *my mother* in the ward. She would be *furious* at being put in a ward."

The nurse gave her a sweeping glance of contempt.

"Sorry, Miss," she said calmly, "it was the only place we had left in the hospital. We are overcrowded as you can easily see."

"Well, then you should have sent her to some other hospital," said Corliss, sounding so much like her mother that Dale looked at her in astonishment.

"That wouldn't have been possible if we wanted to save her life," she said. "She was bleeding profusely, and unable to say where she wanted to go even if we had had time to ask her. There was no one with her of course to answer for her. But anyway we had no other room nor bed."

"Well, you must have her moved at once into a private room. No matter what it costs."

"It isn't a matter of cost, Miss," said the nurse, with another withering glance at the girl. "There *isn't* any other room."

"Then we'll have her taken to another hospital at once," said the spoiled child haughtily.

"That would be impossible," said the nurse stiffly. "She has been operated on, and it would probably be a very serious matter to move her at present. Besides, all the other hospitals are full to overflowing. But anyway you would have to see the doctor. And now, if you want to look in you'll find your mother in the third bed from the far end," and then the nurse turned coldly away and left the three standing alone in the doorway.

It was Dale who went forward, and after an instant of hesitation Powelton followed her, solemnly, walking gravely, as if at a church, feeling that the walk he had to take was miles in length, with all those white staring faces from pillows on each side of him.

But his going left Corliss alone, and Corliss, looking around on the unfamiliar scene, was frightened. Her haughty insolence faded suddenly away and left her trembling and ready to cry. Suddenly the tears came down, and she opened her mouth to scream, but the head nurse appeared at her side and taking firm hold of her arm steered her out into the hall.

"You mustn't make a disturbance in there. There are some very sick women in there, one has just been brought from the operating room. If you frighten her she might die."

Corliss held her scream in the middle, and stared at the

nurse defiantly. "I'd like to see anybody stop me!" she gasped desperately. "How could you stop me?"

The nurse put out her hand and touched a button by the door.

"I have called the orderly. When he gets here, which will be at once, if you haven't stopped, he will muffle your mouth and carry you out instantly. We do not permit anybody in the hospital who cannot control themselves. If you make a disturbance now you will not be admitted to this hospital again."

"But—my—mother—is here!" quivered Corliss.

"It is for your mother's sake, and others, that we make these rules," said the nurse. "You wouldn't like your mother to die because she heard you scream and couldn't get up and go to help you, would you?"

Corliss stared at the nurse with frightened eyes, and then suddenly the elevator in the hall arrived and a man in working uniform came to the head nurse and saluted:

"You sent for me," he said, and his eyes suddenly looked questioningly at the pretty girl with bleary eyes.

"Yes," said the nurse crisply, "I sent for you to carry this weeping girl away. But perhaps she has conquered herself. If she has you won't be needed." The head nurse looked questioningly at Corliss and suddenly Corliss straightened up and lifted her chin bravely.

"Yes, I'll be all right," she quavered.

"Well, that sounds better," said the nurse coldly. "But Jasper, you better stay around and see if she keeps control."

Corliss put on her haughty air and started down the aisle after her brother.

"I'll be all right," she said with much the air her mother assumed to master people, and the head nurse watched her with an amused smile. She was a clever student of human nature and had an aptitude for conquering hysterical women who disturbed the peace.

Powelton and Dale were standing beside that third bed from the far end of the room, and had for the moment forgotten Corliss, else it might have been a lesson to them how to stop Corliss' tantrums another time. But they were not watching and did not see her taking that long solemn walk alone. They were looking down at that still figure on the bed, swathed in bandages, her restless hands wrapped in more bandages, were folded under the sheet, her arrogant face unrecognizable through the sheltering gauze, only her lips visible, and one arrogant eyebrow. It was almost as if she were dead. That was their first impression, for they were so little used to sickness and death. It was a ghastly sight to them to see this woman who had always carried all before her in any situation, lying there so silent, so subdued, so almost frozen in a still helplessness.

Dale was startled to think a few short hours could bring about a phenomenon like this.

But Powelton seemed suddenly to have grown up. His face had lost its spoiled baby-boy roundness and to be graven into a new more dependable maturity. It was as if to him there had been shown a vision of the briefness and solemnity of life and what it was meant for, and a startling revelation of the fact that life wasn't just meant for fun, and one couldn't get away from it no matter how hard you tried.

Then came Corliss, closely but unobtrusively shadowed by the head nurse, with the orderly openly watching her from the doorway. The question was, how would Corliss react to that white still swathed face, that rigid figure.

As Dale looked up and saw them both, she had a vision of what might be ahead for herself and for those two, in fact for those three, if Aunt Blanche came out of this and lived. And yet they had not been told the possibilities, and Dale began to wonder how all this was going to affect her life. Only a few short hours ago she had been planning how to send these relatives away so that she might go on with her plans, and have her home and her school. But it was obvious now that this could not be at once. It might be some time before her aunt was able to leave the hospital, if she recovered at all, and she could not of course refuse refuge to the cousins with such calamity upon them. Her heart sank as she recognized the possibilities ahead. Of course not. And if Aunt Blanche got well what then? There would likely be a time of recuperation, and of course it was natural that she would expect to be cared for by the only relative in that region. There was no use in arguing these matters now, however, or even shrinking from the possibility. This thing had not come upon her through any fault of her own, and being upon her, the teaching of her faith was that whatever came was sent, or at least allowed by the Lord, and therefore was to be accepted sweetly, knowing that there was some purpose in it for her good, and for the Lord's glory. What was that the Bible said about His purpose for each of His children, "that they should be *conformed* to the image of His Son."

So, if that was the Lord's purpose for her, the only way He saw to bring her to be conformed to the image of His Son, then her heart must accept His way, and yield herself to it until His will for her was complete. Meantime she must remember that her business in this world was witnessing for Christ, and that could not be done if her attitude was hostility. Was it then her work for the time being to try to witness to these two unlovely cousins? Well, she would have to learn to love them then, learn not to see all their unloveliness.

So Dale stood and looked at Powelton, and saw the new manliness dawning in the saggy boyish lines of his face, and wondered if it would last, or if every step of the way would have to be a battle.

Then there came the thought of her lover, now far on his way to some unknown destination, someone who belonged to her, and who would pray for her. He might not know what her trials and tests were being, but he would pray for her. He would know it was something hard, even if she did not feel she ought to tell him about all she was going through, but he would pray.

They did not stay long in that awful silence. Down at the other end a woman was wheeled out, and a little later a slight disturbance off at one side showed a new cot being wheeled in. There were other sufferers in this strange new world of a hospital. The new patient was moaning, and a nurse hastened to place a screen around the bed to which she was being transferred. Corliss caught a glimpse of it all, caught her breath, and bit her red lips with her little white teeth, but she did not scream. She had also seen the side view of the head nurse, and cast a quick frightened glance back at the orderly still standing in the doorway. Yes, Corliss had been thoroughly frightened for once in her life.

And then, very soon, the head nurse suggested that they had stayed long enough for now. It would be several hours before their patient would be able to recognize them.

So they walked solemnly back through that awful length of aisle with suffering on every side, leaving a mother behind them, a mother who had never been very motherly toward them, but still had been the only power over them, that had dominated their young lives thus far.

Down at the desk they had a few words with the desk clerk, and then met the doctor who had attended the patient. He spoke gravely, saying it was rather impossible to tell just how serious the injuries had been yet. There was a broken arm, two fractured ribs, and a concussion of course, but it would not be possible to tell further until all the X-rays had been developed. There must be absolute quiet for her for several days, and he hoped there was a good chance of her ultimate recovery, but there must be no excitement whatever of course, absolute, cheerful, quiet when they came to see her, preferably not too often. Meantime they could keep in touch with the nurse, and find out how she was coming on; and in a day or two she would be more able to see them and to recognize them.

It was then that Corliss lifted her phenomenally long golden lashes and used her great beautiful blue eyes on the grave doctor.

"But she'll just hate that ward," she said earnestly. "She won't stand for it for a minute when she comes to herself. She'll simply *have* to have a private room or go to another hospital."

The grave doctor studied the spoiled child a moment and almost smiled.

"My dear young lady," he said almost wearily, "she will have to be satisfied with whatever she *can get!* Every hospital in this city is overcrowded, and they are even putting cots in the main hallways in City Hospital. But even if there were rooms elsewhere the patient would not be able to be moved. It would be as much as her life was worth to attempt it at present."

"Oh!" said Corliss, suddenly drooping like a deflated balloon, and following Dale as they took their way home, in a sad young silence.

12

IT was Corliss who at last broke the silence as they turned into their own street and could see the house just up the hill.

"Well, what are we going to do now?" she asked in a tone more humble than any Dale had ever heard her use before.

"Well," said Dale trying to speak cheerfully, "I think the first thing to do is to get some dinner, don't you? We can't go through hard things without food. And then we've got to sit down and plan just what is to be done next. Do you happen to know what your mother did this morning about her baggage? She said she was going over to the hotel to get it, before she went out. She didn't do it, did she? Because I didn't see any arrive. Although of course I was upstairs and might not have heard a taxi drive up."

"No," said Powelton, "I don't think she did. She told me she was going out to get a cheaper boarding place, that she couldn't stand that hotel any longer, and when she got back I would have to go get the baggage and take it somewhere, or else bring it to the house."

"Well, of course we don't know what she did, and we

can't ask her till she is well enough, so I guess after we have had dinner you better go over to the hotel and get the things. Are they packed in suitcases, do you know, or will you have to go and pack? Corliss, do you know? Did she pack before she came over this morning?"

"No, the things were hanging in the closets, and lying on the bureau."

"Well, then we'll all go over together and get them packed. We'll go just as soon as we've had dinner, or if you aren't too hungry we can go now. It probably won't take long if all of us go."

"Let's go now," said Corliss dolefully.

"All right," said Dale pleasantly, "perhaps that would be best. And anyway Hattie will know to wait dinner for us till we get there."

"I don't want any dinner," said Corliss, her eyes brimming with tears. "I don't ever want to eat again."

"Oh, yes you do, dear," smiled Dale. "You can't go through hard things without food. Come now, don't get to crying. You've been a brave girl. This is something we've got to go through bravely. Courage always helps at a time like this, and we'll try to be just as cheerful as we can."

"But where can we go?" wailed Corliss. "We don't know what place Mom found."

"We'll just go to our house, of course child. You'll stay there till your mother gets well enough to say what she wants to do. You'd like that best, wouldn't you?"

"Yes," said Corliss sadly. "I don't ever want to see that old hotel again."

"Well, here's a taxi," said Dale, "we'll take that and get the packing and moving over at once."

So they went to the hotel, and Powelton marched over to the desk and got the keys.

"He says Mom paid the bill here, and said she'd be back today to check out," he said thoughtfully.

So they went sorrowfully up to the rooms and began their work.

It didn't take long. Aunt Blanche had folded a good many of her things into the suitcases before she left in the morning.

Dale systemized the work.

"You pick up the little things, brushes, combs, powder and so on," she said to Corliss, "and I'll fold up the things that are still hanging in the closet."

So they were soon done and went to help Powelton, but found he was just locking the suitcase. They rang for the porter, and soon were on their way back to the house, quiet and thoughtful, trying to think what was coming next.

"Where am I going to sleep?" Corliss asked. "I don't want that Grandmother's room any more, not since I've seen how Mom looked in the hospital. I said I wanted it, but I don't now. I'm scared of it."

Dale drew a relieved sigh, for she had teared a battle on that subject.

"Why, I think you better take the room where your mother took her naps, don't you? Then Powelton can have the next one, and there's a door between. You can leave it open if you want to."

"Okay," agreed Corliss listlessly, "that will be nice. I'd like that."

"It's okay by me," agreed the newly grown-up brother.

Then they went in to a nice dinner that Hattie had all ready for them, a tasty hot soup and a meat pie, with vegetables. It was hot and appetizing, and there was a peach pie. The young people ate and were heartened, and then arose and offered to help clear off the table. Probably because they felt shy and awkward and did not know what to do next, not feeling in the mood for either games or reading.

Later in the evening Dale telephoned the hospital and got the latest news, that the patient was sleeping quietly,

..nd less restless than she had been. She was doing as well as could be expected at present. So finally the brother and sister went to bed, and were soon asleep, worn out with excitement and worry. And at last Dale was free to go to her own room, read over her precious letter, and go on with the answer she had begun earlier in the day.

Somehow her heart cried out greatly for this newly found lover whom she had known so short a time, and yet who seemed to be the only one to whom she could unburden her heart.

Dale sat down and read over her unfinished letter, and after a moment began to write:

Dear, This is rather late at night. Something happened. We've had an exciting afternoon. My aunt—I think you met her the day of Grandmother's funeral—went out on an errand and was run over by an automobile. They telephoned us from the hospital and we went right over. We saw her but she was still under the ether and didn't see us of course. We came home and got dinner, and now the brother and sister are asleep. The word from the hospital tonight is the patient is doing as well as can be expected. A concussion, a broken arm and ribs, some facial cuts are among the injuries. We don't know all yet of course.

So now I am wondering what is coming next. I think I told you that the aunt has not been easy to get along with, and her children have been rather impossible. But of course now I must be all I can to these cousins, for they haven't anybody else, and I've been thinking that God wouldn't have sent this to me if there hadn't been some good reason. I think perhaps I needed to learn to love them, for I never have, I'm afraid. Of course I haven't seen much of them, but when I have they have always looked down on me, and been just as disagreeable as they could. How-

ever, perhaps some of that may have been my fa
too.

Perhaps I ought not to be telling you all this, fo
you will soon be having enough unpleasant things of
your own to think about. But you are all I have now,
and it is sweet to know I have your sympathy and
prayers. I'm sure God is going somehow to bring
good out of this experience. But for the present at
least, I shall not be able to go ahead with my plans
about the little children till I see the outcome of this.
So I shall be glad to think you will take this to the
Lord for me too.

And now I am going to read your dear letter once
more and pray *for you,* and then I am going to sleep.
God be with you my dear. How I wish I might be
looking forward to your soon coming back to me,
but it will be according to His will. Good night.

DALE

Dale was very tired and was not long in getting to sleep
in spite of all the questions that came up to torment her.
But in the middle of the night she was awakened by a
slender figure in frilly silk pajamas standing by her bed,
and putting a cold little hand on her cheek.

Dale started awake and saw that it was Corliss.

"Why, child, dear!" she said gently, for she saw that the
young girl was trembling like a leaf. "What is the matter?
Haven't you been to sleep?"

"Yes, but I had a terrible dream. I dreamed my mother
was dead. Oh, Dale, do you think my mother will die? She
looked so terrible all done up like that!"

Dale reached out warm comforting hands toward the
erstwhile unpleasant cousin and drew her down on the side
of the bed.

"Why no, dear, I don't think so. You know the nurse
said she was doing as well as could be expected," she said

...ing the cold little hands in her own. But Corliss only ...mbled the more.

"Oh, Dale, I'm —*frightened!*" and the pretty gold head went down on the cold hands and the girl began to cry as if her heart would break.

"I went to my brother but he was sound asleep. He wouldn't wake up."

Then Dale put her arms around the cold trembling shoulders and drew Corliss down close to her.

"Get in my bed with me, Corliss," she said gently. "You are all in a shiver. Let me get you warm. Cuddle up to me and you won't be so frightened. It was only a dream you know."

Corliss promptly slipped inside the covers and shivered up to Dale's inviting arms, and it wasn't a second before she was weeping right into Dale's neck, shaking with great sobs.

Dale let her cry for a while, and presently began to talk in low tones.

"Poor little girl," she whispered. "I'm not much of a substitute for a mother, am I? But you just cry there till you feel better. It will do you good to get all the cry out. Poor little girl!"

"Don't pity me!" cringed the child. "I can't bear to be pitied!"

"Oh, I'm sorry! You see this is something just a little out of my line, and I don't really know you so awfully well yet you know, but you cuddle up close and perhaps I'll learn."

"Oh, you're all right!" gasped the unhappy girl. "I just aren't used to being petted. But—I guess—maybe—it isn't so bad!" Corliss snuggled a little closer, and Dale's arm held her close. How was this coming out, this sudden intimate episode in the middle of the night with this strange abnormal child?

But she began to pat the soft young shoulder, and presently the shivering and trembling ceased, and the hands

she held grew warm. A few more minutes and the b[...]
came softly, regularly. She thought the girl was asl[...]
Should she try to slip away now? No, that seemed t[...]
unfriendly, and if she should waken again she might b[...]
even more frightened. No, she must see this night
through. It might mean all the difference between winning
or losing Corliss. Maybe this was why the Lord had let this
unhappy experience come to them all, to bring them nearer to each other. For after all they were near of kin.

Dale wondered if it was going to be possible for her to
get to sleep again, so close to another. She had always slept
alone. But she too was very weary and it wasn't long until
she was asleep herself.

She awoke very early, and lying still because she did not
wish to waken Corliss, she had the probable day spread
out before her. How was she going to get through with it?
Certainly she could not do it alone. She must have help
from on high. And so lying there with the sleeping Corliss
in her arms she began to pray. And certainly Corliss had
never been so near to prayer in all her rebellious young life.
Would she have been frightened if she could have known
how near she was to an open line to God?

As the morning sun stole in from the window, slanting
across the gold of Corliss' pretty curls, Dale glanced down
at her, and thought how pretty the girl was now, asleep,
with the hard selfish lines erased in slumber, the little
mouth without its illumination, all sweet and innocent.
What a pity the child couldn't be trained to want to be
sweet and pleasant and right. What a pity that in all prob-
ability, if her mother lived, she would have to grow up just
like her mother. Was Aunt Blanche ever sweet and child-
like herself? And would there be any possible way of her
being changed? Of course God could do anything. He
could change what He had made in the first place, although it wasn't likely Aunt Blanche was *born* disagreeable, at least not any more than all humanity was full of sin

173

etermined to go in selfish ways. But how could one get a person like Aunt Blanche, or even one like Corliss, to know their need of God and turn to Him? As far as she herself was concerned it seemed an utterly thankless, useless task to attempt it. It would only bring scorn and derision upon her.

Well, a new day was at hand and what was it to bring forth? There would have to be a visit to the hospital of course, by them all. Judging Corliss by her nervous state last night, there was no telling what she would do. Perhaps she might even be capable of refusing to go to the hospital, which might make trouble with her mother, in case her mother was well enough to know. However she would have to decide that question when she came to it.

The first question that was nearest to Dale's heart just then was whether there might be a letter in her new postoffice box for her, and how she was going to manage to get it without being questioned about why she was going to the office. Really what she ought to do was to somehow manage to slip out of bed without waking Corliss, pick up her clothes and make an escape to the bathroom to dress. Could she do that?

She gave a quick glance around the room to see just what she would need to take with her, for she must plan not to return till time for Corliss to waken. She silently memorized the things she must remember to collect. The garments she had taken off the night before, her shoes, her brush and comb, her purse and keys. Then she gave herself to the task of getting away from Corliss without disturbing her. Almost finger by finger, muscle by muscle she moved, and waited between each stealthy withdrawal, breathless, to see if she had stirred Corliss' deep sleep. But the steady quiet breathing went on, and at last she was free from the covers, and outside of the bed, standing on the carpet, pulling the warm covers up over the girl. Then for an instant Corliss stretched slightly, and drew a single sighing breath, as if the relaxing was a comfort.

Dale stood for several seconds, watching her cousin, thinking again how pretty and really sweet-looking she was in her sleep, and how one could love her if she would only always be like that.

Then carefully she stole across the room and let herself out, closing the door noiselessly. She slid into the bathroom where with swift fingers she donned her garments, hurried downstairs, and went to the kitchen for a word with Hattie who was just beginning to get things ready for breakfast.

"Don't hurry, Hattie," she whispered. "I don't want them to wake up very early, for they can't go to the hospital till visiting hours begin, and it will just be a restless time to get through. I'm running down to the store now to get a few things. I'll be right back, but is there anything else you want besides the yeast you said you needed for hot biscuits tonight?"

"Why yes," said Hattie. "We need mustard and vinegar and cinnamon and salt. Can you bring all those?"

Dale laughed.

"Did you think I had grown weak, Hattie? Sure I can bring them, and a bit of fruit of some kind too. Maybe some grapes. Well then you carry on till I get back. If the cousins wake up tell them I'll be right back and then we'll call up the hospital. It's too early to do it now. But I don't think they'll waken before I'm back."

So she hurried away, and was rewarded by finding a nice thick letter in her new letter box. She went on to the store and got a few necessities, and hurried back to the house.

It was all quiet there yet. Hattie reported that nothing had been heard from the two, who were likely accustomed to sleeping late, and Dale drew a happy sigh of relief and sat down by her desk to read her letter, remembering that she couldn't be sure of long privacy, and so must merely skim over it the first reading, and read it slowly later when she was assured of more time. But as she opened the letter she thrilled anew that he had written again so soon. Her lover! Her letter! It was all so wonderful. So like a fairy story she used to dream when she was but a little girl.

My dearest:

I pause and wonder at myself for daring to write that, but you are mine, aren't you? I rejoice at the thought. It thrills me anew every time I think of it.

And I have been sitting here in the train, flying along to a far and unknown destination, on my way to follow out orders, and as I sit here alone I think of you, and wonder what it would be if you were sitting by my side. How wonderful it would be! And so I try to kid myself that you are here. I turn and look down at where you might be, and smile at you, just vaguely. If any were noticing me they might wonder, but no one in the car would mind. In fact if they knew they would probably all understand. For every fellow in this car has likely left some beloved one behind him.

And when I think of that, and the way I used to feel, looking enviously at the other fellows with snapshots and photographs at which they took furtive glances, I feel triumphant. I used to envy all the other boys, even those who only had sisters, or just friends, and I hadn't even a mother left.

But now I'm filled with joy. For I have a girl who beats them all I'm sure. A girl so beautiful that I wonder any of them could possibly have left her free for me. They just never met her, that's all, I'm quite sure.

Did I ever take time to tell you how beautiful you are to me? You thought perhaps that I never noticed the little details about you, but I did. I was just so

pressed for time on the important things that had to
be said before we parted, that I saved it up to write
about instead. You may think I would have forgotten, but I haven't. I can close my eyes and see your
exquisite face, even the very rose tint of your cheeks,
your lips and chin. The soft unpainted curves of your
sweet lips, the lines they take when you speak, and
when you smile. Even without closing my eyes I can
bring them all back to mind, so that you seem to be
conversing with me, smiling at me. I can see you as
you were sitting against the hemlock green, the sun-
light shining on your hair. It is all dear, very dear. I
can see the little curl at the back of your sweet white
neck when you stooped over to pick up the little
beechnuts that fell at your feet from the beech tree
over at our left. I can see the very color of your dress.
My girl, who says she loves me, and doesn't mind
that we haven't known each other very long, because somehow God has introduced us, and made us
to be sure about one another. After all, that is the
main thing, isn't it? That we both know and love our
Saviour? And when I think of that I find it again so
very wonderful, that I should have walked into that
social center and found you.

I wasn't looking for you then. I wouldn't have
gone to anything with the word "social" belonging
to it to find my dream girl. Because I had found so
many of the girls in such places were just pretty
dressed-up dolls, and that wasn't the kind of girl I
wanted. Not if I never had one, did I want a fashionable doll, no matter how pretty she was.

But now I have found her I defy anyone to find a
more beautiful girl anywhere, than my dear girl. She
thoroughly satisfies me, and I want you to know it.
And I'm sure that wherever I go, and however many
girls I see, whether beautiful or sensible or very

lovely, none will ever look or seem to be as lovely as my girl.

And so I have described to you the girl I love. The girl, who one day, please God, is to be my wife.

There was more of the same sort, deeply sweet and earnest. Wonderful talk which Dale had never dreamed of having written to her. Precious sentences that seemed almost as if they must have been framed in Heaven. At least framed by one to whom Heaven was very real.

And when she had finished reading she folded the letter tenderly and slipped it safely inside the blouse she was wearing. Such letters were not for the public eye, nor for doubtful jeering if one so inclined should come upon it. Precious, precious! She found herself wishing that Grandmother might have known before she went away that this great thing was coming to her life. How glad Grandmother would have been for her!

And then she heard footsteps above stairs, and realized that her day had begun. There was only time to breathe a prayer for help before Powelton came down, and she could hear Corliss hurrying around to follow him.

So she arose and went out to the kitchen to tell Hattie she might as well get ready to serve breakfast.

13

THE young people came down to the dining room very much subdued in manner, and sat down at the table quietly, as those might do who had met with a great awakening of some sort.

Corliss even flung a little shadow of a half smile toward Dale, like pale sunshine, and Dale felt again that wonder that the girl could change so over night. Was it because she remembered her fright of last night? Was she still afraid of that dream of hers?

But Dale sat down cheerily smiling and said, "Good morning," as if she were any hostess.

It certainly was astonishing to see how quietly they ate their breakfast. Though they did not seem so ravenous as they had been before. But there was no complaining, no snarling, no demands for food not on the table. Hattie looked at them wonderingly, and even smiled at Dale when she asked for more cream.

"Have you called the hospital yet?" asked Corliss shrinkingly.

"No, I thought we better wait till the doctor was there. Then we could really find out how things are going. But perhaps I might call now and get the nurse's viewpoint."

Yes," said the boy suddenly. "It seems an awful long me since last night."

"Yes," said Dale springing up. "I'll call right away."

They followed her to the telephone and waited solemnly for the nurse to be called. But when the nurse came there wasn't much news. She said Mrs. Huntley had spent a fairly comfortable night, but she would not be able to give them any definite news until the doctor arrived. Yes, they might come at any time to see her now, but about eleven o'clock would be best. She had of course suffered a good deal of shock from the accident, and they must be prepared to realize that she would not as yet be very responsive. She might not even recognize who they were.

They turned solemnly away from the phone, and Corliss went over to the window and stared out unseeingly. Dale, looking at her furtively, saw her wiping away big tears, and went over to put a comforting arm about her.

"Come on, dear," she said pleasantly, "don't let's worry yet. We'll have to expect she won't be quite herself yet, but the nurse seemed to feel she was doing as well as could be expected. So let's run up and get the beds made. That will help to keep our minds busy, and then we'll get ready to start for the hospital."

The boy stared at her in a troubled way.

"Is there anything you'd like me to do, Dale?" he asked unexpectedly. "I don't suppose I'd be much good making beds."

"Why yes," said Dale brightly. "You can wind the clocks, one in the upper hall, and one in the living room. And there's a door upstairs that needs a drop of oil. It squeaks horribly. Hattie will tell you where the oil can is. It would be well to have all squeaks oiled up before your mother comes home. We don't want anything around to make her nervous."

"Oh," said Corliss brightly, "will she be coming back here, do you think?"

"Why of course," said Dale, trying to make her voi sound cheerful over the thought. "That is, of course I can be sure what *she* will want to do, when she is able to get around again, but I should think this would be her natural haven while she is recovering, and we want to be ready for her."

"Then you think she is really going to recover?" asked the son anxiously.

"Why, I should think so, from what the doctor said last night," said Dale. "He didn't seem to feel there were going to be any serious complications. But of course we can tell better after we have seen him again this morning."

Somehow Powelton seemed to have taken on a new character, silent, subdued, solemn and a bit anxious. Dale rather liked him in his new role. He seemed almost attractive now.

Upstairs Dale and Corliss made lively work of putting the rooms in order, one on each side of a bed, smoothing the covers neatly. Corliss seemed never to have tried bed-making before, and said she thought it was almost fun.

Then they got themselves ready and started for the hospital.

Dale could not help pitying Corliss as she glanced at her while they went up in the elevator. Corliss' hands were gripped viselike and stuffed so tightly into her chic little suit-jacket that the knuckles showed through the material. Poor child. She was frightened again. It wasn't just fear for her mother's safety, was it? She had never *seemed* really to love her mother, although that mother had always given her everything she wanted. But it seemed more a fear of possibilities, gruesome things, like suffering and death.

Corliss' lips were closed tight, her teeth even shut tight, making her soft little mouth into something firm and hard. And her eyes were frightened eyes.

She slipped over to stand by the girl, and slid her hand inside one firmly stiff young arm.

"Don't worry, Corliss," she whispered. "It's going to
be all right pretty soon, I'm sure."

Corliss gave her a troubled searching look.

"Are you *sure,* Dale?" she asked fearsomely.

"Yes, I'm quite sure," said Dale reassuringly.

Then they were at the doorway of that long room filled
with beds, and sick or dying people in those beds. Corliss
gripped Dale's hand as they walked down to her mother's
bed, gripped it so hard that it hurt, but her pursed lips gave
forth no sound. Corliss had really grown a lot in the last
twenty-four hours.

The sick woman lay, almost as yesterday, not seeming
to notice anything, till the nurse came up.

"Well, here are your people come to see you, Mrs.
Huntley," the nurse said in a pleasant tone, and the white
image in the bed turned her eyes toward them and looked
them over oddly as if they were strangers.

The sick woman's quick bright eyes surveyed them one
at a time and there came no welcoming look, nothing but
critical survey.

"You haven't got your tie put on right, Powelton," was
the first thing she said.

The boy's hand went quickly to his tie, but his face got
painfully red, and he cast a quick deploring look about to
see if the nurse or anyone else had noticed his mother.

"Do you feel any better, mother?" asked Corliss in an
unsteady little voice, so evidently trying to say the right
thing, as if she must have thought it out beforehand.

"Better?" snapped her mother. "Why should I feel better? Have I got any reason to feel better? Stuck away in this
great awful white room? My arm all tied up, my face all
tied up, and I can't do anything about it. What does it all
mean, Powelton? Why have you let them do this to me?
After all, I'm your mother you know."

The boy got white around his mouth and stooping tried
to explain in a gentle voice that surprised Dale:

"Mother, there was an accident, and you got hit by an automobile. They had to bring you to the hospital, and they are going to make you get well. You just be patient, and you'll feel better pretty soon."

"Oh, you think you can lecture me, do you? Why, you're nothing but a child! I guess I know when to be patient, and this isn't the time for that. I'll have them to know I won't be kept in this hospital *ward*. I can afford to pay for a private room if I'm really sick, but I don't think I am. They have just got me all tied up this way to amuse themselves, those doctors and nurses."

She chattered on meaninglessly, showing that she was not altogether herself, and then her eyes caught a glimpse of Dale, and she fixed her with a hateful glance:

"Oh, so *you* thought you had to come, too, did you? Well, you can *go!* I don't want you hanging around and gloating over me. And if you do anything unkind to my children before I get back I'll see that you pay for it, do you understand?"

But Corliss coming close whispered earnestly:

"Oh, mother, Dale's been wonderful to us. She's just as sweet and kind as can be! She's taking care of us."

And Powelton came closer on the other side:

"Dale has been awfully good to us," he said firmly. "She has taken us home with her and made us just as comfortable as can be. She couldn't be better. You must not talk that way about her. She is sweet and kind."

"Oh, she *is*, is she? Well it's the first time in her life then," snapped the woman on the pillow. "But she'll turn you out when she gets ready. Don't trust her."

Then the nurse came near and said in a low tone:

"She doesn't rightly know what she is saying yet. She's still under opiates, somewhat, and hasn't got back into the world yet. But I think the next time you come she'll be more like herself."

Oh, thought Dale sadly, she's quite like herself. You

ust don't know her, that is all. But aloud she said: "Of course. I know."

The invalid's sharp eyes had closed, and the visitors began to think it was time for them to leave, but suddenly she opened them and looking straight at her son, she snapped:

"I want to see my lawyer. You go down and explain to him what they are doing to me, keeping me here in this ward, and tell him to come right up and get me out of here. Do you understand?"

The young man looked at his mother disapprovingly.

"I don't think the doctor would approve having your lawyer come to see you now. You will have to wait till you are better. Just be patient mother. It will all come right."

"Oh, you think you can *manage* me, do you? Why, that's ridiculous! Nurse! Help me get up. I've got to get out of this bed right away."

The nurse came quickly, administered a quieting draught, and said gently:

"Just you lie still for a little bit, Mrs. Huntley. Everything's going to be all right."

Then the sick woman turned her eyes toward her daughter.

"Where are you going now Corliss?"

"Why, I think maybe I'll play a little tennis," said Corliss with quick understanding. "You take a nice little sleep, mother, and then we'll come and see you again."

Already the sleeping draught was taking effect, and they were able to slip away without further talk, but the nurse followed them to the hall to reassure them.

"You know she'll be quite different from this in a few days. You needn't feel worried. The doctor seemed to think she was doing as well as could possibly be expected yet."

They got themselves silently out of that hospital and down into the sunlit street, their faces utterly sad and disheartened.

"Now," said Dale suddenly when they were out fro.
any chance of being overheard, "I think we've got to plar
to do something pleasant, don't you? It wasn't just a cheerful session today. In fact I was afraid it would be just that
way, because I've heard before that when people have'had
concussions and shocks they are very vague in their minds.
But they come out of it. Don't you worry. In fact the head
nurse told me that things were going very much as the
doctor had hoped, and he thought if nothing further developed later that we might be very comfortable about the
patient. So, the idea is to try to be as cheerful as possible.
Have you any suggestions? How about it Corliss? You
said something about playing tennis. Is that what you'd
like to do?"

"Oh, I don't know," said Corliss with a desolate look.
"I don't suppose Pow will be willing to. He said the last
time we played that I wasn't playing as well as I used to,
and he was fed up with playing with me."

Powelton turned annoyedly.

"I didn't say just that, Corlie I said we ought to try and
get some others to play with us. I said you were getting
stale just playing with me, and that if we had a foursome
you'd get back to your game."

"Well, isn't that the same thing?" said Corliss sullenly.

"No," said the brother quietly, "Not quite. But anyhow, now, I'm glad to play."

Dale wondered what had come over Powelton, but she
smiled encouragingly.

"That's fine of you, Powelton," she said, "but if you
want a foursome I think I could find one for you. In fact I
might play a while myself if we can't find anybody else and
I'm sure Dick Netherby would help out. He's young but
he's rather a wizard at the game I understand. Anyway,
let's try it. I'll call him up and see if he's free."

Neither of the cousins was particularly overjoyed at the
idea of strangers, but they were on their good behavior

t now, it seemed, so they said nothing, except "Oh, all ght," and Dale went to the telephone. When she came back she said it was all right, that Dick could come, and he was going to bring over another racket for her to use, so they would all be able to play.

"Who is this Dick?" asked Corliss rather grimly. "Is he just a kid? Because kids can't really play our game."

"Wait till you see," said Dale smiling. "They send for him everywhere to play because he's really a sort of champion. But suppose we come on and eat our lunch now, and be ready when Dick comes. He may not be able to stay long this time. He's working somewhere in late afternoons."

So they went in to the nice lunch that Hattie had ready for them, and the atmosphere became a trifle less doleful.

But Dick as a tennis player turned out to be a great success. He arrived early, and they heard his sharp whistle while they sat waiting for him. They went off happily together, Corliss studying this bright-faced homely boy with the engaging grin, and wondering why it was she couldn't seem to make him look at her admiringly, the way the high school boys at home did. But there was a sort of a dignity about Dick that in spite of his youth made him seem older than he really was. Hattie watched them going off together, Dale swinging her racket as gaily as any of them, and she said to herself:

"Miss Dale, she is a real livin' saint, that's what she is! Just fancy her goin' off to play with them brats after the way they treated her before this."

14

IT was a golden day in the late fall, and as they started out for the tennis courts the leaves of the trees seemed just beginning to flame into deeper color, especially the maples, some of which had brought out a lovely real coral pink, that seemed almost as if they were trying to aim at the new fall fashionable shades. Dale took it all in, to paint it over again in words for David when she had an opportunity to be by herself and write him again. Up in a tall tree a little late bird was voicing his joy in the continued mildness of the weather, and announcing his intention of going South soon for the winter.

Somehow the problems of the immediate future grew less staggering to her mind as she went out into the sunshine to try and help two other despairing souls to keep their footing in their new uncertain world.

But there was something else besides the sunshine and the singing of birds that gave Dale a song in her heart as she went forth for a real playtime; and that was her lover, going somewhere—out into danger far away from her—but *loving* her, with a love that she felt would last even into another life, if God willed that he might not come back in

..s one. But oh how she prayed that he might come back!
..nd so David in mind went out with her, and she thought
..much about him, and perhaps played the better because of
her thought of him.

That afternoon set the pace for a sane steady life for the
two, little-more-than-children, who were thus suddenly
cast upon the mercy of a heretofore unloved cousin. They
all had a good time, even the girl who was giving up of her
time and thought to help the two cousins.

They came home to another good dinner. Hattie was all
for this that her young mistress was doing now. These
wild young visitors were showing some sense and allow-
ing themselves to be led in right ways. Well, she would
help all she could. So the dinner was full of little pleasant
surprises, that only Hattie knew how to make, and yet it
had not been costly, either in money or ration stamps.

That evening Dale got out a large fine picture puzzle,
and so well had she proved herself an equal in tennis playing that the other two were interested to inspect the puzzle.
Before long they were all working away happily at it,
spurred on by trying to get their portions finished as soon
as their cousin finished hers, which proved to be some
contest, for Dale was skillful at picture puzzles as well as
tennis.

Dale hustled them off to bed at ten, realizing she had a
letter to write yet before she slept, and wondering if Corliss would repeat last night's act again. She asked her if she
would like to sleep with her again, but Corliss sheepishly
declined. Dale had caught a glance between the brother
and sister, showing that the brother had been making fun
of his sister for what she did the night before, probably
scolding her. "I'll be all right," she said with a pale little
smile, and then added, "but thank you just the same."

"All right," said Dale in a matter-of-fact tone, "but
come in any time, night or day, when you feel you need
company," and a smile passed between the two girls that

was far different from any glance they had ever shared before.

The picture puzzle, left on the table in a corner all night, proved an incentive to get up early next day and go at it and Dale began to feel that if she could just keep these two busy, and a little interested, half her problems would be solved.

So the days fell into a pleasant routine, the visits to the hospital beginning each day, sometimes another in the late afternoon, all brief, and bringing very little satisfaction.

As the mother recovered, more and more she fell into the habit of bewailing her fate, and somehow trying to blame Dale for her accident. If Dale hadn't been so trying she said, she was sure she would never have gotten so confused as to let herself get run over.

Dale avoided such issues as much as possible, and responded by bringing a few lovely late blossoms from the garden, until Aunt Blanche waved them away one day and called them weeds. "Take those weeds away!" she snarled disagreeably. "They give me the creeps. They make me sneeze, and they might have worms on them." So then Dale brought a few roses from the florist's and made Corliss give them to her mother. But it made little difference in the woman's attitude. She was determined to complain. She took a dislike to all the nurses and demanded others. She kept up a continual outcry about being put in the ward, and kept demanding a private room. But no private room was given her. There was the same excuse, "We have no private room to spare. The private rooms are now occupied by two or three patients at least, because of war conditions."

But that kind of talk had never stopped Aunt Blanche, and she kept right at it, harping on it whenever her children came to see her. Blaming Dale for not doing something about it. But the utmost Dale could say was that she would speak to the doctor about it.

And then she began to clamor again to see her lawyer. But when the nurse tried to reach him he was always out of town. The plain truth being that he did not want to see her, for, having gotten all the money out of her that he reasonably could, he felt it was time to be away from the vicinity. And neither Dale nor the children made any response to Mrs. Huntley's requests to see her lawyer. They were not in sympathy with her on this subject. The son, at least, had reached the stage where he began to see just what kind of a man this lawyer was. He could not argue with his mother now, while she was sick and unable to leave the hospital and look after her affairs, so he said nothing. That had been his habit in dealing with things he did not like in the past, always to ignore them, so now his mother was not surprised at his attitude. But she spoke to him bitterly about his unwillingness to help her, and sometimes Dale could see that it was very hard for him to hear her fault-findings. Just once he did say:

"Mother, I don't have much faith in that lawyer," but his remark brought about such a torrent of abuse and scorn that he did not venture to oppose her again. Dale could see he shrank from hearing his mother shriek out "Powelton! Stop! How dare you speak that way of my lawyer?"

It was on the day that that happened first that the boy was very silent on the way home, until they got quite near to the house, and then he said quietly: "I wish you folks would begin to call me by my right name. I just hate that name Powelton! I wasn't rightly named that anyway. Dad wanted me named after himself, George Harold, and I want to use George now. It sounds more like something real, and not that sissy name of Powelton."

"All right," said Dale. "I'll call you George. I like that name. But—will your mother mind?"

"I expect she will," he said bitterly. "Powelton was her maiden name. But I'd rather have my father's whole name."

"I think you have a right to be called what you want to," said Corliss unexpectedly. "I know mother used to want to call me Clarissa, and I wouldn't stand for it. But now she seems to like Corliss. Anyhow, I think you can do what you like. Mother won't be around for a while till we get used to it. I like George best, too."

The lad looked pleased, and nothing more was said, but they were careful after that to call him George.

After dinner that night Dale brought out a new picture puzzle and they grew almost gay at times as they worked over it. They were beginning to really enjoy each other's society, and since the mother was away there was no one to find fault.

So the days settled into a quiet routine, and it was well for Dale that she had something pleasant to occupy her mind, for David's last letter had intimated that he was being sent off on some mission from which he would not be able to write to her, perhaps for a long time.

Nightly she read over that last precious letter, and prayed for him, wondering where he was, trusting him to the care of the Heavenly Father, and then reading a few verses in the Bible, verses they had agreed together to read at night while he was gone.

So they got through the days, wondering always what was coming when the invalid recovered and was able to walk. Would she come to the house that Dale owned, where they were staying? And what would it be like if she did?

It is safe to say that all three of these young people thought a great deal about this subject. Dale knew that of course she must invite her aunt if she seemed to want to come, but that it would bring dissension on every side. Corliss and George both knew that this quiet time while they were waiting for the recovery of the mother, was heaven compared to what it would be if she returned. Then there was the subject of a nurse. Corliss knew *she* would never be able to take care of her mother, for there would be no satisfying her ever with anything. Oh, it was all a sore subject, and none of them liked to think about it. And only Dale could throw it off by laying it all in the keeping of her Heavenly Father. "All through the night," and all through the days, also.

Of course Dale was the one who dreaded it most, perhaps, for she would be the butt of all the fault-finding, and she would be the one who would have to be sweet and bear it as if it were nothing. Could she do it? Yes, but not in her own strength. In the strength of her Lord she could lie back and take it sweetly, remembering that it was not herself who was bearing the responsibility, but her Lord who had promised to undertake for her. She had put her all in His hands, and she must only be careful that she did not intrude herself into the matter, but let her Lord manage it all for her.

It was very still in the room for a few minutes, with only the soft sound of the flickering flames in the fireplace, where a quiet wood fire brightened the dusk in the corners of the room, mingling with the silvery beam of the new moon stealing across the floor as if to meet and caress the firelight.

Troublous thoughts were going through the minds of the young people as they sat working over the new picture puzzle. At last Corliss broke the silence.

"What are we going to do, Dale, when mother begins to get well? I tried to ask her today while you went to speak to the nurse, but she looked at me so strangely, and just said *'Stop!* Don't torment me with questions like that when I'm sick.' And then you came back with the nurse and I couldn't say anything more, but what *are* we going to do?"

"I think the way will open somehow when the time comes," said Dale with a sweet smile. "There's really nothing to worry about, you know. There will be a way."

"Yes, but we can't stay here," said the boy. "You are

wanting to start a school or something, and we are taking up all your time and your house. And goodness knows it will be worse when Mom comes here with a nurse in the bargain. We ought not to put you out this way."

It was a manly speech and it thrilled Dale's heart to think her cousin had had kindly thoughts for her comfort.

"But I'm not worried, George," she said pleasantly. "Maybe that school wasn't in God's plan for me just now, and certainly having you here was, for the present, anyway. And somehow I think it was nice that you stayed here and we got better acquainted with each other, don't you?"

"Swell!" said George heartily. "I never knew you were so nice, and I'll always be glad I got to know you. You've been wonderful to Corrie and me. You couldn't have been better. But all the same that's another reason why we ought to get out and let you have your house to yourself."

"No," said Dale earnestly. "You mustn't think that way. I'm just glad you are here, and I know we're going to have a nice time together, in spite of worry and anxieties, and maybe some discomforts in the days ahead. But I'm sure there's something good coming out of it all."

"What makes you so sure?" asked the boy curiously.

Dale hesitated for an instant. Should she tell him? Would he understand? Yet she felt she must.

"Because my Heavenly Father is managing it all, and I have trusted my life with Him. I know He will work it out right for our best good. You see what he wants for us all is to make us like His Son, Jesus Christ, and if He sees that hard things will accomplish that for us in a better, quicker way than anything else would, then that is what He will do for us. I know, for I have told Him I want to rest my life with Him entirely."

"But you couldn't have any fun or good times that way, could you?" asked Corliss in wonder.

"Oh, yes, definitely so," said Dale. "You know He

loves us, and wants us to be happy in Him. So He would want to give us happiness as well as hard things. And I believe He truly loves me. He has given me a great deal of joy in many ways. Sometimes my heart is just thrilled to running over with the things He has handed out to me."

Corliss looked at her curiously, studied the radiant look on her sweet face, and wondered at it.

"Well, I wish I could feel that way about missing things, and seeing uncomfortable things coming ahead. But I can't," she said.

"Well, perhaps that is because you do not know my Lord Jesus yet. That makes all the difference in the world. When you know somebody well you know whether you can trust Him or not. Do you see?"

"No, I'm not sure I see at all," said the girl. "What about all those people over in the war, and all those people in Europe? Don't you suppose there are any of those who know God? Don't *they* pray and trust Him? And He doesn't do anything for them, does He?"

"Oh yes," said Dale quickly. "There are a lot of God's children over there, and a lot who are trusting Him, too, I know. I have a few friends, some among the fighters, some among the people who have lost their homes, and their dear ones, and they are just *resting* in the Lord and waiting patiently for Him to set the world right. They believe He will do it. And while they are suffering, they are trusting too, and they understand that this is all going to work out in the end for righteousness, and for good to all."

"Well, I don't see that," said Corliss. "I couldn't trust that way, not with things going wrong the way they are. It doesn't seem kind in God."

"But you see, dear, you just don't know Him, and you don't understand what He is working out for the world. There is the question of sin that is everywhere, sin that has to be conquered. Sin from which He died to make a way for us to escape. And just as if *He* had sinned instead of us, He deliberately took our sins upon Himself, and bore their punishment as if they had been His sins. We've nothing left to do but believe that He did it, and accept what He did, and take Him as our personal Saviour, and we are free from it all."

The boy had stopped working with the puzzle and was looking at her, taking in all that she said, weighing it, pondering it.

"I'd like to hear more about that," he said at last as he turned back to his puzzle. "It sounds reasonable, but not very likely. I don't know anybody that would do that for people. *Die* for them. Is all that in the Bible? That's a book I've never read. Just heard a snatch or two now and then read in school. But does it have real things like that in it?"

"Oh, yes," said Dale with shining eyes. "I'd be glad to show you some of them if you would be interested."

"I think I would," said the boy.

And then suddenly the doorbell rang and Dale went to see who had come, although both the young people started up anxiously as if they thought they should go, and Dale realized that they were always having in the back of their seemingly light minds the possibility of some change coming to their mother, the anxiety of what might be happening next.

"It's all right, George," she said as she hurried to the door. "Probably some neighbor. I would likely have to go anyway." But they followed to the hall and hovered in the shadow till they heard it was a special delivery letter, and as they couldn't possibly figure out how that could have anything to do with their affairs, they retired to the picture puzzle again.

They heard Dale tear open the envelope, saw through the doorway how she paused eagerly to read the brief missive, and they looked up curiously to see the bright color in her cheeks, and the glad, yet sorry, look in her eyes. But she went quietly over to her chair, and sat down.

"It's only a note from a dear friend who is probably being sent overseas, or somewhere, on a dangerous mission. He wanted me to know that he was starting, though he cannot tell me where. It is just a sort of a good-by, for the time being."

The two young people were very quiet for a long time, and the picture puzzle grew into a semblance of the story it was to tell when finished. At last Corliss asked a question.

"Does he—the one who wrote that letter—know God?"

Dale looked up with a bright smile.

"Oh, yes," she said happily. "He knows Him *very well,* and he is trusting in the Lord to help him through, whatever way He will, either to bring him back home, or to his Heavenly Home."

"Do you mean there is any fighter, a *young* man, who feels that way about war and dying and all that?"

"Yes, I know a good many. Some who didn't really trust God before they went over, but who have come to need Him, and cry out for Him, since they have been surrounded by death and terror. But this man especially really knows and trusts and is *happy* in the Lord."

It was just at that point that the kitchen door opened and Hattie walked in with a tray bearing three cups of hot chocolate topped with whipped cream, and a heaping plate of delicious sandwiches. The young people pounced upon the food eagerly, and the subject for the time being was forgotten. Or was it? Did the two cousins, after they had retired for the night, lie awake pondering these things which they had never known or thought of before? And Dale knelt long beside her bed praying for them.

But once more before she turned out her light she read the precious letter over again, then folding it she put it under her pillow before she lay down.

The letter was very short.

Dearest:

Only a minute to write. Orders have just come through. We are about to leave for an unknown port and probably no opportunity to write again for sometime. Be praying, and so will I. Remember, "All through the night," our Saviour will be watching over us, and "Joy cometh in the morning." Trust on, beloved.

DAVID

So when she lay down and closed here eyes, the bright words of faith from that letter illumined her dark room. Out there beyond her window was the dark night, and the hovering images of fears that might be imperiling her beloved, but those words of trust made the difference in what might have been a message full of fear. So Dale, trusting, slept sweetly, in spite of tomorrow, and more tomorrows, looming large and portentous ahead in a dreadful future, which yet could not disturb her sleep, because her faith was fixed upon the Rock, Christ Jesus.

15

AND while they slept, a long way off, a great ship slid out upon the ocean, beginning its perilous way into the night.

David Kenyon had not expected this change to the new duties to which he had been transferred. He was ready to be an unimportant cog in the machinery of this war to which he had already given many weary months, and much bravery for the cause of righteousness. But to be put into a position of trust in place of a notable man whose health had failed in a crucial time, had not been within the possibilities of his thought. Yet here he was, ordered to have charge, for the time, of a convoy transport, which there was every reason to suppose would be followed and bombed by the enemy from both under and on, and over the sea. He had not known definitely just what his orders were to be when he wrote that note to Dale, yet now as he thought about it with the full responsibility of the new duties upon him, he was glad he had written as he had. It was his farewell to her for the time, and together they would be praying and trusting their all.

He watched the dim lights of the harbor disappear into blackness and wondered if he would ever see them again.

...ned a solemn time to him, almost like standing at his ... deathbed, watching himself die. It was going to be his ...y, presently, to watch for the enemy. Would he be ...ual to the task? He thought of the lives that would be ...ependent upon him, of the responsibility that would be his, and then as he went below to the bunk room to prepare for the night's duties, it presently came to him that it was not only his own deathbed that he might be set to watch, but that of all the others who were his comrades. He did not know them all very well yet, for he had been with the most of them but a few hours, on the train across the country, but those other fellows were his responsibility too. It might be their deathbeds also, as well as his own. And were they ready to die? With him it was right either way, for his heart was fixed on the Eternal.

He cast his eyes about on the fellows in the bunk room. It was comparatively quiet. Only an occasional attempt at a joke, for all seemed thoughtful, suddenly brought to realize what might be before them that night. They were all getting into suitable garb for their coming duty, a night on deck.

Some of their young faces looked hard and bitter, some careless, trying to whistle and laugh off the solemn thoughts that must come at a time of stepping into a night of peril.

There was one, a young lad, younger than any of them, who had recently come among them, and he looked exceedingly blue. The others had been kidding him, trying to find out what made him look like that, but the boy's face grew only more desperate. Somehow it reminded David of the way he used to feel when he had his first taste of danger. The other fellows had all had experience too, though he could see that some of them were grave with apprehension even yet, whenever they were still long enough to let their thoughts get the ascendancy. But this young lad touched David's heart deeply.

"What's the matter, kid?" he asked pleasantly. "Scared?"

He spoke with a quiet heartening grin, but the boy lifted that desperate face to him and did not smile.

"Sure!" he said solemnly. "Aren't you?"

"No," said David firmly, "not scared. Feeling a little solemn perhaps, because this thing we're in is real, not just a game that doesn't matter, and of course death is stalking these waters, underneath and overhead as well. But we knew that would come sooner or later when we joined up with the outfit, and I don't feel that God is dead. I know He's looking after me."

"How'll that help you when the bombs begin to fall?" asked the boy. "I guess they're all good and scared, if they'd just own it, aren't you fellows?"

Several of the men lowered their glances and gave a shamed assent.

"What I'd like to know," said the boy, looking straight at David, "is why you're not scared? Is it just because you've been in battles before? Have you got used to it, and don't mind it any more, or what?"

David shook his head.

"No, Phil," he said gently. "It's because I have a Saviour in whom I trust. I know He'll do the best for me, whatever comes. He's wise and powerful, and He's watching over me continually."

"Aw, that's all bunk," sneered an older man. "Nobody that was a God would be bothered watching over a lot of tough fellows that didn't give a hang about Him, or never had paid any attention to Him. You just got brought up that way, Dave, and swallowed a lot of old traditions, that's all. But you can't tell me when you see bombs coming your way that you ever think about God, or that your beliefs ever help you get by without being scared stiff."

"But it isn't like that, fellows," said David earnestly. "You got it all wrong. In the first place it isn't a lot of traditions. It's a Person Whom I know and love, and

Whose love has been with me through a good many years, in a lot of other troubles, so I know He'll not forget me now, and whatever He does for me will be the best that *could* come to me."

"Yes, but you see I haven't got any such friend as that," said Phil, in a sort of contemptuous quiver. "I wasn't brought up with traditions. My folks never even went to church. And you can't just rest down and trust somebody you don't know, and you're sure don't care a hang for you."

"Oh, but He does. He cares very much for you, Phil."

"What gives you that idea?" sneered the boy.

"Because He's said so, and all you have to do is believe it. He loved you so much that He gave His life for you, so that you might know you could be saved forever."

"I don't know how you could possibly know that."

"Because He has said so in the Bible and I believe it. 'For God so loved the world that *whosoever* believeth in Him should not perish, but have everlasting life.' Then, here's another, 'He that heareth my word, and *believeth* on Him that sent me, *hath* everlasting life, and *shall not* come into judgment, but is passed from death into life.' There are a lot of other proofs. I can show them to you if you care to read them, but aren't those enough for a start?"

"I suppose so, if I was sure He said it. If I was sure He was God and able to carry out His promise," said the kid miserably.

"Yes—well," said David thoughtfully, "if you were driving through an unknown country and lost your way, and you came to a road that had a sign on it directing you to the place of your destination would you stand there and debate, and say, 'How do I know this is the right way? How do I know but somebody put this sign up just to fool me? Just to lead me into trouble? Or how do I know but it was just a joke somebody is trying to play on me?' Would you go around looking for another road? Or would you

turn down the road and try it out and see if it led to y
city?"

"Well, I don't know. Maybe I'd looked for another roa
first."

"So?" said David. "Well, have you looked for another
road yet? Is there any other way in a time like this when
danger is on the way? Do you know any other way to meet
God and not be afraid?"

"I suppose you can just trust to luck," said another
young fellow dismally. "I suppose if you're going to get
through you will, and if you aren't there's nothing you can
do about it."

"That doesn't sound very hopeful Sam, do you think it
does? Just swing out into the blackness and trust to *luck?*"

The boys sat earnestly thoughtful, their heads bent. One
caught his breath in something that sounded like a sup-
pressed sob.

"Luck's no good. It's nothing to trust to," said another
gloomily.

"Well, at home I used to go to Sunday School every
Sunday for years, and just before I left home I joined the
church to please my mother," said another tall boy with a
tentative question in his voice.

They were all looking at David, so after a minute he
answered·

"Are you satisfied to offer that as your entrance ticket
into eternity, Jim?"

The tall fellow sank down on his bunk and collapsed,
burying his face in his crossed arms. "Oh, I don't know,"
he answered. "I don't feel sure about anything."

"Isn't it safer to take the condition Christ offers? He
says, 'He that *believeth* ' If you're going to trust something
better get the conditions straight. Couldn't you just accept
that offer of His and swing off and trust *Him,* and let Him
prove it to you? That's what trust or belief really is. Letting
God have the chance to prove it to you. I took it that way

ver since He's given me peace. He'll give it to you too
ou'll take Him, and try Him out."

There was a great silence for a long moment broken by
ne distant sound of an explosion. They had been hearing
those at intervals, all day, but somehow this one seemed to
deepen the silence.

"We may not have much time ahead to accept that offer," suggested David.

The lad called Phil suddenly looked up, his eyes wild
with fright.

"*I'll* do it," he said with sudden conviction. "What do
you have to do?"

"Just tell Him so," said David, coming close to the boy
and drawing him down on his knees beside the bunk,
kneeling with his arm around the lad, and so he began to
pray for him:

"Oh God, our Creator, Who loved us all, and sent Your
own Son to take our sin upon Himself and die the penalty
for it, as if He had been Himself the sinner, we are coming
to You, because You have said You love us, and want to
save us, and we do not know any other way to be saved
except to believe what You have said. We know that we
are going out in a few minutes into what may be sudden
death for us all, and we know no power on earth can help
us. So we are casting ourselves on You knowing that You
will do the best for us that can be, because You love us, and
have died for us. So take us, and make us, whether in life or
in death, Yours to all eternity, because You have promised
and we have believed that promise and are trusting ourselves to it."

There was a brief pause and David sat quietly, "Now,
Phil, will you tell Him you accept Him as your personal
Saviour?"

Another pause, and then Phil's low solemn voice,
scarcely heard above the sounds of engine and waves:

"Lord, I'm believing You, and I'm taking You for my

Saviour now and forever. I've done a lot of sinning, b
You said You'd take care of that with Your blood. Than.
You. And now, whatever comes, I'm Yours, Lord.
Amen."

It had been very still there in the dim narrow bunk
room. But one by one the other five fellows that were
there had knelt down, in a kind of group, with their faces
buried in their folded arms. And as the two remained
kneeling after their prayers, there came other voices.

"Lord, take me too. I want my sins forgiven!"

"Lord, I'm afraid to die. Stay with me. Help me!"

"O God, I haven't been very good. I haven't pleased
You, but won't You forgive me too?"

"Lord, I'm scared stiff! Get me ready to die too, please."

The man called Jim who had said he had no friend in
God, was the last to kneel down, and when he tried to
speak his voice was broken with sobs:

"Lord, I've been an awful sinner, and I've never believed or thought anything about You before, but here I
am, and if you can do anything with me, Lord, take me!"

Then David's clear voice took up the prayer:

"Lord, we believe. Help our unbelief, and save us in the
midst of all this terror. To live, or die, Lord, we commit
ourselves to You."

Then from above them came a signal. It was time to go
on duty. They all sprang up, a new look on their solemn
faces, almost a smile on the face of the lad Phil as he
brushed away a tear and gripped David's hand, saying
fervently, "Thank you!" and dashed away to take his place
in the line of duty.

And the others, with frank tears still on their faces, came
by David Kenyon and gripped his hand. "Thanks, old
man," said one, "I'm all right now." And they all felt, as
they moved out to meet what the night had in store for
them, that there was a bond between those seven that
nothing would ever break, in time or in eternity.

And suddenly a great joy came to David, such as he had not dreamed there could be on a night of peril like this one. He felt as if the blessing of the Lord had been bestowed upon him. For there had never been a joy like this one, to know the wonder of leading those needy souls to know Him, to know what it was to have the Lord with them. The joy that came to his own soul as well to have all fear of death removed, and then to know that, living or dying, all was well with those other fellows too. Was that what was meant by "the joy of the Lord" in the Bible? Was it that He allowed His children to share in His own joy in saved souls who had accepted His so wonderful salvation? His heart thrilled and thrilled again as he took his way out to the place where duty called him, praying as he went, "Oh Lord, help me to give the right orders at the right time. Show me how to do my whole duty tonight. And do You please order the outcome according to Your will."

16

ALL that night the boys were out on duty under the sky,
looking for enemy lights, and thinking. Now and again
they looked up into the sky and sent their thoughts out to
find God, to wonder at Him for making a way for them to
be safe forever.

They walked the deck as if it were a sanctuary, and God
were there. For some of them it was the first realization of
a personal God that had ever come to their consciousness.
As they met one another on duty bound there was a grave
shy smile in their eyes, as if they belonged to some secret
order. And later, before they took their rest toward dawning, they knelt in the dimness of the bunk room, and then
lay down to sleep, over the enemy-infested sea, with a
quietness in their hearts that they had not known before.

Late in the next day the enemy was sighted more than
once, and when night came there were distant flashes,
sounds of planes, vanishing, and coming again.

The night was very dark. As the hours dragged by not
even a single star could be seen in the blackness above.
David Kenyon, alone for the moment looking down at the
deck, saw his comrades pacing back and forth and his heart

to think of them as they had knelt to His Christ.
they had all meant it, he was sure. Now, whatever
e, he felt sure of seeing them all in the Father's house
ve. His thoughts paused tenderly when he remem-
ered that someday he might tell this all in a letter to Dale.
Or perhaps tell her face to face if it pleased God to let him
go home. Just now of course there was no opportunity to
even send letters. His duty was imperative and all-
absorbing. But how he would enjoy telling of those buddies of his, and their surrender to his Saviour!

Suddenly there was a signal. A light! A sound! A plane
coming on! More lights! More sounds! More planes! The
enemy was here at last, and coming strong!

With one swift look above David turned to give com-
mands, lifting a quick prayer, with a passing wonder what
it was going to be like to be suddenly ushered into the
presence of God. He was conscious of a lifting of his heart,
as he went quickly into action to meet the oncoming test.

"God by my side," he said softly to himself, "All
through the night."

Suddenly bombs splintered the blackness of the night, a
shudder came from the sea beneath. Great geysers of water
spouting within a hundred yards, downpouring, flooding
the decks, drenching everything, then sucking resistlessly
back to the sea, taking all in its way with it. It washed the
men from their feet, sending them sprawling against the
rails, barely saving themselves. Oh, God, are You there?
Yes. Thank You! Seven men all safe so far. Phil? Yes,
clinging to the mast yonder. *Boom!* Another blast! This
was the night they had known was coming when they first
prayed. The night they had trusted the Lord to be with
them. To live or die! Unafraid? Unafraid, because God
was there!

David gave his orders in firm crisp tones as the noise
died out for an instant. His men looked up and their eyes
answered his. What would it be like in Heaven, if that was

where they were going now? Yet, they would all
liked to finish their job for victory before they left.
God had His plans. Ready Lord! What will You have n
to do?

There came another bomb! And another of those shud-
dering undersea attacks! Another geyser more torrential
than before. David called a sharp order for his men's pro-
tection, and the enemy came again.

More planes overhead, more bombs dropped. Then a
terrific explosion and the forward part of their ship was
shot away, *gone!* He could scarcely believe his eyes. Absolutely sliced off and disappeared! That meant the men that
were on that part were down under the sea? Who were
they? And the radio? *Gone—!* The smoke and storm ob-
scured the atmosphere. It was of no use to look for his
buddies even if he could see through the smoke. There was
no time. It was only a question of moments, seconds even,
perhaps, before they would all go now.

There came another geyser. A great plume of water
close at hand plunging down, greater than any before. A
real inundation. Even David was swept over, though he
had tried to anchor himself. And when it was past he
looked around for the rest of his seven. The fellows that
just a little before this happened had been kneeling together to commit themselves again to the care of the Al-
mighty. Where were they? And as he looked the wash
came back violently from the top side of the tilted ship, and
the men with it, and swept them all into the sea! *His men!*
He looked aghast. Down into that inferno of burning oil
and tossing water! His men! Going into glory by *fire!* The
boys he had been working with. The boys who had
prayed with him that morning. Somehow they had all
seemed to feel this day was the end of things.

The enemy was coming in thick and fast now. There
was fire in either end of the ship. Some of the brave men
were putting it out and fighting also, and David as he cast

to give an order, saw the enemy coming on again in
force. Planes and ships, and submarines working to-
her against them. Was there time for one more effort
efore he too must go? He called an order that instantly
started what guns they had left. Oh God, keep us true.
Make us brave to the end.

Another great explosion, two more geysers shot up almost beside him, and descended in torrential floods. His
six buddies were gone, washed out to that awful frothing
flaming sea, and disappeared! Bless God, they had gone
Home! But there were still some gunners left. Another
chance before all was over.

He gave the command and the guns spoke sharply,
quickly.

Something struck David on his head. Fire and darkness
came upon him. He did not see the enemy turn to flee in
panic. He did not know that his last effort had turned the
tide of battle. He felt the ship turning over, and he reached
out to take hold of something, anything that he could hold
to, as he went down to join those buddies of his whom he
had led to know his Lord. This was God's will, now, that
he should go. God's will was best, and he was content.

For an instant he roused to remember Dale. If only he
might have written her farewell. But she would know
where he was gone. It would be hard for her. But perhaps
they would find the little note he had written and fastened
in his Testament over his heart, a note he wrote when he
first started on this unknown expedition. A last word in
case he did not come back. God keep her, his dear girl!

Once he roused enough to know someone was trying to
lift him. He tried to tell them not to bother. It was too late,
and then all got black again. The explosions seemed very
far away. He was now definitely on his way to God.

Did it always take so long to die, or was it but a moment
after all? So many thoughts could press upon his brain and
flash a meaning to his fading soul. His ship! What of his

ship? He was responsible for what was left of his ship! Shouldn't he do something about that, or was it too late? He had distinctly felt it turning over, hadn't he? Felt the sea beside him, close beside him so that he could touch it, or was that the hallucination of an abnormal brain under strain? But would God look after his ship for him? Yes, of course, if God was taking him Home. It was God's ship, and he would be answerable to God now, not even to the navy. God was above the navy. Only he wanted to have done his duty bravely, in his fight for righteousness. But God was the captain, and God would look after the outcome of the battle. Would perhaps explain it all to him when he got over there at Home with his Captain.

Then he drifted into a dream of Dale, sitting against the hemlocks, holding his hand, and giving sweet promises, her lips upon his, her smile for his eyes. Dear Dale! Perhaps one day up above they could talk this all over and understand why it had been this way. Dear Dale! She would be praying for him, now, perhaps.

The sea was very close to him now. He felt as if he were riding Home. Would he be meeting his comrades, perhaps before they entered glory? Would they all go in together? Well, it would be all right however it was. They had taken his Lord for Saviour. They would not be shy meeting Him. And it was very dark now. The end! There would be glory presently, and no more regrets. All peace and blessedness. Dale would be coming too, someday. Good night! God would be with her all through the night.

And back in his own country Dale was kneeling *then,* praying that God would be with him wherever he was, on land or sea, perhaps by some strange telepathic influence feeling that he was in special peril.

When the morning came there was another day, with its own problems, so far remote from the exaltation of the night before when she had felt for a time so very near to David.

Now, this morning David was far away somewhere on the sea probably, going through hard things, in peril, perhaps. He had expected that if he was sent out again. And she, Dale, had homely duties to perform, common details to look after, sordid questions to settle. There for instance was that meeting in her church that she had promised to attend. It was a meeting sponsored by her Sunday School class of girls. They would feel aggrieved if she was not there, and there were little details that they would expect her to advise them about. Yet how could she conscientiously leave her cousins? They were desolate and seemed to depend on her. Of course they could go to the movies again, probably, but somehow she felt that was not the place for them, now in their uneasy restless state of mind. They were just beginning to be strangely dependent upon her, to look to her for entertainment, and a way to while the anxious hours away. Little by little she was growing to feel that their unhappiness was not altogether on account of their mother's illness. They had come to believe what the doctor had told them, that she would presently be well again, and quite all right. But there was something more to their uneasiness she was sure. She must find out what it was if possible and try to discover a remedy for it. She must not lose her weak hold over them, now when they were just beginning to turn to her and trust her. What was she going to do about it?

In the end she went to her Lord in prayer and laid the whole burden down at His feet.

"Dear Lord, here's something I just can't do anything about. Please manage it for me."

Then she went downstairs and found the two cousins working hard at the puzzle they had not quite finished the night before, and they greeted her cheerfully, quite as if she was a real pal. She marveled at the change that had come upon them in these few short days, while they were going through trying times.

They had a cheery breakfast, and while they ate the telephone rang. It was one of Dale's Sunday School class, consulting her about the meeting that night, and with her mind still undecided about whether she ought to go she answered the girl briefly.

"Yes, Doris, I *hope* it is going to be possible for me to be there. I have been trying to plan all the week for it. But Doris, if I *shouldn't* be able to make it I'll be sure to call you beforehand. And if that should happen suppose you get Margaret Dulles to take my place and greet them."

"Oh, Miss Huntley!" came a dismayed voice over the telephone, so loud in protest that the two cousins could not help but hear. "We can't possibly get along without you. And besides Margaret Dulles has gone to her cousin's wedding in New York, and she won't be back for over a week. You just *must* come. There isn't anybody else to take your place. That old Mrs. Gromley will want to take over, and she always makes everybody so mad. It just won't do!"

"Well, why not take it all in your own hands, Doris? I'm sure you could be a very nice hostess."

"Me? Oh! *No!* I never could do it! I should just die if I had to take over responsibility that way. I really *won't*. And you know all the girls would be deadly jealous. They always say I try to get in the limelight. Miss Huntley it'll be a regular flop if you don't come. What's the reason you can't? You aren't *sick,* are you?"

"No," said Dale thoughtfully, "I'm not sick, but you know my aunt had an accident and is in the hospital, and my two cousins are here. I really don't like to leave them just now when they are under such a strain."

"Oh, but can't you bring them along? I'm sure they would enjoy it. The speaker they are bringing is perfectly marvelous they say. He's been in all the major battles in the Pacific, and he tells about it very vividly. And the singing will be swell. I've heard the quartette myself, and it's perfectly spiffy. Would it do any good if I were to come around and invite them? I think I could get time."

"Oh, that's kind of you, Doris, but I don't think that will be necessary. I'll see what I can do about it. I'll let you know later. I'll arrange *something* for you, anyway. Don't worry."

When Dale came back to the table the cousins looked up.

"What is it, Dale? Anything we can do for you?" asked George.

Dale's eyes brightened.

"Why, that's awfully thoughtful of you, George," she said. "There *is* something you could help me out with if you don't mind, but I'm afraid it might bore you."

"What is it, Dale?" asked Corliss eagerly. "You've done a lot of things for us that must have bored you. I guess we could stand being bored a couple of hours or so for your sake. Is there really something you want us to do? It might even be interesting, you know."

"Yes, that's quite true," said Dale thoughtfully. "I'm told the program is very fine. But of course they will all be strangers to you. Though I don't want to leave you here without anything to do a whole evening."

"Forget it!" said George loftily. "We aren't infants. And anyway, what is it? We can stand anything once."

"Well, you see our church is interested in a young college that has only been going a few years, and my Sunday School class of girls has undertaken to have their college quartette and glee club come and give us a program, and tell a few words about the college. You see one of our own boys from the Sunday School has been studying there for three years, and now he's overseas, and everybody wants to help his Alma Mater for Jan Hooper's sake. So this is the night they are coming, and I promised to be there and meet them, and perhaps say a few words about our boy who is now in combat. But I was going to try and get somebody else to take my place. Since your mother was hurt I didn't feel as if I wanted to leave you alone."

"Leave us alone, *nothing!* We're *going,* Cousin Dale," said Corliss unexpectedly. "We'll go with you of course, won't we George?"

"Sure we will," said George. "Besides, if you're going to speak we wouldn't miss it for the world. Even if your program isn't good. Tell us about it. What time do we go?"

"Well, that's certainly nice of you," said Dale appreciatively. "The meeting is eight o'clock. We'd have to leave here around seven. Well that takes a load off my mind. I'll call Doris and tell her it is all right. I'll be there. And now I think it's about time for us to go to the hospital."

But when they reached the hospital they found the patient in a most trying mood.

"Powelton, I want you to go down to the city right away and find that lawyer of mine. I positively *will not* be put off *another hour.* I've simply *got* to see him. It's very important, and you'll be responsible for making me a lot worse if you don't get hold of him at once. Do you understand? And don't let them put you off by any of these stories they've been telling the nurse, that he is out of the city, because I'm sure he's not, and I won't stand for his treating me this way another day. Now that's your job, Powelton, and I want you to start at once."

The lad gave his cousin one despairing look and then quietly answered his mother,

"Why, yes, mother, I'll do the best I can. But I still think you are making a great mistake getting messed up with a man like that. I don't believe he is an honest man. He doesn't sound like it to me."

"Be still, Powelton, and do as you're told. You're not grown-up enough to be a suitable judge of people, and anyway this is my affair Go!"

"Very well, mother," said Powelton, with so little of his

usual disagreement that his mother stared at him in surprise. "Shall I report back here after my errand is done?"

"Why certainly! You may bring the lawyer back with you just as soon as possible."

Without another word, and with only a sweeping glance toward Dale and Corliss, George turned and marched out of the hospital, and the two girls by Mrs. Huntley's bed stood silently, with averted gaze, both understanding just how unpleasant this errand was going to be for the boy for he had expressed his views about the lawyer more than once.

It was finally Corliss who broke the silence after George left.

"Mamma, when are you coming back to the house? Aren't they letting you get up pretty soon? What has the doctor said?"

The mother looked at Corliss languidly.

"The doctor? Oh, he never says anything. Just tells me I'm getting along as well as could be expected. I've told him again and again that I never shall get better until I have a room to myself, but he says that's something they don't expect to have in this hospital, not till the war is over. That's ridiculous of course. They're just trying to get me to offer some enormous sum for a private room, but they've overstepped themselves. I shall not offer a single cent more until they actually moved me to a good big room. That stuff about not having a room is ridiculous. In a great big institution like this, and no private room for a woman who is willing to pay for the best they have."

"But mother, you're mistaken. We know for we've been all over the hospital, and every nook and cranny is filled with cots and patients even in the hallways. We came in the back door today, and we could hardly get by to the elevator."

"That may be true about the common halls where the

poor people are put, but you didn't open the doors and look into all the private rooms, did you?"

"Why, yes, mother," said Corliss eagerly, "Dale and I talked it over, and we thought we would just go around all the halls and see if we could discover a room that wasn't occupied, so we did. You see we thought perhaps somebody was being moved home or something, and we went all around and looked in all the rooms, for you see this was the time when most of the doors are standing wide open, or if they are not we could ask a nurse. But mother there wasn't a single one empty, and *all* of them had two beds and sometimes three in them. And there were three emergency cases came in this morning, accidents, and they don't know where to put them. There isn't another spot where they can put another bed, and I heard the head nurse say there was nothing else to do but to send a few cases home before they were supposed to go. That's the reason I asked you whether the doctor had any idea of sending you home today."

"Well, I certainly am not going to let them send me home until it's time. I'm not going to be cheated out of my rights by some petty accident case. That certainly wouldn't be fair. Besides, I haven't any home to go to. I couldn't of course go back out west when I am not able to take care of myself yet, could I? And I've no other place to go. I have been distinctly told by Dale that I'm no longer welcome in what she calls *her* house, so until I can get some sort of settlement about that house from my lawyer I couldn't leave here at present."

"Oh, but Aunt Blanche," said Dale earnestly, "you are mistaken. I did not *ask* you to leave. I told you I was going to have a school, and I was afraid it would not be comfortable for you with a lot of children in the house. But that is all changed now. I have given up the idea of having the school for the present. I have found another girl who has taken it over, and so we shall have plenty of room for you as long as it is convenient for you to stay, and we will of course do our best to take care of you and make you as comfortable as possible. And I have only been waiting until you were feeling a little better, and able to make your plans, to tell you this. My cousins and I have been getting on very pleasantly together, and I'm sure we have all been looking forward to your coming back to us as soon as you are able. There will be room for a nurse too, as long as you need her. I thought maybe we should be inquiring about that, for they say nurses are very hard to get, and I know they have been terribly short on nurses here. Of course if worst comes to worst Corliss and I might be able to make you comfortable. I'm not exactly ignorant about nursing, for I've had a short course in it, and then of course I've had a good deal of experience taking care of Grandmother. But I suppose you will be a little happier if you can induce one of the regular nurses here to be with you, at least for the first few days of your home-coming. Have you spoken to your nurse yet to see if that would be possible?"

"Spoken to her? No, certainly not. I wouldn't have one of these nurses on any account. They are abominable. But of course you would be no better. I fancy that taking care of your grandmother was a very trifling matter compared with my case. And in any event I shouldn't think of troubling you. Not after what you said. I certainly could not be comfortable there, not after the way you have treated me and my children."

"Mother! You mustn't say that," put in Corliss, "Dale has been perfectly wonderful to us all through this horrible experience. She has been just lovely. She's played games with us, and bought picture puzzles for us, and we've had a grand time. If it hadn't been for you being sick and us not knowing what was going to happen, we would really have had a lovely time. I like this place. I really do."

"That will do, Corliss. Don't go into hysterics about

this. If you could enjoy yourself while I was suffering I suppose I ought to feel glad, but I can't say I relish your attitude. And no, certainly I'm not coming to that house! As soon as the doctor comes I will ask him if he can't send us up to your Aunt Evelyn's in Connecticut. We'll take a nurse along, maybe two, for the journey. I'll risk it but I can get plenty of nurses when I get up, and I think I shall get up today. I'm not going to be kept down any longer!"

Corliss gave Dale a frightened look. What had she done by starting this subject? But perhaps the doctor would be able to straighten her mother out on a few things.

Then the nurse came in and announced that it was time for the patient to take a nap.

"But I'm expecting my lawyer," snapped the patient. "I simply can't take a nap till I get my business settled. After that I'm going away, and you can't tell me any more when to take a nap for I'll be my own mistress again."

But the nurse went quietly about her duties, gave the patient her medicine, arranged the bed clothing, plumped up the pillows, and adjusted the screen about the bed. And in the meantime Dale and Corliss slipped away and went home.

17

VERY solemnly the two girls walked along, not talking until they were some distance from the hospital. At last Corliss spoke.

"Why do you suppose my mother acts like that, Dale? Is she sort of out of her head, do you think?"

Dale gave a troubled sigh.

"No, I don't think so, dear. I think she's probably just hurt and worried with a lot of things. I'm afraid I hurt her by telling her about my school. I didn't mean to of course, but I just didn't know how to plan, and I had promised the committee I would start the school."

"Of course," said Corliss. "And now you have given it all up just for us, and mamma talked that way to you! I can't bear to think *my mother* would be that way to you after you've been so nice and kind to us."

"Well, don't worry any more about it, dear. I guess I must have been to blame the way I spoke. I should have waited till she got ready to tell me what she was going to do, only I had to tell the ladies before they had their next meeting. I guess I didn't tell the Lord about it and ask Him to look out for it. When I don't do that I usually get into trouble."

Corliss looked at her in wonder.

"Do you always talk to God about everything you do?" she asked

"I should," said Dale, "but sometimes I get going my own plans and forget that the Lord knows better what He wants me to do. I'll have to ask Him to straighten this out for me."

"I suppose that would be a wonderful way to live," said Corliss thoughtfully. "I always plan to do what *I* want, and not bother about anything else. But I guess maybe that's why I always get into so much trouble. I wonder if my mother knows how to live this way. Sometime maybe I'll tell her about it, but I don't know. It might only make her furious. She never likes me to know anything she doesn't know."

"Well, but we can pray for her, that God will show her. After all that might be better than telling her about it now, though sometime God may show you a way to tell it. And now I'm wondering how George got along with his errand. I wonder if he found the lawyer at home, and persuaded him to come to your mother. If he didn't I'm afraid George will have a pretty bad time when he gets back. But never mind. We'll pray about that too."

"Do you think my prayers would do any good?" asked Corliss after a minute of silence. "I've never been very good myself, and I'm sure God doesn't think much of me."

"Oh yes, God loves you. He wants you to take what He has done for you in dying on the cross and taking your sins on Himself, and if you'll take Him as your Saviour that means you are born again, and are His child. Surely, pray, but first pray for yourself, tell Him that you are sorry for your sins, and that you will accept Him as your Saviour. Then when You are His child you can ask Him for other things. Now, here we are at home, and probably lunch is ready. Shall we wait for George or do you think he will get lunch in the city?"

"He won't bother to wait for lunch. He'll get back to the hospital and then come home. And perhaps mother'll be asleep when he gets there so he won't have to wait. I think he'll be here soon. But let's sit down when Hattie is ready. I can save something for him if he doesn't come in time."

But George arrived soon after they had sat down. He was breathless from a rapid walk, and his eyes were troubled.

"I didn't go back to the hospital," he said worriedly. "That lawyer is not to be found. They say he is gone up to Canada on business and won't be back for several weeks. I don't much believe it. I think he doesn't want to talk with mom any more, and he just tells his secretary to say that. I even went to his apartment, but the housekeeper had the same tale, and they wouldn't even give me his address. They said he was off for his health and couldn't be bothered with business. So there! What was I to do? I knew if I went back to the hospital I'd have all kinds of time with mom, so I just telephoned the nurse and told her about it. Told her to ask mom what I should do. But she said mom was asleep and she shouldn't waken her now, but she would tell her after she had had her lunch, and phone us if there was any message. I don't know if I did the right thing or not, but I couldn't help being glad that bum wasn't there. I don't trust him. I think he is putting it all over on mom."

"Yes," said Dale. "He hasn't a very good reputation. But perhaps your mother will forget about it this afternoon and there will be a little more time to work this out."

"She says she is going to write Aunt Evelyn, George, and we are all going there as soon as she is able to get up."

"Not *me!*" said George. "That's an aunt I never want to see again if I can help it. She is worse than mom about finding fault and she thinks I'm the world's worst. I simply won't go there!"

"Well, don't worry about that now, George. Wait till the time comes and maybe there'll be a way to work it out," said Dale.

"There sure will as far as I'm concerned," said George.

"What if we go upstairs for an hour or so and see how we can fix up a nice room for your mother to come back to as soon as she is done at the hospital. Then we can tell her it's all arranged, and maybe she will be pleased," Dale suggested.

"Oh *yeah?*" said George unbelievingly, "I never saw her pleased yet at anything anybody did for her. But of course we can try it."

"George, you ought not to be so hard on your mother," said Dale, with a troubled look. "After all she's your mother, and she's sick and suffering."

"Okay, I know it," said George penitently. "I guess I'm a sort of a heel, but it certainly makes me mad the way she finds fault with everybody. That pretty little nurse at the hospital was almost in tears about her when I talked to her on the phone. But I guess I shouldn't act this way of course. Only nobody is going to make me go to Aunt Evelyn's, not on yer life they aren't."

"No," said Corliss, "and I won't go either. But we'll have to wait till mamma is better before we can say anything about that. Maybe she'll be pleased after all if we fix up a room here, only it will be hard on Dale."

"No," said Dale, "I *want* her to come. I wouldn't feel right if she didn't, and perhaps if she comes we can make her have a nice time and get a better feeling between us all."

George grinned.

"Wishful thinking!" he commented, and then added, "Well, mebbe! I sure hope so."

"Listen!" said Dale. "Let's make a game of this, and get

really interested in it. Let's go upstairs right away and see what you think about which room we should prepare."

"Oh, I know which room she will want, if she takes any," said Corliss. "She'll want the room you gave to me, the one where she used to take her naps, and George's room would be just right for the nurse while she is here. George and I can park anywhere, down in the living room on the couches, if you don't mind."

"Oh, that won't be necessary," said Dale. "You can come in my room with me, Corliss, and George can go up in the front third-story room if he doesn't mind. It isn't very large, but there is a comfortable bed up there. I used to sleep there myself sometimes when Grandmother had company. There is a bureau, too, and a chair, so I guess you could be comfortable."

"Sure, I can. I'll get along anywhere. That will be swell."

"Well, come on up and see what you think," said Dale, and they trooped happily upstairs.

"You can put your things in the hall closet, Corliss. It's all empty. I took everything out of it yesterday and packed them away in trunks in the storeroom upstairs, and Hattie cleaned it, so it's all ready for you. Do you want to move your things now? I think it might cheer your mother up if she knew we had everything ready for her and the nurse."

"Sure, I'll move them right away. I think this is going to be fun," said Corliss. "Are you going to move upstairs now, George?"

"Okay," said George. "It *might* have some effect on mom if she knew everything was all fixed. And we could get used to it. Then Hattie can get everything ready for mom and the nurse."

"All right, but there is something else I want to tell you first," said Dale. "There is Grandmother's room of course, and if you think your mother would rather have that I can take Grandmother's things out of the room and pack them away, and I will if you think your mother would prefer that. Or, if either of you would rather have it than the other plans I suggested."

"But I thought you said you didn't want anybody to have that room, Dale. I thought you said you wanted to keep everything just as she had left it." This came from Corliss, spoken thoughtfully.

"I know. I did want to keep it just as she left it for a while," said Dale. "But perhaps I was wrong to feel that way. If you think I should give it up I'll be glad to do so. I want your mother to be comfortable. Or, Corliss, if *you* still would like to have that room, I can arrange that. I don't want to be selfish."

"No," said Corliss sharply. "I don't want the room, and I don't much think mother would. Anyway I don't think she should have it, not after the way she's acted to you."

"No," said George. "She shouldn't and neither should Corliss. You have been awfully good to us, and you have a right to do what you want to with your own house. No, I think the other arrangement is much better."

"Wait," said Dale, taking a key out of her breast pocket. "I want to show you the room, and perhaps you will understand why I felt almost as if it was a sacred place. But I guess that was silly, and if Grandmother's room is going to make things easier, why here it is, and it shall be up to you who is to have it."

Dale put the key into the lock and flung the door open, and the two cousins stood solemnly in the doorway and looked around, wide-eyed and interested.

"Why, it's sweet," said Corliss, two great tears gathering in her eyes. "I don't wonder you didn't want me to come barging into this room. It looks just like I remember Grandmother."

Suddenly Dale reached over and kissed Corliss softly on her forehead.

"You're a dear!" she said. "I'm so glad you feel that

way. I was afraid you would want to make fun of the quaint old-fashioned things and I just couldn't stand that. And now, since you feel this way, I don't mind if you come in here to sleep. I really don't, Corliss. And I think Grandmother would like it too. That will likely be more comfortable for you than sleeping with me."

"No," said Corliss shrinking back, "I love to sleep with you. I really do. I like it a lot. But I'm glad you let me see this room. It somehow seems to be a real place, and I think I understand you better for seeing it."

"Yes," said George, huskily, "I'm glad you showed it to us. And I don't blame you for wanting to keep it as she left it. I know just how you feel about it. And I'm glad Corrie thinks so, too. If anybody sleeps there it ought to be you, Dale. Grandmother would like that better I'm sure. But anyway, mom wouldn't choose it for herself I know, because she told me that other room where she took her naps was the nicest in the house she thought. It wasn't so noisy as Grandmother's. That fronts on the street and she said you could hear all the children crying and shouting and playing. No, Dale, you better just keep that room as it was. Open it up sometimes if you want to, but don't give it to any of us. Not now. Come on and let's get mom's room fixed. Anything you want carried anywhere, Dale? I'm strong and able."

"Thank you," smiled Dale. "We'll see. Now, let's take your mother's room first. What needs moving out? Corliss, have you heard your mother say she didn't like anything in this room?"

Corliss looked around with troubled eyes.

"Well, yes," she said reluctantly. "Mother never liked that bureau. She said the one in the room you intend for the nurse was much larger and more roomy. She liked the big mirror, too."

"Why that is easily changed," said Dale. "Come on George, let's get to work. We'll move the other one out of the way and then there will be a place to put this. And Corliss, what else did she want changed?"

"Well, she said she'd rather have one of the overstuffed chairs from the living room, instead of that straight-up-and-down one that had long rockers to fall over. But I don't think you ought to change that. The big chair belongs in the living room, and this rocker wouldn't fit there."

"Oh, nonsense," said Dale. "What difference does that make? A chair is a chair, and they are easily changed. Anything else?"

"No," laughed Corliss, "only that engraving of the Lord's prayer in the gold frame. She said she didn't like it, and she always turned it around to face the wall when she lay down. She said she didn't want to always be confronted by religion. I'm ashamed to tell you this, but you asked me."

"That's all right, Corliss. We'll have those things changed in a jiffy. Are you sure there was nothing else she didn't like?"

"No, that's all except the big pincushion. She said it was all out of style to have cushions like that."

"Well," said Dale laughing, "if that's all I guess we can get by."

"But I don't think this is right, Dale," said George, "to make all this trouble for you, and when she may not come after all. I don't think it is a bit polite of moms to want it."

"There, there, George. We want to get this room so she will like it, don't we? Well, don't let's stop on little things like that. Let's make it nice for her, the way she wants it, and maybe she will be happy about coming. And say, I've been thinking. Suppose you two go to the hospital without me now, and then you can tell her about it and not feel hampered with having me around. Then she can tell you just what she really wants. I think that will be better, don't you?"

"But we'd rather you went along," said Corliss.

"Next time, dear," promised Dale. "Besides, I have to go to that committee meeting about the school and tell them what I had planned, and introduce the girl who is to take my place. It really is better this way just for this time. Now come, let's get this furniture in place and get it done so it looks pretty and you can draw a word-picture of it for your mother."

The young people worked with a will, and soon had the two rooms in lovely order. Dale went to her store of pretty linens and selected two of her nicest bureau scarfs, and some of her best towels and the rooms looked pretty as pictures.

"We'll get a rosebud or two for the bureau, and I'll put my bud vase in here," said Dale as they stood surveying it all when it was finished. And even Hattie came to stand in the doorway and look.

"I'll take the curtains down, Miss Dale, and wash 'em," said Hattie. "It won't take long to iron 'em and get 'em up and when you come back you'll be surprised."

"Thank you Hattie," said George suddenly. "And Dale, I'll take that steel engraving up to my room. Do you mind? I seem to feel I'd like to have it where I can look at it for a while. It's very old, isn't it?"

"Yes," said Dale. "It belonged to great-grandfather, Allan Dale, and that's one reason why I have always liked it. Yes, take it to your room. I'll be glad to think you are looking at it sometimes. And now, it's getting late and you two ought to be going. Remember you have a very important mission, and I'll be praying for you while you are gone. Good-by."

They separated and the brother and sister went solemnly on their way, planning together their campaign.

"We'll have to settle that matter of her old rat of a lawyer first," said George. "I'll have to make her understand that he is gone absolutely, and we can't possibly get hold of him, and then you can start in and tell her about the room if you want to, Corrie, and what we've been helping Dale to do. Don't forget to tell her how she offered you Grandma's room if you wanted it. That'll make a big hit with mom."

"I don't know as she'll listen to anything I say about the room. She got pretty mad at me this morning when I tried to ask her when she was coming back home. She said she had no home to come to, and a lot of things, and then Dale spoke up and told her she never meant to hurry her away, and that of course she wanted her to come here now, that this was the proper place for her to be getting well, and she was as nice as could be. But it didn't do a bit of good. She just told me I needn't get into hysterics on that subject, and you know, all that old stuff she always shuts me up with."

"Well, never mind, you go ahead, Corrie. I'll back you up, and we'll try to work it out."

"All right, I'll try again," sighed the girl, and they walked discouragedly up the steps of the hospital to their appointed task.

18

WHEN the two walked timidly into the hospital and up to their mother's bed, she was partly sitting up against her pillows, and eyeing them as if they were a couple of criminals plotting to keep her from her rights.

"Well," she said, looking sharply at George, "where is my lawyer? I thought I told you to bring him with you. Where is he?"

The boy braced up bravely and looked his mother courageously in the eye, a slightly apologetic smile on his lips.

"Sorry, mother," he said courteously, "so far as I can find out he has gone out of the country. The nearest suggestion I could get from his office or his home either, is that he went to Canada to spend a few months in the woods and try to recover from a severe nervous breakdown. And he has ordered his secretary, and what there is left of his family, not to disclose his address to anybody. I've done my best to get some other answer, but there doesn't seem to be any way to get any further information."

Mrs. Huntley's face was stony cold and the look she gave her children was as if she suspected them of making up this story. But after a few minutes of characteristic storming and questioning she began to cry. Just big stormy tears pelting down her angry cheeks, and her lips trembling almost pitifully.

Corliss looked around with a worried expression to see if the nurse was near, for if she was she would undoubtedly send them away for making her patient weep, and this really must be stopped.

Corliss got out a crisp little clean handkerchief, softly wiping her mother's tears away, as gently as if she had been a baby, and the mother looked up astonished, the action was so unprecedented. Corliss had never been known to do the like before.

Then Corliss began to talk, softly, quietly, as a mother might comfort a little child.

"There, mamma, don't feel bad. There'll be some other way. Don't you worry. Listen. We've got some nice things to tell you. We're getting ready for you to come home to the house. Dale and my brother and I have been working at it ever since lunch, and we've fixed it all up so prettily. We've moved the bureau you didn't like, and got the nice big chair in your room, and taken the old rocker out and the picture you didn't like is gone too. We had a lot of fun doing it. Dale didn't mind at all. In fact she thinks it looks lots better. And she got out her very prettiest bureau scarfs. And the curtains are being washed, all crisp and nice, and everything is going to be lovely. And we've fixed up the next room for your nurse, and we wondered if you couldn't be allowed to come home in a day or two. It would be lots nicer for you there, and then we could talk about plans and things without having a lot of people listening the way they do here."

Then the son spoke up.

"Yes, moms, I think that would be better. I thought I'd go down now and have a talk with the doctor, and see what he says, and then we could get the ambulance and take you very comfortably."

"No, no, *no!*" exclaimed the sick woman. "I can't go till I see my lawyer. He's taken all my money and he hasn't done anything about it."

"Never mind moms, we'll see about that after we get you to the house—" The mother stared at this boy who had always been bored at any planning for herself, and didn't know what to make of it all.

"But I can't go to Dale's," she mourned, more tears coming down.

Corliss got up and dabbed at the tears again.

"Don't worry, mamma," she said coaxingly, "we're looking after you, and yes, you *can* go to Dale's house. She *wants* you. She really does. If you could have seen her going around with her eyes so bright, smiling and planning to put pretty things in your room you would be sure she wants you. You'll like it there. And Hattie has been planning to make some spoon bread for you. Come on, cheer up, muv, and let's have a happy time. And when we get you home and you're really well then we can talk over plans for what we'll do next."

So they kept on coaxing, and the mother, amazed to have some real loving comfort offered her, finally settled down and ceased her objections. George, delighted at the outcome, began to think of Dale's promise when they came away, to be praying for them. Did prayer really ever do any good?

The two young people were greatly comforted themselves that they did not have to go back with ugly refusals ringing in their ears. The nurse had told them she thought the doctor would think their mother might be well enough to be moved in a very few days now, and the mother almost put on a watery little smile for them. Was that the effect of Dale's prayers?

So they went home to Hattie's nice dinner, and then hurriedly to Dale's meeting with her, wondering whether they really hadn't made a mistake promising to go with Dale. Would they be bored, after all? But they had promised and they couldn't go back on Dale after all she had tried to do for them.

They started early, for Dale had duties to perform before the talent arrived, and while she was organizing her girls who were to be ushers, the brother and sister sat together conversing in low tones about what their mother would likely to do after she was well enough to travel, and what *they* wanted to do.

"There's one thing I *won't* do," said Corliss stubbornly, "I won't go near Aunt Evelyn's. You've got to back me up in that, brother. If you don't I'll run away and make you all a lot of trouble."

"Sure, I'll back you, and it's equally true that I'm not going to Aunt Evelyn's. Do you know what I'm going to do? I'm going to college somewhere if I can manage it, or else I'll get me a job in some defense plant."

So they quietly and unhappily plotted, knowing that any plan they could make would likely be swiftly overthrown by their mother when she got back to her normal self.

Then presently the talent arrived, several young men and girls, and Dale brought them over and introduced them to her cousins.

George was interested at once, and Corliss sat looking them over, filled with interest. They all were bright-faced and well dressed, though plainly, and she couldn't quite place them socially. There were a few in uniform, some soldiers and some sailors. One was introduced as the dean of the college, though he seemed quite young, also, and he and George fell at once into conversation. Corliss wondered what it could be about. Something about the college she judged, though she caught only a word or two of their conversation.

Then the meeting began, with a burst of song from the audience, followed by a chorus from the glee club, and a number by the quartette, who were publicly and informally introduced to the audience. George and Corliss were interested from the start.

There was a brief talk from the young dean about the college, especially stressing its Christian character, which for the moment somewhat dampened George's ardor. But he soon forgot that aspect and grew interested in the personality of the different speakers and singers. For the young men sang solos and gave testimonies about what the college had done for them, until George grew deeply interested. Religion of course wasn't his specialty, yet these fellows didn't look like sissies.

Then suddenly a very tall sailor from the navy was introduced as the speaker of the evening, and immediately the audience was breathless, enthralled with the young man's story.

He had been a student in the college before he enlisted in the navy. Three years he had been out in active duty on the sea, and had participated in all but one of the great naval battles.

Simply, unostentatiously, he told his story, and made those terrible battles live before his audience.

And the strange thing about this story was that the young man constantly spoke of the Lord as his companion all the way through. And he talked so naturally and easily and enthusiastically that one could not possibly think he was proud of his own achievements, or even that he was dragging in the religious aspect.

He spoke of his first impressions of the college, and how surprised he was that every day began with prayer, prayer meetings of groups in their rooms, an atmosphere of prayer and dependence upon God. It opened a new view of life to the brother and sister who sat listening in wonder.

When the service was over they all gathered about the young talent, and talked especially with the young navy man who had spoken. Corliss lingered in the offing listening to every word he said. Corliss had never heard a young man talk this way, as if he knew the Lord personally, and yet wasn't afraid of Him.

But George was talking to the dean, asking questions, accepting a bunch of printed matter, looking at the papers in his hand and then asking more questions, and when they all finally parted at the church door the dean and George seemed like old friends, and the dean's last word was, "Well, Huntley, glad we met, and I'll be looking for you next week. Good night."

It was on the way home that George spoke:

"I'm all kinds of glad, Dale, that you took us to that meeting tonight. I'm going to that college! What do you think of that?"

"I think it is simply wonderful, George! I couldn't ask anything better for you. I've known a lot about that institution, and it's great!"

"Oh," said Corliss aghast, "but—what will mamma say? Will she let you go? And what will you do for money? She'll never let you have any if she doesn't like the college."

George was still for a moment, and then he said:

"I'm not going to ask mother, not till I get everything arranged. I'm going to *work* my way through. The dean said they had an arrangement for that, and that speaker said he did, you know. That's what I'm going to do."

"Oh, but George, you can't go away and leave me," said Corliss pitifully, "I just can't stand it! You know I can't. You know mamma won't let me do a thing if you're not with me, or else she'll send me away to some stuffy girls' school, and I'd *die*. I'd just *die* without you."

"Mebbe you could go to this same college, kid? Girls go there you know. There were all those girls there in the glee club. Don't girls go there, Dale?"

"Oh, yes, but would your mother let you go there? Perhaps she does not believe in co-educational schools."

"No, I don't believe she does," said Corliss. "And besides, I never finished the last year of high school. You can't go into college without credits. You know that."

"Oh, we can fix that up somehow. You can get a tutor and catch up. There are always things you can do. We'll see. But don't you say anything about this, not to mom, or anybody else, till we find out more. I'm going down to that college and see that dean again, and I'm going to telephone to my old principal at high school and get him to send me my credentials. And then you know Grandmother left me that thousand dollars. I suppose I could use that in a pinch, couldn't I? Dale, don't you think Grandmother would like me to use it that way?"

"Why, yes, I think she would. But George, I don't just know how that was left. Haven't you a guardian or something? Perhaps you could get his permission. We might ask Mr. Granniss. He drew up the will. Probably he could tell us all about it."

"Yes, would you mind doing that?"

"Not at all. Mr. Granniss is very nice. If there is any way you can use it he will know. When are you of age, George?"

"Oh, bother. Not for two years yet. But when that comes, then I'd have to go into service if the war's still on. Of course I wouldn't mind that, but that's the reason mom wouldn't want me out of her sight. She wants to keep me young so they can't get me. But I've been figuring to get into the marines somehow and then be with that crowd who are in college at first, until they are called. I tried to get mom to let me go into a college that way. But she had nine fits. She doesn't want me to go to war, and she says anyway it will soon be over," the boy said glumly.

"Well, don't worry. We'll find out just what rights you have and then when your mother comes here perhaps there will be a way to get her consent."

"Consent nothing!" said the boy. "She'll never do that. But she can't tie me to her apron strings all the rest of my life. I've got to be a *man!*"

"There'll be a way, George," said Dale comfortingly. "Don't let's worry about it tonight. But I can't tell you how glad I am that you feel this way about this grand college. You don't know what it will do for you if you go there. I've known a lot of boys and girls, too, who have gone there and they have all been rather wonderful."

Corliss looked up sadly.

"Yes, Dale, I can see it is a wonderful place, but just for that reason mamma wouldn't like it. She would never consent, not for anything."

"Well, Corliss, dear, suppose we hand this over to the Lord and see if He will do anything about it for you. Meantime, George, when are you going down to the college?"

"Next Tuesday. I hope that's not the day the doctor picks out to send mom home. I'd like to get this settled before she gets here, for something tells me there won't be much chance after she comes. She'd find some other college right away. She wouldn't think this was swell enough I'm afraid," said George dejectedly.

"Well, don't worry about it. Things may work out your way yet," said Dale cheerily.

"Fat chance!" said Corliss dejectedly.

But George set his lips firmly.

"They are *going* to work out the way *I* want them for *me,* any way," he said. "I think I'm old enough to say where I'll go to college, and I mean to do it. If I have to work my way through, why then all right, but *I'll* choose the college, see? This is the first college I ever heard of that appealed to me, and I don't mean to let it go for any other, no matter how noted the other is."

Dale smiled quietly to herself. This was better than she had hoped. If George did get to go to such a college he would surely learn what the Lord could do for him in his life. But then, on the other hand, it might make a lot of trouble for him in his home life, and would she be blamed for it? Probably. But what of that if it worked out for George's good? Well, this was one more thing to be prayed about and put in God's keeping.

Dale sat up a little while that night after the others had retired. Somehow she felt as if she must write and tell David about what had happened that day. He might not get the letter for weeks or even months, and of course he might not ever get it on this earth, but still it helped her to bear the long absence and the terrible possibilities if she kept in touch with him by writing, even if he could not answer her. That she was prepared for. He had told her it might probably be a very long time before he could send a letter out to her. But it comforted her to talk to him on paper.

So she wrote a long letter, telling of all the problems about her aunt, and how she hoped some of them were working out. Thanking him for the prayers she knew he was putting up in their behalf. And then she wrote of the wonderful Christian college and the interest her young, almost-heathen cousins, were taking in it. Another item for his prayers. Perhaps the Holy Spirit would guide his prayers for her problems.

It was quite late when the letter was finished, and she stole quietly into her room and got into bed so quickly and silently that she hoped she had not wakened Corliss. But after she had cautiously settled herself in her bed Corliss' hand came stealing over and clasped hers, squeezing her fingers, and then Corliss whispered:

"Oh, Dale, this has been a perfectly wonderful evening.

I'm so glad you took us. And oh, I do so want to go to that college!"

"Dear child!" said Dale tenderly, "I hope you can."

"I was thinking, Dale, if mamma should go up to Aunt Evelyn's perhaps, just *perhaps,* she might let me stay here a little while and study. Wouldn't there be a tutor around here I could get, or couldn't *you* help me get ready to pass an examination so I could go to that college too? I could get a job somewhere that would only take part time and I could pay you for teaching me—"

"Corliss, dear! I wouldn't want any pay, if I would be good enough. We'd have to find out about that of course, dear, in case there was such a chance. But you wouldn't need to get a job. I could give you one. Not a very lucrative one of course, but one that would give you a little spending money. I thought perhaps you could help me with that little school I'm likely taking over when the way is clear. How would you like that?"

"I'd love it. Wouldn't I really be in your way, Dale? Wouldn't you hate having me here for several months till I was allowed to go to college?"

"No, dear, I wouldn't hate it. I would love it. You have grown to be very dear to me since we have been through so much together, and I'd love having you. But of course that would all have to depend on your mother and what she is willing for you to do. But I'd love teaching you if I know enough. I'd have to find out the requirements of course, maybe I could. If I couldn't there would be somebody else I'm sure."

Talking quietly their voices presently faded into silence and then Dale heard the soft even breathing of Corliss and knew she was asleep and for the time being out of her perplexities. It was strange wasn't it, how pleasant it had been to have Corliss want to stay with her? And such a few short days before, what a trial it would have been. She wondered what had made the difference. Was it because she had been trying to make it pleasant for them, and how she seemed to have come to love them?

Ruminating over the wonder of a God-given love where there had been natural dislike, it was not unlike the God-given love of a hitherto unknown lover. Softly she fell asleep praying for that lover so very far away. What would she have thought could she have known that her lover was now alone on a wide turbulent sea, tossing in a little toy of a lifeboat, and that the man who had rescued him and put him there had gone back for some cans of provisions and met a bomb instead. A rescuer who had lost his life! And a rescued man who had been struck by a falling spar, was delirious, alone, on the wide ocean, under a dark starless sky, burning with fever, with no provisions and no companion, with a wounded shoulder, full of pain, too far gone to know his own situation. Now and again a scrap of a song from out of his past floated out hoarsely from the little boat into the night. "All through the night, all through the night, my Saviour has been watching over me."

Was David taking his last journey, on his way to meet his God?

19

IT was a sunny bright day when they brought Mrs. Huntley from the hospital, in the very best ambulance the institution boasted, with two of the choicest nurses in charge. The nurses had not been the choice of the hospital, but the patient had made such a terrific uproar about the matter, that rather than have the uproar kept up, the hospital arranged to give her what she wanted on the way over. However, the nurse who was to remain with her for a week or two was not the one she had asked for, and expected to have, but a younger nurse, a recent comer into training, because they could not spare the best nurses from the busy institution. The nurse who was to remain was sitting in front quite meekly with the driver, and pledged to say nothing about it until the patient was well settled in the new bed, and the other two had disappeared around the corner where the ambulance was in waiting for them. Then she was to arrive at the bedside and take up her duties. It was not going to be easy for either the nurse, or the family, to say nothing about the patient.

So Mrs. Huntley, arriving back in the house she had made so uncomfortable before she left, a little weary from the excitement of moving and the trip, was settled comfortably in the delightful guest bed that had been the pride of dear Grandmother's heart. She rested back on the smooth shining linen, away at last from the hated sights and sounds of the hospital, closed her eyes and without intending it, fell into a delightful sleep, and never knew until her waking that she was now at the mercy of an entirely new nurse.

The afternoon waned, and the family tiptoed about carefully, to preserve the utmost quiet. A single rosebud in a clear glass bud vase touched the atmosphere with delicate luxurious fragrance, and later there came stealing through the house the delicious odors of fresh baked bread, and roasting meat, even penetrating to that quiet room upstairs and speaking to the sleeping senses of the woman who for long weeks had been on hospital fare. Of course it had been a fine hospital with the best of fare, but that was not exactly home cooking, and certainly not Hattie's cooking. And strange to say after all her grumbling, here was Hattie working hard, determined to do her best for the woman whom she had despised, and to have such a dinner as would tempt the appetite of the most particular guest. She was at least determined not to let her dear Miss Dale outdo her in kindliness toward the woman who in her heart she looked upon as the hatefulest of enemies. And yet she was doing her best to produce a delightful dinner that would interest and tempt an invalid's appetite.

It was later when the invalid at last awoke, the new nurse standing by her side and offering a cool wash cloth, and a spoonful of medicine, and then arranging the delightful tray that Dale brought up with a smile.

Mrs. Huntley did not at once discover that the nurse was new. She was just a trifle bewildered at being in a strange bed, and having a new situation about her, Dale coming in so smilingly, her children there as if they really enjoyed having her. Perhaps it was something as Heaven may surprise some of us who have not been living in great antici-pation of it. But at least she did not rise to her usual rebel-lious attitude, and George and Corliss began to hope that perhaps things were going to be different now, and mother was going to live a happy life like other people and not find fault with everything.

Corliss hovered about her and offered to feed her the dessert, which was Hattie's specialty, a confection of eggs and gelatine and cream in a most delectable form of char-lotte russe, and was eaten with cream and crimson rasp-berry jelly. The invalid in a kind of wonder accepted her daughter's ministrations, a bit ungraciously perhaps, but still accepted them. So all went smoothly until it was time to prepare the invalid for the night and the new nurse ap-peared on the scene again and began to get her ready for sleep. Then she recognized her strangeness, and demanded the other two nurses, and when she was told that they had gone back to the hospital, as they could not be spared any longer, she raved wildly, declined to let the nurse touch her, and demanded that her daughter telephone to the hos-pital and have those nurses sent back to her. When the son and daughter both declined to accept that commission, saying that the head nurse had told them it would be im-possible, she went into a storm of tears, and mourned her helplessness, and the cruelty of the doctors and nurses, and declared she would make that institution known as a dreadful place form one end of the country to the other, so that they would have no patients any more. And at last she sent for Dale.

Dale, with a heart lifted for help went quietly in to her aunt and tried to reason with her, and when she found that did no good, she offered to do the nursing herself, but that too was most summarily declined. On the whole it was very late that night before the invalid was at last composed and drifting off to sleep and the family could take heart of hope and try to get a little rest themselves.

Dale's last thought as she drifted off to sleep was for her lover far away, "Oh Lord, keep him safely all through the night," and as she closed her eyes and fought back the weary tears that stung to blind her she wondered when, if ever, she would see him again.

It was two days later, hard days every hour of them, that the message came from the War Department that Captain David Kenyon, naval bomber pilot of note, and recently transferred to the command of an army transport, was missing in action.

Somehow it seemed to Dale at first as if she could not bear to see the sun shine when she thought of her lover, with that calm trust in his eyes, that sunny smile on his lips, gone from her. Dead perhaps, or even something worse. Missing in action! Didn't that usually mean that they were taken prisoner? Oh, it seemed as if her heart would break. Yet of course she mustn't let it. She had known when he went away that this might happen. He had known it too. And they had the sure knowledge that they would meet again. They both were saved, born-again-ones, and they were going Home to meet. She must not give way to this awful goneness that crept through her very being. She had work to do, souls to win, guests to make comfortable. And they did not know of her loss. She must not betray her sorrow. She must go on about her duties knowing that her Lord was keeping her, and would live her life for her if she would only let Him. So, not even sorrow must be able to get her down.

And she could not weep even at night. Corliss was sleeping with her and she must not let her know she was in trouble. Corliss did not know she had had a lover.

Then the thought would come that perhaps he was not dead. Sometimes those who were missing in action were found, sometimes they were able to escape from their prison camps. At least she could pray, and her Savior would be watching over her lover, day and night, and he was beloved of her Lord. He would not let anything harmful come to David. She remembered how they had prayed together "in life or in death Lord." Yes, she must be brave. She must be as brave as if she too were fighting in action.

Then it came to her that she had a home front to fight right here in her house. She had to try to win her household to know the Lord.

But neither did life in the home move smoothly. It was hard for everybody. The invalid, when she found the nurses of her choice were out of the question, accepted the new one only under protest, and made the poor thing's life miserable with millions of unnecessary errands, demanding this and that which could not be had, and making many outcries and protests when she was frustrated; and she made the lives of her son and daughter very unhappy.

Perhaps it was thus that Corliss began to see herself as she had been, selfish and proud and cruel, and began to try to have some self-control.

George meanwhile had made a couple of trips to the college of his choice, and secured all the necessary details about what would be necessary for both himself, and perhaps later for Corliss, also, to enter, though they had no present inkling of how this wish of theirs was going to be carried out.

But Corliss, as soon as she found a little free time when her mother would not suspect, went downtown and procured certain books upon which she would have to be examined if she tried to enter college. With Dale's encouragement she began to do a little study by herself helped out by suggestions from Dale, who was busy indeed just at present assisting the rather inefficient nurse, and taking her turn with the invalid whenever it seemed wise to do so.

Life was looking pretty bleak to Dale just now, with the heavy burden of anxiety upon her heart, the thrilling joy that had been hers suddenly turned into fear and sorrow, and a lingering anxiety. It seemed to her as if her every breath was a prayer.

The days dragged by, each moment filled with some difficult duty, or some knotty problem to solve. Sometimes as she passed the door of her grandmother's room, which stood open always now, like some glimpse into a quiet prayer room, her thoughts went back longingly to the sweet days when Grandmother had been there, slipping from her quietly day by day. But they seemed in contast with this hectic time like a little glimpse into Heaven. Still, she had had no precious lover in those loved days, and now whether he was dead or alive he was hers. If still on this earth she might still pray for him, and his return. But if in Glory, surely he was doubly hers then. So she must not be despondent. Besides the rest of the people in the house knew nothing of her own special heartache, and so she must carry a sunny face always. They must know that she had a Lord who was able to keep her from falling. Able to give her a sunny smile in the midst of trying circumstances.

Yet in the midst of these hard days, often as she sought the quiet of her grandmother's room for a little while to pray, she gradually became possessed with the thought that she must pray with all her heart for David. She had a strong feeling that "missing" in this case might not mean death, or even imprisonment. There were stories coming in now and then of those who had been sent out on missions and their ships had been lost, but somehow they had floated for days and finally been picked up. There was one notable case like this, a man who had found God through those days of panic and almost death. Might not David be somewhere safe in God's keeping?

Meantime the date of the opening of George's college was coming on, and George was determined to begin if possible. They got hold of Mr. Granniss and at his suggestion called up George's guardian who had charge of his finances, and found that he could and would give consent to the arrangement until such time as the boy's mother should be able to look after his affairs more carefully. So George arranged to go down to the college and start, returning usually at evening to talk with his mother and keep her satisfied that he was all right. She never had been one to greatly concern herself over the daily doings of her children. If they were enjoying themselves somewhere she was usually satisfied. So for the present George was able to say he was getting acquainted with the surrounding neighborhood, or he was reading or studying, and she did not question further. Although they all knew this could not go on indefinitely, and he would soon have to account for his absences.

Corliss, meantime, spent as much time with her mother as seemed acceptable, always with a book at hand, trying to study when her mother slept. And more and more Mrs. Huntley was becoming dependent upon Dale and Corliss for attention, preferring to have their ministrations rather than the nurse's to whom she had taken a dislike.

And so the days settled uneasily down to a routine, and the invalid seemed a bit more content than when she was in the hospital, but kept on with her daily demand for the lawyer. Then one day she asked Dale if she supposed her Granniss-lawyer might be prevailed upon to come and talk with her about trying to get back the money she had paid the fraud of a lawyer, Buffington.

Mr. Granniss very kindly came, and let her talk, but told her that he was afraid, since she had given cash both times in paying him, and had received no receipt for the amount, that it was hopeless to try and get it back. She had nothing to show for the transaction, and that lawyer had the reputation of conducting such affairs in a shady manner. After he went away Mrs. Huntley wore a desperate look, and Corliss found her crying when she came to give her her supper that night.

The girls did all they could to cheer her up, told her she didn't need the money now. When she got well she would have another check due from her regular income, and so why bother? But the lady did not cheer up easily. And the bills began to come in from the hospital, and the doctor, and finally the doctor told her that he wished she would go for a few weeks to a certain sanitarium up in the mountains. That he felt it would not only build her up wonderfully, but that she might even find help for a more rapid recovery through a noted specialist who was working up there. And when she told him she could not afford it, he told her that his sister was driving up that way to take another patient and they would be glad to have her go with them. There would be a nurse along, and it need not be such a hard trip, nor very expensive, and she need not be in a hurry about paying his bill.

He was very kind and most surprisingly the invalid was intrigued by the idea and decided to go.

So, the household was all in a twitter getting her ready, and off. She even sat up for an hour or two and felt no worse for it.

And then Dale came to her with a check for five hundred dollars.

"Aunt Blanche," she said earnestly, "I want you to take this to pay your bills, and perhaps have a little over for necessary expenses when you get there."

Tears sprang unbidden to the invalid's eyes, and she stared at Dale, unable to believe that Dale wasn't doing this for some disagreeable reason

"I can't take your money, Dale," she said in a broken voice. "I'm afraid I haven't been very pleasant to you about the house."

"Oh, that's all right," said Dale happily. "I'm glad I

have the money to help you out. Your own money won't be here in time you said, and there's no reason why you shouldn't use mine, for the present at least. I don't need it just now."

"But you are taking care of my children, Dale, and that has cost you something. And I really ought not to go away now. I ought to arrange to send my children home, or put them in a school somewhere before I leave."

Dale caught at the idea.

"Oh, don't worry about that now. Just you go and get well," she said. "Corliss and her brother will be all right here, and I'll promise to find a school for them both where they will be interested till you come back for them. You wouldn't need to worry at all on that score. What you should do is to get well first, and then everything can be settled up."

"But they could go up to my sister Evelyn's, only they both dislike her so much they will make a terrible fuss about it."

"Well, never mind. I think they'll enjoy it here more, and I'll love to have them."

Her aunt looked at her for a minute in wonder. Then she said thoughtfully, "But you wanted to start a school."

"Well, perhaps I will later, and if I do I'll let Corliss help me teach perhaps. Anyway we'll manage nicely."

And so, though there wasn't much gratitude expressed openly, the matter was arranged, and the next morning saw the aunt carried carefully out to the big comfortable hospital car in the arms of a strong man, one of the hospital nurses, who knew how to handle broken bones without hurting. The family stood on the sidewalk and watched her happily away.

"Now," said George, "do you figure it was all our prayers that brought this about, so I could go on to that college without expecting a hurricane every time I came back?"

"I shouldn't wonder," said Dale, smiling. "And now Corliss, we can really get to work at your studies so you will be able to take those examinations sooner. Perhaps if you are both already entered in that college when your mother gets back she may consent to let you stay. At any rate you can have a chance to find out if you really like it."

"Oh, I like it all right," said George, "and I'm sure Corrie will too."

"Of course," said Corliss. "Oh, Dale, I think you've been perfectly wonderful to bring all this about for us."

"There, there," smiled Dale. "Forget it, and come let's get to work. What comes first? Latin or mathematics?"

"Latin!" said Corliss. "I simply adore that, and I like to get the easiest things out of the way first."

So they settled down to regular life, doing good work, and being fairly happy.

It wasn't really very different from Dale's life the last few years, perhaps, but she hugged the thought of her wonderful lover to her heart, and still prayed for him day by day, hoping against hope that some word might someday come from him.

And every night when George came home to dinner he had pleasant things to tell of his college, and she could fairly see him grow into another person from day to day.

DALE was getting to be a good teacher. She was enjoying the study herself, and enjoying Corliss' quick mind, enjoying the game of getting her ready for a quick examination. But while she was working with her hands here and there about the house she was continually praying for David, that if it were God's will he might come home to her sometime. That she might not have to live out her life without him.

Now and again the world read in the paper that some soldier or sailor boy who had been reported missing had come home, and her heart would leap, over the thought of what joy his people must be having on his return. Would such joy ever come to her?

It was as if she were living his life out with him wherever he was, in prison, or suffering, or distress of any kind. Her Saviour watching over David, and she keeping continual watch for answer to her prayers. Of course most people would tell her she was a fool to keep on hoping, for now days and weeks had passed since the word had come, and nothing further came. She was glad that nobody knew of her lover, for now they could not pity her. She would hate to be pitied. For they would not understand what was strengthening her in such a mortal sorrow. They would think she did not care, and she could not bear that. And they would never understand how an idea, a trust in an Unseen Being could keep her bright and sunny. She must not bring her Lord into shame by not trusting Him, and she knew He was able to keep her, even though He did not see fit to give her back her lover.

There came letters from Aunt Blanche, not written by her own hand, because her arm and wrist had not yet recovered strength to write, or at least she thought they hadn't, which amounted to the same thing. But she had found a nice nurse who for a consideration would write very neat letters, and she described the sanitarium where she was, and all its lovely views, and the people, some pleasant and some disagreeable. But she said that she had found a few friends who were very good bridge players, and therefore she was happy, for she simply adored bridge.

She said that her usual check had come through and she was sending Dale twenty-five of what she owed her, and would hope to be able to repay her in full before too long. Meantime she thanked her for being so kind to the children, and she was so glad that they had found suitable schools where they were happy, and she hoped they would do their best to behave and not get into trouble anywhere as she wasn't there to get them out.

Dale did not wonder that neither of her cousins mourned much for the absence of their mother. They had been greatly broken up when she was hurt, but more because they were afraid of suffering and death, than because of any deep love for her. Nevertheless they were greatly glad that their mother was happy and had decided to stay where she was for several months, until she was thoroughly well and could go home and attend to her own affairs as usual, for they were both very much in love with their college, and wanted above all things not to be taken away against their wills.

At last Corliss was ready for her examinations, and was hoping to be allowed to get into classes before the year was over. And suddenly Dale felt that if she did, life was really going to be quite dull for herself without either of her bright young cousins. For now they had all grown to be very dear to each other, and whenever there was a chance for George to get away from his work he would run home for an hour or two to report on how things were going with him. And then one day he came in a great hurry and said he couldn't stay but a minute, that he was coaching another fellow in geometry and had promised to be back before supper to help him.

"But there is something I want to tell you, Dale. I knew you'd be interested, maybe Corliss too. Anyway, *I've found the Lord,* and I thought you'd be glad! It's wonderful to know I'm saved, and I never was so happy in my life. I don't know what mother would say to it. Sometime I'll have to tell her, when I've had a chance to live it a little and let her see I'm different. It isn't a thing I'd know how to write to her about. She'd be taking me right away from here and sending me to some worldly college. She's horribly afraid of anybody getting religious. But now, Corrie, I'm praying for you, and I want you to get saved, and then we'll begin to pray for moms."

He scarcely gave them opportunity to tell him how glad they were. Even Corliss seemed glad, though she didn't altogether understand the matter, and after that day often asked Dale many questions, and sometimes consented to read the Bible with her. But Corliss was more interested to pass her examinations now, and she was working very hard.

And at last she did pass them, and Dale went with her to enter the college and they were all very happy about it.

But when Dale went back to the empty house it seemed

very desolate without either of her cousins, and she wondered if she ought not to think about taking over her school, although it seemed to be getting on nicely without her, and she wondered if that was what the Lord would want her to be doing now. She seemed to have arrived at a place of pause, where she must think things through, and know how she was going to order her days.

And then that very night there came a letter from the War Department that Captain David Kenyon had been found, and brought back to a base hospital, where he was under the best of care. A letter was enclosed that had been found in his Testament in his breast pocket. He had been wounded and was not yet in condition to tell all that had happened to him, but it was known that he had floated for a number of days on the ocean in one of the small rubber boats, that he had been picked up by a flyer who had seen him far from land and had taken him to his own outfit. He was wounded and not in very good physical condition when found, but now the doctor gave every hope that he would eventually recover.

There followed an address where she could write, and Dale, the tears of joy streaming down her face, hurried up to her lonely room and began to write a letter. Perhaps he would not be able yet to read much of a letter, but she would put what was in her heart for him just in a few words at first. And later she would write all that she had wanted to say for all the lonely weeks he had been away.

But the first letter she wrote came from the depths of her heart.

My precious David:

The letter has just come that says you have been found. After all these weeks when you were missing in action, now you are *found,* and in the hands of nurses and doctors who can help you.

My darling, I cannot thank God enough that you

are safe, and I can know where you are. I've been praying hourly for you. I know you were always safe, because our Saviour has been watching over you.

Now I shall get this down to the postoffice at once so that you may have word from me as soon as you are able to understand it, but I'll be writing all the time now, every day, and if they are too much, just let the nurse put them away to keep for you till you are well.

> Good night, beloved,
> DALE

She looked up to find Hattie standing in the doorway looking at her with troubled eyes.

"Why, Hattie, I thought you had gone to bed," she said.

"No'm, Miss Dale, I couldn't go to bed nohow else I knowed you was all right and ready to rest. I thought you'd be lonesome, mebbe. But you look real happified, Miss Dale. Are you glad you got rid of them children?"

"Oh, no, Hattie. I love the children, and I shall miss them very much of course, but I am happified, Hattie. Something wonderful has just happened to me. You heard the bell ring a little while ago? Well, it was a special delivery letter from the War Department, telling me that a dear friend of mine whom I love very much and who has been missing in action for several weeks now, has been found. He was floating for a long time, several days perhaps, on the ocean in a little boat, and a flyer saw him from the sky and picked him up and took him to a base hospital. They are taking care of him, and they think he may get well. Yes, I'm happy, oh, so happy and thankful to God."

"That's great, Miss Dale. And do I know that man?"

"Why, I'm not sure. He was here several times. Do you remember a man in naval uniform at Grandmother's funeral?"

"Man with gold bar on his shoulder and gold wings on his breast?"

"Yes, that's the one, Hattie. His name is David Kenyon, and we were engaged before he went away. He's been made a lieutenant commander now. Oh, Hattie, I'm so happy!"

"Well, you got a good man I am positive. He's the very handsomest man I ever saw, and that's certain. Does anybody else know about this?"

"No, Hattie. You're the first one. I'll want to tell the cousins of course when they come back for the week end. But how I wish I could tell Grandmother. How she would love it!"

"Don't you reckum she already knows it, Miss Dale?"

"I think perhaps she does," said Dale softly, with a golden look in her eyes.

After that Dale wrote every day to her beloved, who perhaps was not yet able to even hear the letters read, but she had to write them, else her heart might have burst with the messages it contained.

And when the cousins came home for their first week end, they looked at her for a minute and then they said:

"What's the matter? What's happened? You look as if something wonderful had come to pass."

"It has," said Dale with a great illumination in her face. "My very dear commander, to whom I am engaged, and who has been missing in action for a long time, has been found and is in the hospital, with a very good hope that he may get well and come back to me."

Then Corliss lifted up her voice, a new, happy voice, and screamed for joy.

"Oh, Dale, you darling Dale, I'm so very glad for you," she cried, and caught her cousin around the neck and administered some very definite kisses. "Who is he, Dale? Is it that perfectly darling uniformed man that came to Grandma's funeral? David Kenyon, wasn't that his name?

Oh, I'm so glad, so *glad*. I thought he was wonderful!"

And then George spoke.

"Well, I'll say you put one over on us all this time. You never let on all these weeks that we've been so close to you! And you didn't wear a ring or anything."

Dale laughed.

"We didn't have time to think of rings or anything but each other, he had to go away so soon."

"That's the talk," said the boy. "Rings are just do–dabs anyway. And besides, in wartime, people aren't thinking of things like that. Say, but I'm glad for you Dale, only I hope you won't go far away from us where we can't see you any more. You don't know what you mean to Corrie and me. We were talking about it on the way up today. You are 'own folks' to us now, and I don't know how we'd ever get through all of life that's ahead if you go so far we can't get to see you often. You can just tell cousin Dave that we won't stand for him taking you away to China or anywhere far off, and that's not mebbe."

Dale laughed.

"I'll tell him," she said happily. "But you might as well know that your cousin David is very much interested in you, and has been praying for you while he was away. Yes, he has, and I've written him a lot about you, too, although I'm not sure he ever got those last letters, for he wasn't allowed to write after he went off on this last assignment."

They sat down and wanted to know all about him, and Dale got out her pictures. They really got acquainted with their new cousin, and quite approved him.

And then after a time they got back to talking about their college and all the things that had been happening there, and how they enjoyed the Christian fellowship.

"And Corrie does too," said George eagerly. "I guess you'll find she's saved now, too!"

Corliss nodded her head.

"Yes," she said, "one couldn't stay there very long and not be. They all just live in an atmosphere of salvation. And it begins little by little to seem more and more real to you, till you want it for yourself."

"Oh, I'm so glad!" said Dale. "So very, very glad!"

And then all three cousins knelt down and thanked God for His so-wonderful salvation.

21

DAY after day Dale watched for more news, though her common sense told her that there might be a long delay. The first announcement had left her to suppose that David's condition was more critical, and if he was still delirious of course he would not know what message had been sent her, nor have strength to frame a personal message to her. How long would she have to wait, she wondered? Of course until he could talk to the nurse, or to some comrade, no one would know how to get in contact with her, except the War Department, and they had already done their duty in letting her know her man had been found, and was doing as well as could be expected.

Night after night she went to bed praying, and morning after morning she arose with new hope in her heart that there might be some word that day. Hattie, too, was on the qui vive every time the telephone rang, or every time the doorbell sounded.

Dale laughed as she met her rushing to the front door in answer to a ring, and called out:

"He couldn't be coming yet, Hattie," she said. "He's away on the other side of the world somewhere, and he's been too sick to even send a personal word, so there is no use in expecting him to come and ring the doorbell."

"Aw, but Miss Dale. He might have flewed, mightn't he?"

"Well, not likely in the condition they gave me to understand he was in."

"Aw, well, you can't always tell what may happen in wah times," said Hattie, nimbly excusing herself, and grinning at her mistress.

Dale grinned back, and thanked God in her prayers that night for good cheerful Hattie, among the other blessings He had granted her.

Three days later there came a telegram, brief and to the point, but from David himself.

> Beloved Dale:
> Safe in His Care. All my love, David

Dale sat down and laughed and cried for joy into that telegram. It told so much and yet so little. He must be better or he could not have worded it. It rejoiced with her and bade her rejoice with him that he had been saved from great peril through their Saviour who had watched over them "All through the night." It told all his love. He had not forgotten her, and she apparently was his first thought when he came back to life and self again.

She had much to tell the cousins when they came again, and they all rejoiced together that David was getting well. For there presently came letters from David's nurse, and from a comrade now and again, giving a few more details of his progress. His shoulder was healing nicely. His hands were getting stronger. The sprained wrists were so much better he would soon be able to write her a letter "under his own power," and not have to wait for a secretary to take dictation.

There was nothing about the hardships he had gone

through, except one sentence, "I'll tell you all about it when I get home. God speed the day. Joy cometh in the morning."

The two eager young cousins who were so interested in her romance exulted in all these messages, which Dale let them read because she enjoyed having someone to talk them over with. And they just reveled in knowing what a wonderful man was coming back to their dear Dale someday.

But now brief letters in his own hand began to come oftener, and Dale began to take new heart of hope that soon he might be coming home. He hinted now and then that there might be a chance, though the doctor had not yet told him his release was coming soon.

Of course like all soldiers and sailors who had been in combat David wanted to go back and finish up the job, but when he suggested it his doctors and nurses shook their heads. Definitely no. He had been through too hard a time, and his physical strength was not up to such things yet, perhaps never would be. He had earned his ribbons and his stars and other decorations, what else did he want, they asked him. And so he let his heart relax, and began to look forward to seeing his beloved once more. Oh, would she think the same of him? He asked himself that a thousand times a day, yet kept on praying and hoping.

But Dale began definitely to get ready for his coming.

She wanted the house to be in perfect order, though with Hattie's willing help there wasn't so much to be done in that way. The house was always in order, for Hattie took pride in keeping it so. But there were a few curtains to be renewed, a few little things that needed mending, and it was happy work to be doing, in between the Red Cross work she was doing now, and the occasional groups of children she supervised during part of each day, while their mothers were away at war work. Some of Grandmother's geraniums and pots of ivy needed trimming and coaxing into early bloom, that the house might be gay and attractive when he came.

And often as she sat sewing, or reading, only half her attention was on her work. She was remembering her lover as he had been with her on that one long beautiful day among the hemlocks out under God's wide sky before he went away. And now was it really true that he was coming back to her? *He* had hoped that God would let him, *she* had hoped and prayed about it, and given up her will about it again and again. But God had been so very gracious to save him from that awful fate alone on the sea. No, not alone, but alone with God on the sea. But it was God's sea, and the sea could not harm him when God was watching over him.

Again and again precious thoughts like these went through her mind until her heart became a continual paean of praise. And now she was so often watching for his coming, for he had at last told her his coming might be soon, and unannounced. He might be brought home in a plane when there was opportunity. There were so many things that had to be considered in sending wounded soldiers home, so many men to be sent back and forth.

Quite often now, when Dale was alone sitting at her desk or under the light reading, or resting in a comfortable chair, she would get up and go out on the porch, just to look down the road, and see if anyone was walking up the street, just to look up to the night sky and fancy how he would be coming, like that great plane that sailed across the house above her at a certain time each night. And sometimes the moon would be rising, a lovely golden crescent, or later in the month a great round full silver orb in the wide deep blue of a sky punctuated here and there with white stars, and she would think, "What if he should come now, tonight, while I am standing here, and we could be here together watching this night. Sometime we will perhaps. Sometime he will be here, and will not go away, but we shall be together, shall *belong* together. How great and wonderful that would be!"

She went over all her pretty anticipations. How she would telephone Corliss and George to come home and meet him. Or stay—perhaps it would be better for David to take her down to the college. Ah, that was something that must wait until he came, to see how well he was, and whether he was able to take trips like that.

Then she would chide herself for planning so far ahead when she was not even sure yet that he was to be allowed to come home at all at this time. He might even be considered well enough to be sent on another assignment, and there might be another long period of waiting and trusting ahead of her yet. Well, even so, the war must be won, and if their Lord had planned it that way they must be content.

Then she would chide herself for making up so many possible disappointments when it was all in her Lord's hands, and she could perfectly trust that He would do His best for her and for David.

One night she came down to supper in a little new frock all bright and gay with small knots of giddy little flowers scattered over its white sheeny surface, and outlined here and there with cords of scarlet among the bright knots of flowers. It was a pretty dress and she wished he were there to see it. And then she got up and went out to take her nightly observation of the sky and see if there were any planes coming over the house, just to carry out her whimsical fantasy.

She had looked long into the face of that great moon, and counted the stars about it, and finally turned away. And then, suddenly she heard a car. It was coming up their street. It came on quickly. It was the town taxi, and it was coming straight to her door! Could it be? Oh, it wasn't Aunt Blanche come back to take her cousins away from their beloved college was it? For an instant her heart stood still and foreboding but then she saw a tall man in uniform was getting out, paying the driver, picking up his bag from the curb where he had dropped it while he hunted out his change. He turned and looked toward the house, saw her standing there, her little gay dress fluttering in the evening breeze, the moonlight on her beautiful hair, and then she knew him. It was not just a fantasy of her imagination. He was there in reality. She could hear the taxi that had brought him going down the street, turning into the highway below. It was all real, and David had come home!

It was then she turned and flew down the steps and went to meet him, went straight into his arms, right there in the dusk of the evening, with all the neighbors' quiet little houses around her watching, holding their breath to tell it to the nightingales.

And David dropped his bag and folded her in his arms, laying his cheek against her own.

"Dale, my darling! Oh, I have you in my arms once more. God has answered my prayer and brought me back to you again!"

And Dale nestled into his arms just as she had been dreaming she would do, and felt her heart overflowing with gladness and thanksgiving.

There was another watcher besides those neighboring houses. Hattie had heard the taxi, and Hattie had tip-toed softly into Grandma's room, and peeked out between the curtains. She caught the gleam of the street lamp on the bright bars of the uniform, she saw the bag, she measured the stranger's height, and knew the lost had returned at last! And then Hattie went back to her room, got dressed in a jiffy, and went to brewing among her pots and pans, till she evolved a tray of delightful tempting edibles, topped by cups of fragrant tea, and little delectable frosted cakes with cherries on them. Little sandwiches and scrambled eggs such as no one but Hattie could make and season just right. And then quite innocently she came sailing into the living room with her tray, as if a bell had sounded and she had been sent for.

"I thought you might like a little bite to eat, Miss Dale," she said wistfully, and then paused and eyed the tall uniformed man, liked his face, and heartily approved of him.

So Dale roused smiling, drew a little away from the strong arm that encircled her shoulders, and spoke:

"Oh, thank you Hattie, that was nice of you. David, this is Hattie. She's a part of us, you know, and she has been helping me watch for you."

"Oh, yes, I've heard of Hattie, and I'm glad to meet her at last!" said David as he got up from the couch where he had been sitting and took Hattie's two work-hardened hands in his own big ones, and gave them a warm pressure.

"Oh, thank you suh," said Hattie with her best bow. "And now you children set down an' eat your 'freshments 'fore they get cold. I sure is glad you have come at last, Mr. Captain, and I hope they gets this war over now you've come back so you won't have to go away no more."

Laughing and happy they sat down to the ample tray and ate as they had not eaten since that day on the mountain top that seemed so very long ago. And yet now that David was here, was only the other day.

They had eaten it all, every crumb, and Hattie had taken the tray away and left them to a happy talk. Then quite suddenly there was the sound of a car, a clatter of young feet on the walk outside, coming up the steps, and there came the cousins, barging in gaily. They paused an instant at the doorway abashed, then George roused to the occasion.

"Oh, excuse us, Dale. Are we interrupting? A fellow was coming up for the week end and we got a chance to ride up with him in his car. We thought you wouldn't mind. But gee, we didn't know you had company. If we're in the way we'll go back. But, say, isn't this Cousin David? How are you, David? We're glad you've come at last, and we hope you'll like us. We like you a lot already just from your picture you know."

Then David Kenyon got to his feet again and took the two new cousins by the hand, one hand in each of his own.

"Well, I certainly like that," he said genially. "That's the nicest welcome you could have given me, and I sure am going to like you two just as much. I've been hearing all about you in letters, you know. And I'm so glad you both are saved and we can all be happy together!"

"There! See that?" said George to his wide-eyed sister, "I said he was all right, and he is, Corrie, and I guess we've got about the greatest family a fellow and a girl could have. How about it, Dale? Do you mind our coming home this first night he's here?"

"Oh, no, I'm glad you've come. I want you to know him right from the start."

Then Hattie appeared in the doorway and summoned the younger ones.

"They all had a little suppah," she said, "but they done et it all up, so I guess you two bettah come out in the kitchen and tell me what you want to eat, and I'll fix it up for you."

So laughingly the two disappeared into the kitchen, and Hattie felt she had accomplished great things to leave the dear girl and her returned lover alone together.

Promptly David's arms went about Dale, and drew her close to him, her head on his shoulder, her face against his, where just their lips could touch.

"My darling!" David said, and drew a long deep breath of satisfaction. "Oh, it is so good to be with you again!"

Once more his face went down to her and his lips met hers, and then he raised his head and looked into her eyes.

"How soon can we be married?" he asked her earnestly. "I want you for my own for always. I kept wishing all the time I was gone that we had had time to get married before I left. But of course I couldn't help it that we were going so soon. But how soon, dearest?"

"Why, right away," said Dale joyously, with a lilt in her tone. "The sooner the better."

"That's perfect," said David. "We'll hunt up a license tomorrow. How long do you have to wait to get a license in this state?"

"Why, I really don't know, but what matters a little bit of time like a day or two? You are here now and all time will go fast. But I'd like the cousins to be here."

"Of course," said David. "They're rare! I'm glad they are near by. But oh, my darling! To think I have you in my arms at last! It seems too good to be true." He drew her close again and touched his lips to her eyelids.

"My precious!" he said. "What did I tell you, 'Joy cometh in the morning,' This is our morning."

Dale smiled softly, and then added in a low tone,

"And my Saviour kept you safely all through the night."

About the Author

Grace Livingston Hill is well known as one of the most prolific writers of romantic fiction. Her personal life was fraught with joys and sorrows not unlike those experienced by many of her fictional heroines.

Born in Wellsville, New York, Grace nearly died during the first hours of life. But her loving parents and friends turned to God in prayer. She survived miraculously, thus her thankful father named her Grace.

Grace was always close to her father, a Presbyterian minister, and her mother, a published writer. It was from them that she learned the art of storytelling. When Grace was twelve, a close aunt surprised her with a hardbound, illustrated copy of one of Grace's stories. This was the beginning of Grace's journey into being a published author.

In 1892 Grace married Fred Hill, a young minister, and they soon had two lovely young daughters. Then came 1901, a difficult year for Grace—the year when, within months of each other, both her father and husband died. Suddenly Grace had to find a new place to live (her home was owned by the church where her husband had been pastor). It was a struggle for Grace to raise her young daughters alone, but through everything she kept writing. In 1902 she produced *The Angel of His Presence, The Story of a Whim,* and *An Unwilling Guest.* In 1903 her two books *According to the Pattern* and *Because of Stephen* were published.

It wasn't long before Grace was a well-known author, but she wanted to go beyond just entertaining her readers. She soon included the message of God's salvation through Jesus Christ in each of her books. For Grace, the most important thing she did was not write books but share the message of salvation, a message she felt God wanted her to share through the abilities he had given her.

In all, Grace Livingston Hill wrote more than one hundred books, all of which have sold thousands of copies and have touched the lives of readers around the world with their message of "enduring love" and the true way to lasting happiness: a relationship with God through his Son, Jesus Christ.

In an interview shortly before her death, Grace's devotion to her Lord still shone clear. She commented that whatever she had accomplished had been God's doing. She was only his servant, one who had tried to follow his teaching in all her thoughts and writing.